NEXT EXIT HOME

What Reviewers Say
About Dena Blake's Work

Kiss Me Every Day

"This book was SUCH a fun read!! ...This was such a fun, interesting book to read and I thoroughly enjoyed it; the characters were super easy to like, the romance was super cute and I loved seeing each little thing that Wynn changed every day!"—*Sasha & Amber Read*

"Such a fun and an exciting book filled with so much love! This book is just packed with fun and memorable moments I was thinking about for days after reading it. This is one hundred per cent my new favourite Dena Blake book. The pace of the book was excellent, and I felt I was along for the fantastic ride."—*Les Rêveur*

"The sweetest moment in the book is when the titular phrase is uttered. ...This well written book is an interesting read because of the whole premise of getting repeated opportunities to right wrongs."—*Best Lesfic Reviews*

"Wynn's journey of self-discovery is wonderful to witness. She develops compassion, love and finds happiness. Her character development is phenomenal. ...If you're looking for a stunning romance book with a female/female romance, then this is definitely the one for you. I highly recommend."—*Literatureaesthetic*

Perfect Timing

"The chemistry between Lynn and Maggie is fantastic...the writing is totally engrossing."—*Best Lesfic Reviews*

"This book is the kind of book you sit down to on a Sunday morning with a cup of tea and the sun shining in your bedroom only to realise at 5 pm you've not left your bed because it was too good to stop reading."—*Les Rêveur*

"The relationship between Lynn and Maggie developed at an organic pace. I loved all the flirting going on between Maggie and Lynn. I love a good flirty conversation! …I haven't read this author before but I look forward to trying more of her titles."—Marcia Hull, Librarian (Ponca City Library, Oklahoma)

Racing Hearts

"I particularly liked Drew with her sexy rough exterior and soft heart. …Sex scenes are definitely getting hotter and I think this might be the hottest by Dena Blake to date…"—*Les Rêveur*

Just One Moment

"One of the things I liked is that the story is set after the glorious days of falling in love, after the time when everything is exciting. It shows how sometimes, trying to make life better really makes it more complicated. …It's also, and mainly, a reminder of how important communication is between partners, and that as solid as trust seems between two lovers, misunderstandings happen very easily."—*Jude in the Stars*

"Blake does angst particularly well and she's wrung every possible ounce out of this one. …I found myself getting sucked right into the story—I do love a good bit of angst and enjoy the copious amounts of drama on occasion."—*C-Spot Reviews*

Friends Without Benefits

"This is the book when the Friends to Lovers trope doesn't work out. When you tell your best friend you are in love with her and she doesn't return your feelings. This book is real life and I think I loved it more for that…"—*Les Rêveur*

A Country Girl's Heart

"Dena Blake just goes from strength to strength."—*Les Rêveur*

"Literally couldn't put this book down, and can't give enough praise for how good this was!!! One of my favourite reads, and I highly recommend to anyone who loves a fantastically clever, intriguing, and exciting romance."—*LESBIreviewed*

Unchained Memories

"There is a lot of angst and the book covers some difficult topics but it does that well. The writing is gripping and the plot flows."
—Melina Bickard, Librarian, Waterloo Library (UK)

"This story had me cycling between lovely romantic scenes to white-knuckle gripping, on the edge of the seat (or in my case, the bed) scenarios. This story had me rooting for a sequel and I can certainly place my stamp of approval on this novel as a must read book."—*Lesbian Review*

"The pace and character development was perfect for such an involved story line, I couldn't help but turn each page. This book has so many wonderful plot twists that you will be in suspense with every chapter that follows."—*Les Rêveur*

Where the Light Glows

"From first time author, Dena Blake, *Where the Light Glows* is a sure winner…"—*A Bookworm's Loft*

"[T]he vivid descriptions of the Pacific Northwest will make readers hungry for food and travel. The chemistry between Mel and Izzy is palpable…"—*RT Book Reviews*

"I'm still shocked this was Dena Blake's first novel. …It was fantastic. …It was written extremely well and more than once I wondered if this was a true account of someone close to the author because it was really raw and realistic. It seemed to flow very naturally and I am truly surprised that this is the author's first novel as it reads like a seasoned writer…"—*Les Rêveur*

Visit us at www.boldstrokesbooks.com

By the Author

Where the Light Glows

Unchained Memories

A Country Girl's Heart

Racing Hearts

Friends Without Benefits

Just One Moment

Perfect Timing

Kiss Me Every Day

Next Exit Home

NEXT EXIT HOME

by
Dena Blake

2021

Credits
Editor: Shelley Thrasher
Production Design: Susan Ramundo
Cover Design By Jeanine Henning

Acknowledgments

Some people say that their high school years were some of the best of their lives. That statement is one I cannot make. It was three years filled with emotions I don't care to relive. Happiness, sadness, and a whole lot of anxiety. In that same regard, it was part of a path that shaped me into who I am today. Hopefully, I'm a better person because of it.

Radclyffe and Sandy Lowe brought me into this publishing family four years ago and I have never looked back. Bold Strokes Books is the elite of publishers, from my exceptional editor, Shelley Thrasher, to the stellar production crew. I could not have asked for more. You all make my stories shine.

My writing family is the best. High school would have been much better had you all been there with me. I'm so happy to be included in this talented crew.

Kate—you are my rock. Thank you for always being there for both the good and the bad. Wes and Haley, my full-grown babies, I hope to always make you as proud of me as I am of you.

Thanks to all you readers out there. Without you my stories would forever remain in my head.

Dedication

To everyone who has ever felt different.
You are not alone.

CHAPTER ONE

Harper had her hands full when she pushed open the door. Daisy, her recently adopted red, cocker spaniel barked and sped around the corner, probably from Eden's room. Daisy slid on the hardwood floor as she crashed into Harper's legs and sat on her foot.

She laughed at the usual greeting. "Hang on, baby. Let me put the food down." She walked around her to the kitchen. "Eden. I brought dinner." She dropped the to-go containers on the counter as well as her phone, then squatted to pet Daisy, who tried her best to bathe her face with doggy kisses. She stood and went back out to get the rest of the bags from the errands she'd run on the way home, as well as her laptop from her Explorer in the driveway. Her daughter, Eden, was nowhere to be seen yet, but Daisy met her at the door again, with the same excitement, which made her smile. At least someone loved her.

She was ready to drop. Her day at the clinic had been busy and long, plus she'd had to make several stops on the way home to pick up a few items she needed for their drive to Blueridge. She probably hadn't needed to wash the white Ford SUV, but it was something she did before a road trip. She had no idea how long she'd been running errands. It had seemed to take forever, and the food wasn't ready when she reached the restaurant.

Eden rushed into the room, took the top off both containers, and settled on the chicken and broccoli pasta, her favorite. That left the usual side salad and boneless hot wings for Harper. She told herself that if she threw in a salad with her fried foods, they would be healthier somehow. The ten extra pounds she'd put on since her breakup with Vanessa this past year hadn't proved that theory.

After shedding her parka, which she hadn't really needed today due to this unseasonably warm February in Denver, she dropped it on the kitchen chair. She filled Daisy's empty dish with dog food, and now, with all the evening responsibilities done, she reached into the refrigerator and took out a vanilla porter. One of the three left from the Breckenridge Brewery six-pack she'd bought over the weekend. She wasn't a huge drinker but did indulge in a beer or a glass of wine on occasion. Since she'd found out about her father's heart condition last week, the occasion had become more like routine.

Before she could sit down, her phone rang on the counter. It was the clinic. She hit the green button and pressed it to her ear. "What's up?"

"Sorry, Dr. H, but an emergency's coming in, and I can't reach Dr. V." Jeremy wouldn't have called if it wasn't absolutely necessary.

Damn it. "She's supposed to cover tonight. She knows I'm going out of town."

"She's aware. I reminded her myself earlier today."

"I'll be there in ten." Her ex-girlfriend, Vanessa, always left the emergencies to her, since she lived closer. Even when they'd lived together, V deferred to her whenever something came up after hours. She hadn't minded then, but now that they were separated, split, or whatever they were, it was different. She minded a whole lot, especially since V was aware of her plans.

She should've known better than to get involved with V in the first place. She never failed to flirt with every pretty girl in sight, including their mutual friends. At first, she'd written it off as insecurity, constantly eliciting compliments from anyone who would provide a boost to her ego.

After they got together, she suspected, on more than one occasion, that something had gone on between V and another woman. When she'd questioned V about it, she'd just blown it off—acted like she was out of her mind—told her to get her jealousy in check.

She'd gotten it in check enough to not see the blindside when it hit her. She'd never suspected the affair that was going on between V and one of their closest friends—neither had her friend's wife. It seemed V's charm and money were hard to resist.

She was still kicking herself for accepting V into the clinic as her partner. Now it seemed she'd never be rid of her, and she'd still be doing all the work to keep the clinic running.

She slipped the porter back into the six-pack, then slid the hot wings and salad into the refrigerator next to it and headed down the hallway to Eden's room.

"I have to go back to the clinic."

"Okay." Eden didn't veer her eyes from the show she was watching.

"Are you packed?"

Eden nodded as she twirled a forkful of pasta and stuffed it into her mouth.

"Hopefully I won't be long." No response to that. She turned and headed to the door. Daisy followed her, and her sad eyes told Harper she wanted her to stay. She squatted, rubbed her ear, and kissed her nose. "I'll be back in a little while." She probably could take her with her, but she didn't know what kind of emergency she'd be walking into.

Harper paced the lab area of the clinic waiting for the emergency to come in. She'd be the first to admit she'd drunk way too much coffee today, as usual, and it was making her as jittery as a jackrabbit running from a coyote. Given the amount of caffeine in her system, she had no doubt she'd be able to outrun a whole pack of them right now. She glanced at the clock on the wall, then at her watch. It had been almost thirty minutes since she'd received the call from Jeremy for the emergency. She'd already pulled the dog's chart and read that Birdie didn't have any major health concerns. *Where the hell do they live? Is the dog better? Worse?*

"What's the woman's number?" she shouted to Jeremy at the front as she reached for the clinic phone on the wall. Before she received a response, she heard, then saw, the women as they entered the clinic, a blonde and a brunette. They were frantically describing the dog's symptoms as they came farther inside, their voices growing louder, echoing in the hallway as Jeremy led them to the exam room. The brunette held the tri-colored papillon in her arms while the blonde looked at Harper in terror.

She stroked the dog's cheek. "So what do we have going on with little Miss Birdie here?" She could see the skittering in the dog's eyes as well as the disorientation right away.

"I let her outside to go to the bathroom, and she just fell over. Then when she got back to her feet, she did it again." The brunette looked terrified, her eyes wide like she was remembering the incident. "I thought maybe something was wrong with her leg. I checked, and it looks okay." She started to cry.

As Harper continued stroking Birdie's cheek, she examined each of her paws, applying slight pressure to the pads, which didn't draw any kind of distress from the pup. "How old is she?"

"Twelve, and we're not ready to lose her." The brunette's lip trembled as she spoke.

"She'll be okay, baby." The blonde rubbed her partner on the back. "When we helped her up, she tried to stand, but she fell on her side." The fear in their eyes was palpable.

Harper patted the exam table, which she covered with a towel to give Birdie some traction. "Why don't we see if she can stand now?"

The woman placed Birdie on the table and reluctantly let go. She immediately fell to one side. Harper caught her with one hand and gently let her rest on the table.

"Oh my God. Do you think she had a stroke?"

"I'm not sure." It was definitely a vestibular system issue, and she couldn't rule out a stroke at this point. "I don't see in her records where she's been sick lately. Has she been shaking her head at all? Like maybe her ears have been bothering her?"

The women looked at each other and shook their heads. "Not that we've noticed."

She took an otoscope from the drawer behind her, fastened one of the smallest plastic cones on the end of the light, and looked in Birdie's right ear, and then the left. "Her ears look good."

"Then what is it?" The urgency in the woman's voice was clear.

She popped off the disposable cone and dropped it into the trash before she continued to stroke the frightened pup and gently feel the glands on her neck. "I need to take some X-rays of her head, draw some blood, and run a few tests to make sure something isn't going on with her thyroid." She leaned against the counter and crossed her arms. "Is there anything she might have eaten or gotten in to that might harm her? Chocolate, grapes, raisins, macadamia nuts?"

"No. She'll eat just about anything, so we're very careful about keeping those foods put away in places she can't get to."

She tilted her head to make eye contact with Birdie. "Has her head always tilted to the side like this?"

"No. Not at all. That's new."

"We need to move her to the back to get the X-ray and take the blood. You can carry her if you'd like." She hated separating owners from their animals. All that did was make both of them more anxious.

"You go," the brunette said to the blonde as she loved on Birdie. "I don't think I can watch them take blood."

The blonde nodded and waited patiently for her partner to give the pup a kiss on the head. She gathered Birdie into her arms and followed Harper through the door to the clinical area of the office for the tests.

Jeremy came into the room and led them to the X-ray machine in the corner of the area, where he guided the blonde to lay Birdie on her side and keep her calm as she draped a protective vest across the front of her. Once they'd taken the X-ray, they moved her to the exam table. The pup appeared calm as Harper slid the catheter into her front leg and drew the blood. Even though she was shaking, Birdie seemed to understand she was trying to help her.

"I'll run some tests, and then we'll know what's going on, or at least what's *not* going on." She smiled, trying to reassure the blonde. Harper wasn't sure at this point, but she didn't think Birdie was experiencing anything they couldn't control. They wouldn't know that for sure until she finished the tests.

Jeremy led the blonde through the door and back into the exam room.

"What do you think it is?" Jeremy watched as she prepared to test the blood.

"She's an older dog, with sudden onset of peripheral vestibular signs with no detectable cause—no signs of outer- or middle-ear infection, ototoxicity, trauma, hypothyroidism, infectious disease, etc." She continued processing the blood. "I think the blood will come out normal, but I could be wrong."

Once the results were ready, Harper was glad to see she was right. The only thing that was going to cure Birdie was time. She went back into the exam room.

"Birdie has something we call vestibular disease. Also known as old dog syndrome."

"What does that mean?"

"It means something has gone wrong somewhere in her nervous system, but we can't quite pinpoint it. It's kind of a wait-and-see situation. What we can do is give her something to help combat any nausea or motion sickness, but she doesn't need antibiotics since I don't see any signs of infection."

"What about steroids? Will they help?"

"There's no evidence that they will, and I don't want to give her anything she doesn't need. It might do more harm than good." She petted Birdie lightly. "The signs for vestibular disease are usually most severe during the first twenty-four to forty-eight hours, and many times the pets improve within seventy-two. The head tilt might stay with her, but usually that and the stumbling will resolve over a seven- to ten-day period."

"So, we should just let her rest?"

"Yes. Help her tonight when she needs to go to the bathroom. I think you'll see some improvement by tomorrow morning. Just comfort her and be patient."

As the brunette held Birdie in her arms, both women seemed to have calmed down, but she could still see the concern in their eyes. She took a clinic business card from the holder on the small sink counter and jotted her cell number on it, then handed it to the blonde. "That's my cell. You can call anytime if you have concerns." She usually didn't hand out her cell number but felt it would make them feel better to have it just in case.

"Thank you." The brunette slipped the card into her back pocket. "We really appreciate you coming back in and working late for us like this." She opened the door, and they walked toward the front.

"You're welcome." She stood in the doorway of the exam room and waited as Jeremy unlocked the front door and let them out.

"Hopefully she'll be better tomorrow," he said.

"Hopefully." She glanced at her watch before she took her key fob from her pocket. "I gave them my cell number, but let me know if they have questions and call the clinic number instead." She headed for the back door. "I need to get home and pack, so I can get on the road. I'll call tomorrow."

"Will do, Dr. H. Have a safe trip." Jeremy closed the back door as she got into her Explorer.

She fully believed Birdie was going to be all right, though convincing her owners had been more difficult than she'd anticipated. Nevertheless, this was not the way she wanted to start her trip. Being out of town when one of her patients was sick wasn't relaxing. It only added to the stress she was feeling about the drive to Blueridge. She was definitely going to get off to a later start than she'd planned.

After being greeted at the door by Daisy and giving her a thousand pets, Harper went into the kitchen, pulled open the refrigerator, and searched for the food she'd dropped off earlier. Gone. "Eden. Where's my food?"

One of Eden's friends, a boy—not a boyfriend—appeared from the hallway. "I'm sorry, Dr. H. I didn't know that was yours." He held up a container. "There's still some salad left."

She bit her tongue but screamed inside. She'd really wanted those wings tonight. "It's okay. I'll find something in the freezer." She yanked open the door, took out a Lean Cuisine frozen dinner, and popped it into the microwave.

She picked up the phone and called Pete, her best friend since childhood, whom she still talked to weekly. Thank God for unlimited call and text plans. He picked up on the first ring.

"Are you sitting on the phone?" She smiled.

"Oh, that would be jarring—possibly exciting. A definite new meaning for booty call." Pete was always quick with the jokes.

She laughed. "Stop. I will *never* call your booty for anything like that."

"What time will you be here? I have a nice bottle of wine to share with you."

Pete was sort of her welcome wagon whenever she went to Blueridge. He had a way of easing her into the indifference of it all since she'd detached herself from her hometown long ago.

"I'm afraid that will have to wait until tomorrow night." She sighed. "We had an emergency at the clinic, and I'm not even on the road yet."

"I hope the little bugger is okay." Pete was more compassionate than Harper sometimes.

"She's fine. Just a little off balance."

"Like me." He chuckled. "Maybe you should bring her to me."

"Absolutely not. You have trouble remembering to feed a fish, much less a dog."

"You can't keep judging me for something that happened so long ago."

"It wasn't that long ago, and yes, I can."

"Fine. No pets for me. I'll just continue to love on the ones at your dad's clinic."

She heard the cork pop through the phone. Probably drinking the wine without her. "How are things there since Dad had surgery?"

"Disorganized." He sighed. "Your dad can only handle so much over the phone. A couple people have actually gone out to the house and avoided the clinic altogether."

"Dad probably loves that." That wasn't good. The doctor had specifically ordered no stress and lots of rest.

"You know him. He's so easy."

"Yes. I guess he is."

"Anyway. Get your asses in the car and get on the road. Let me know when you're here. We'll have breakfast."

"Won't your spidey senses let you know that?" This was one of the never-ending jokes she'd used on Pete during the past decade. He didn't care much for them from others, but tolerated them from her.

He laughed. "Haven't heard that one in a long time. My senses are nil when it comes to you at this point, but we'll remedy that while you're in town. I want to hear everything about what's going and not going on with V."

"I'm afraid that might be a longer and messier story than you want to hear."

"I have time and napkins."

"Sounds good. I'll check in when we get close."

Peter Parker had been Harper's best friend since the second grade, when he and his family had moved to Blueridge. He always said he'd get out of there someday, but then he met Olive, the sweetest woman both of them knew, and found himself smitten. He went where Olive went, and she wasn't going anywhere out of Blueridge. Her family owned the sporting goods store in town, where Pete managed the business and Olive handled the books. Pete made the best of small-town life and seemed to be doing a great job at staying happy.

Harper could probably learn a thing or two about happiness from him. The next coming weeks would prove that.

CHAPTER TWO

It was just about seven when Addison got into her Subaru Outback and headed for Happy Tails. She was thrilled she was going to catch this morning's sunrise as it crept over the mountains. It was like fire dancing in the sky and made her wonder what it was burning from—what was on the other side. She'd been to the top of those mountains many times and already knew what was there. Always a beautiful sight—one she didn't want to ever live without.

During both the summer and winter months, she'd spent many mornings hiking up the mountains at sunrise to take in all the serenity. Of course she never went up alone and, in winter, always made sure someone with a snowmobile was waiting at the top. She'd never been much of a skier and didn't have time to improve her skills. Skiing down the mountain after hiking up required a ridiculous amount of endurance and mad skiing skills, neither of which she had.

Addison parked behind the clinic and went inside. She was the first one there, as usual. It had been a little lonely since Jim had been home after his heart attack. With both him and her mother at home rather than at the clinic, the usual social interaction she craved had been missing. Her friend Gemma's daughter, Jessie, the part-time college student they employed, didn't usually arrive until around ten or eleven o'clock, at least two to three hours after the clinic opened. Jessie had graduated high school the year before and was taking several online classes, some with morning lectures, but was usually there to work afternoons and sometimes on Saturday mornings, if they needed her.

The first thing she usually did, after getting inside and locking the door behind her, was to relieve the night watch and check every animal they'd kept overnight in the clinic, whether it had come in for surgery or wasn't feeling well from the night before. Then she'd perform physical exams on each one, so the information would be available for Jim, Dr. Sims, to create a treatment plan and note any findings before the patient was released to go home.

She took off her coat and scarf, then hung them on one of the pegs on the wall. Besides her and Jim, they had several qualified volunteers, but no one was there to relieve today. They didn't currently have any pets in for surgery or emergencies, which was good, since Jim was still at home recovering from his heart attack. If there were, he would insist on checking them himself. The man never stopped working. She'd been able to handle the routine visits herself, except for one that she'd called him about last week, and he'd guided her through it. She still had so much to learn.

She went to the office and turned on the computer to check the message board for questions. She could check it from the computer up front too, since all the computers had internet connections, but if she sat down behind the counter in the reception area, someone would probably tap on the glass door and scare the living daylights out of her. There were only one or two messages. She'd specifically set up the message board to field questions for people who couldn't make it into the clinic or didn't want to call. She was surprised at how many people didn't actually like to talk to people.

She glanced at her watch and headed out to the front of the clinic to open the door. Mrs. Cooper, the first appointment for the day, was already there, in her car outside. She opened the door and waited as Mrs. Cooper gathered up Chester, her five-pound Yorkie, from the front seat and came inside. Mrs. Cooper was always dressed as though she was going out to a special event—long coat, black slacks, and a silk scarf. Addison had never seen her wear jeans.

"How is Chester today?" She smiled and gave him a soft scratch on the cheek below his ear.

"Just here for his rabies shot."

"And I'm ready for him." She led the woman into an exam room and patted the exam table. "Hold him right here for me." She read through his history and then took Chester's vitals, listened to his heart and lungs, and felt along his tiny body for anything abnormal, like a mass or lump. "Everything looks good." She added her notes to his chart and flipped the folder closed. "I'll be right back."

She went through the door across the room into the lab area in the back, closing the door behind her, found the bottle of rabies vaccine in the refrigerator, and took a syringe from the drawer before she went back into the exam room. There, she held up the vial for Mrs. Cooper to check. She always brought the vial with her and showed it to the customer to prevent any unwanted mistakes, a practice she would probably be more comfortable with in time.

"Chester's so well behaved." The dog sat perfectly still on the exam table as she turned to the counter behind her and filled the syringe with the appropriate dosage.

"Are you going to give him all that? He's not very big."

"The dosage is the same for all breeds and sizes." She pinched the loose skin around his neck and administered the shot. "I won't give him several different vaccinations at the same time, but don't worry. He'll be fine with this one today."

Mrs. Cooper gathered Chester into her arms. "I certainly hope so." She petted his neck softly.

Addison opened the door and let Mrs. Cooper lead the way out, not bothering to try to collect payment. Mrs. Cooper had been a longtime customer and preferred to be billed, so that's what they did. She sat at the front counter and took out one of her veterinary books. She'd had plenty of time to study while Dr. Sims was recovering.

Her morning was going to be slow and repetitive, as she was only doing checkups and vaccinations. She thought so, anyway, until Kevin Ryan rushed through the door with his dog Munch.

"What's up, Kevin?"

"I think he ate a scraper. I was using it this morning to bake a cake before I set it on the counter, and when I went back to clean up, I couldn't locate it."

"How big was the scraper?"

He held his fingers about six inches apart. "It was plastic with a rubber tip, and you know how he likes to chew things."

She did know that. Kevin had brought Munch in several times before for the same issue. It was unlikely that he'd swallowed it whole, since it was so large. "Okay. Let's bring him back for an X-ray."

She led him to the corner of the lab area, where the digital X-ray equipment was located, and he lifted Munch onto the table without direction. He knew the drill. She took a vest from the holder, slipped it over her head, and handed one to Kevin, holding Munch while he put it on, then adjusted the camera. "Keep him steady until I tell you it's okay." She went to the computer console arm of the machine, adjusted the grid to the area of Munch's stomach, and clicked a few images.

She didn't see any major objects, but she would send the images to Jim so he could take a look at them. "I don't see anything that he wouldn't be able to pass normally. Your scraper might have ended up somewhere else. Hopefully not in the cake."

His eyes widened. "Oh, shoot." He chuckled. "At least I was baking at home and not at the restaurant."

Kevin owned the best Italian restaurant in town—the only Italian restaurant in town. It was one of Addison's favorites, and she loved his special ravioli, which he always made for her even if it wasn't on the menu.

"I'll send these to Dr. Sims to make sure, but I think Munch has gotten a bad rap on this one."

"Thanks so much for fitting us in." He led Munch back into the empty waiting room.

"You bet. Any time." It had been the highlight of her day so far. She watched him leave and stood by the front window, glancing from side to side to see if anyone else was pulling into the lot. The temporary veterinarian was supposed to arrive sometime this morning and was scheduled to start tomorrow. She was kind of excited at the thought of learning from someone else, but she hoped they didn't do things too differently. That might cause problems with some of the patient care when Dr. Sims returned.

After seeing several more patients, including a miniature schnauzer with worms, a cocker spaniel that needed an ear cleaning, and a pair of adult Labrador retrievers, she tended to one with possible joint issues and another with several hot spots that had appeared recently. In addition to that, she'd vaccinated three different puppies, which meant she had almost completed the morning appointments, and it was only ten thirty.

The afternoon schedule was very light, and Jessie would be there to help out, which meant she'd be able to study quite a bit. She was grateful to have the tech position at the clinic. It gave her the opportunity to get hands-on experience. When she'd gone back to school, she hadn't realized how difficult it would be—how much less her mind could absorb. Completing online classes to get her veterinary-technician degree and working full-time was taxing at best, and being a full-time parent in addition made everything exhausting.

She planned to attend veterinary school at Colorado State University in the future, if she ever finished her associate degree. She hadn't quite figured out all the logistics with living in Blueridge, which was a solid seven hours away from the college in Fort Collins, but when the time came, she would make it work somehow.

Jim had offered to help her with her studying, but that hadn't worked out as well as she'd hoped. He was very good at practicing veterinary medicine, but a lot had changed since he went to school. If she posed the question to him in just the right way, he usually was able to answer it. If not, she usually got a lengthy story with an example from a patient about something that had happened somewhere along the way during his career. Although interesting, those stories burned up a lot of her study time, so she'd learned to limit her questions.

❖

Harper's knuckles were white as she gripped the steering wheel. Her anxiety was going through the roof, and her rumbling stomach was only making it worse. She thought she was over her past insecurities, but everything had kicked in as soon as she'd seen the town of Blueridge emerge in the distance. Even the sunrise couldn't calm her as it usually did. By the time she pulled up in front of the clinic, she was ready to turn the car around and get the hell out of town. But that wasn't possible this time. She tried to put the pain aside, compartmentalize it, as she always did, and gain her courage. She hadn't been back since her mom's funeral, and that whole trip had caused a cluster of feelings she hadn't wanted to experience, and clearly hadn't dealt with.

Everything had changed so much since then. Her dad had moved the clinic from the small space in the middle of town to the edge bordering the highway that led to another isolated Colorado ski-resort town, which didn't have a veterinary clinic. After he'd lost her mother, bringing in more business seemed to be his focus, so being located next to the feed store didn't hurt.

He worked more hours, which made him ignore his health issues, which in turn had caused his heart attack. She'd thought it was his way of coping for the loss until, in one of their phone conversations, he'd mentioned his feelings for Patty Foster. That's when their contact had lessened. She hadn't taken that news well—it was too soon. Her mother had been gone for only a little over a year when they got involved, and she couldn't understand how he could move on so quickly. Attending the small wedding a year later was out of the question. No way could she see her father marry someone else. She didn't have it in her to watch everything change—for him to move on from her mother.

Now she didn't have a choice in the matter. Her dad was sick, and she had to step up to help, whether she liked it or not. That's what her mom would want her to do, right?

She glanced over at Eden, who was fast asleep with her cell phone in her lap and had been for most of the drive. Was it normal for a sixteen-year-old to be so engrossed in social media? So concerned about what others were doing—what others thought about what she was doing? It had been the same when Harper grew up in this little town, only social media hadn't been necessary. Gossip had spread like wildfire throughout the high school, and no one ever had the chance for rebuttal. Her stomach clenched as she thought about it.

She checked her reflection in the visor mirror. No mistaking the dark circles under her eyes. If she'd stuck to her original plan instead of leaving last night, they'd have been just starting the drive about now. But she'd had that late emergency call and drunk way too much caffeine to get her through it. By the time she'd gotten home, she'd been wired up like a greyhound puppy. Eden was already packed, but she had to do a load of laundry before she could finish. Once that was done, she loaded the car, and they got on the road.

Daisy leapt from the backseat onto her lap. "I guess you need to get out again." She was sure Daisy had to go to the bathroom, since she'd had to stop only once on the way here. She fastened the leash to Daisy's collar, took in a deep breath, and opened the car door. It was now or never.

CHAPTER THREE

Addison watched from the window in front of her desk as the white, late-model Ford Explorer drove up. "Who is that?" she said to the empty waiting room as a woman got out. She was the most gorgeous creature she'd ever seen. She vaulted from her chair to get a better look and watched as she lifted a cocker spaniel from the SUV. "Oh my God, she's coming here." She pulled a small compact from her desk drawer, looked at her reflection, and tossed it back into the drawer.

She sped down the hallway past Jessie, whom she hadn't heard come in through the back. "Thank God you're here early. I'll be right back." She rushed to the bathroom, tugged a brush through her blond hair, and fastened it into a ponytail. Then she straightened her favorite hoodie with the faded logo on the front. Right about now she was wishing she'd taken a little more time getting ready this morning. She pinched her cheeks, moistened her lips, and went back out front.

"Good morning." *Really. Is that all you can think of to say?* The woman wasn't wearing a jacket, so she couldn't stop her gaze from roaming from her red-and-black plaid flannel shirt, tucked neatly in at the waist, to her form-fitting skinny jeans. She was only a few inches taller than Addison, but the short heel of her boots made the discrepancy seem so much larger.

The woman smiled slightly and said, "I'm looking for Dr. Sims."

"He's not in yet this morning. Is there something I can help you with?"

"No. Not really. Is he at home?"

"He doesn't usually see patients at home."

The woman kept eye contact as she nodded and pulled her lips into a half smile. "That's good to know."

She craned her neck and looked around the woman to the Explorer parked out front. "Do you have a pet in the car?" She knew fully well she did. She'd seen her take the dog out before she'd run to the bathroom.

"Thank you for your time. I'll catch him later." The woman plucked her Ray-Ban sunglasses from her head, where they were nestled in her thick, dark hair, and slid them on before she turned and went out the door.

"But…" The woman was gone before she could say anything. Was this the temporary veterinarian she was expecting? From her last discussion with Jim, she'd thought the fill-in was a man.

Addison's feet seemed to be glued to the floor, but then she noticed someone waiting in the car for the woman. She immediately rounded the counter and sped to the window to get a better look. It was a young girl—one who looked a lot like the woman, but much more familiar. The car had Colorado plates, which meant she was local, right? Blueridge was somewhat of a tourist town, and they didn't get many new locals needing a veterinarian this early in the ski season. Her stomach dipped as the woman's electric-blue eyes flashed through her mind. Who was she? Who were they? Why hadn't she seen her around town before? And why didn't she bring her dog inside if she was looking for a veterinarian?

She rushed to the counter, picked up the phone, and called her mother at the house. "Some brunette's here looking for Jim." She fanned herself with a piece of mail from the desk. Not just some brunette, a gorgeous one with dark hair and light eyes. That perfect combination hit her hard.

"Oh, she's early." Patty's voice became muffled. "She's here, Jimmy."

"Mom—Mom! I can't hear you. What are you saying?"

"I'm sorry, honey. I had to tell Jimmy. We weren't expecting her until later this afternoon."

"Who, Mom?" She dropped the mail and gripped the counter. "Who weren't you expecting?"

"Harper. Didn't you recognize her?"

"Harper, as in Jim's daughter?" She dropped into the desk chair. That couldn't have been Harper Sims. She was too...perfect. "No way. She has a teenager with her."

"Her daughter, Eden."

This news was certainly going to throw a monkey wrench into her life. "Why didn't you tell me she was coming?"

"Well, we weren't really sure she would. We planned to bring in someone else, but after Jimmy talked to her, they decided that she'll help out at the clinic while he's recovering."

"I'm taking care of the clinic just fine. I've been working with Jim long enough to know how to do most everything he does."

"Yes. You have. But you're not a licensed veterinarian yet. There are some things you can't legally do without him there."

"People are fine with putting off elective surgeries for their pets until he gets back."

"We need to be able to handle emergencies if they arise, and Harper is licensed. She offered to help and Jimmy accepted."

"What the hell, Mom. She hasn't been back in over five years, and now you're going to let her take over?"

"Listen. Jimmy misses her. He needs this opportunity to make things better between them, so don't get in the way of that."

She ground her teeth together. "Fine. But you could've at least told me."

"I didn't think you'd care. You weren't really friends with her, were you?"

"No. But I'm keeping this clinic running."

"You're right. I'm sorry. Maybe this will free up some of your time for studying."

"Yeah. Maybe." The bell on the front door chimed, and she glanced up to see the postal worker delivering the mail. "I've gotta go. Talk to you later." She didn't wait for her mom's usual "I love you" at the end of the call. She was angry and didn't want to hear it right now. She hadn't really been friends with Harper when they were younger. In fact, she'd been crueler to Harper than she could ever admit, especially to her own mother. She dropped the phone into its cradle and paced the room. "I'll be back in a little while." She brushed past Jessie and took off out the door—she had to get out of this place and figure out what to do about this development.

Her system was on fire, reacting the same way it had so many years ago when they'd played Seven Minutes in Heaven at Harper's sixteenth birthday party. She'd been so pissed at Gemma, her so-called friend, for throwing Harper's name out there. Everyone knew she was gay, and no one had volunteered to go into the closet with her. It was cruel, and Addison hadn't been raised to be that way. Heat overtook her neck as the boys made shitty comments. She crossed the circle of jerks, took Harper's hand, tugged her into the closet, and shut the door.

She closed her eyes as she remembered the encounter and let the heat overtake her, just as it had then. Harper had told her nothing needed to happen. At that time, Addison had dated boys, and she'd never really considered dating girls. But she knew Harper had a crush on her, and it *was* Harper's birthday, after all.

"Thank you for not making fun of me like everyone else." Harper backed up and leaned against the closet wall. *"We don't have to do anything."*

"I know. I'm sorry about Gemma. She's an ass."

"She totally is, and she has a big mouth." Harper laughed. "I doubt anyone will chance one second in this closet with her."

The sound of Harper's unfiltered laugh did something to her— made her want to tell everyone to fuck off and stop worrying about what they thought. Not possible. They were all standing right outside the door just waiting for juicy gossip to spread. "If they do, it'll be all over school."

"In light speed." They both giggled, and Harper's voice became soft. "Why do you hang out with her?"

"You know how long we've been friends. If I stop now, I'll be the target of all the lies she spreads." She took in a breath and couldn't help but take in the scent of Harper's strawberry shampoo. She always smelled so good.

"I guess I can take the heat for you."

"You shouldn't have to take it either." Sadness filled her as she recognized the connection between them she'd never acknowledged before. Insecurity wasn't reserved for her alone. She just wasn't brave enough to face it. Not like Harper did—every day.

"I'm used to it."

She couldn't see Harper's eyes, only the faint outline of her jaw in the darkness as Harper stared at the door, probably counting down the minutes until they were released from this prison. She had to be dreading the trashy comments that would be made when they opened the door and exited.

"Happy birthday." She had no idea what had come over her, but she closed the distance between them, took Harper's face in her hands, and kissed her with everything she had. When Harper snaked her hands around Addison's waist and pressed against her, Addison hadn't expected the thrill rushing her—every inch of her awakened as their hips met. Suddenly she was on fire, and her groin was throbbing like it never had before—like she never knew it could. She surprised herself by deepening the kiss, grabbing hold of Harper and enjoying this new awareness circling through her. Seven minutes was way too short for the marvelous sensations engulfing her. When the kiss was over, she grabbed hold of something—anything to keep her balance, and ended up on the floor of the closet, pulling several coats off the rack as she descended. They both laughed, and Harper sat on the floor facing her.

When the door swung open, thankfully, all the other kids joined the laughter. The closet bar had been pulled loose, and everything in the closet was under them—on them—everywhere. It was the perfect cover for a few moments in time she would never forget. Definitely heaven.

She'd let the kiss happen—actually made it happen. She just hadn't expected to enjoy it so much. It was like someone had doused her with pixie dust, and she suddenly realized why she never liked to kiss boys. After that, she'd thought life in high school as she knew it was over. Harper would tell someone, who would tell someone else, and so on. Word traveled like wildfire amongst her clique. All the other kids would know soon enough, and she would be the talk of the school. But nothing changed. Harper had kissed her exquisitely in the closet that night—left her completely stunned and aroused, and didn't tell a single soul.

Gemma had grilled her, and Addison had denied anything had happened during those seven minutes. Harper had followed her lead and said the same. She was so turned on, and her face had to have been brighter than red, that it was a miracle everyone believed them, including Gemma. It was simply out of the question that, prim and proper, Addison Foster would delve into the unknown with publicly out Harper Sims. On one hand she was relieved she didn't have to endure the ridicule from the other kids, and on the other she was disappointed she hadn't been freed from the shackles this new discovery placed on her. She had locked herself inside a self-imposed prison that kept her from pursuing the amazing experience she'd shared with Harper.

After high school, Harper had moved to Denver, not a long distance away, only a little over six hours' travel time, five in good traffic. She'd been to Denver many times since then, but never had the courage to contact Harper. Still, after that night, Addison had never thought being with Harper was completely off the table. In fact, she'd always hoped for a second chance to make things right—for both of them. To at least become friends.

Now Harper was here, back in Blueridge, and all those feelings were resurfacing like a raging blizzard, the kind that makes you lose all sense of direction—the blinding kind with no end in sight. Just the thought of kissing Harper again made her wet beyond comprehension, and she definitely understood that fact now and wanted to act on it. Admittedly, she hadn't experienced a kiss so arousing since that night in the closet with Harper. Why hadn't she recognized that about herself back then sooner? Why had it taken her so long to find out how wonderfully sweet another woman's body could taste? Why hadn't she gone to Denver after Harper Sims when she'd realized it? Because Harper had moved on, and she was a fucking chicken. That was why.

CHAPTER FOUR

Harper hadn't expected to see Addison Foster within the first hour of arriving in Blueridge, and definitely not working at her father's clinic. Why hadn't her father mentioned that fact? She'd thought Addison was off in some other city living her happily-ever-after life. That's where she'd been when Harper returned for her mother's funeral. Harper knew that for sure because she'd asked Pete. Why the hell hadn't Pete told her Addison was back?

She took in a deep breath as she headed to her car. Addison was still gorgeous—even hotter now than she'd been in high school. Was that even possible? Even without makeup she was stunning, and it looked like she'd gained a few pounds, which made her even more sexy—at least to Harper. Practically stole the breath right from her lungs. There was something to be said for women with soft curves and swells. Why did high-school crushes never die? They only got stronger.

As Harper slid into the car, Eden hit the button and moved the seat back straight from the reclining position. "What's wrong?"

"Nothing's wrong." She glanced at Eden. "Why?"

"Your face is all red."

Damn it. Was it like that when she was inside with Addison? "They have the heat turned up way too high in the clinic." She had no idea how Addison could still get to her this way. She'd thought she was over that teenage crush long ago.

"Is Grampy there?"

"Nope. He's at the house." Still trying to clear the vision of Addison's amber eyes from her mind, she started the car and backed out of the parking space. Addison's eyes could always mesmerize her, and that fact hadn't seemed to change. Maybe coming home for a few weeks wouldn't be so bad after all. "We'll head out there after we have breakfast with Uncle Pete."

Eden smiled. "Cool. I'm starving."

She hadn't seen a ring on Addison's finger. Was she still married? Was she involved with someone? Was she still straight? All questions she shouldn't ask, hadn't intended to ask or pursue, but damn. She wanted to know all the answers. She was in no state of mind to learn any of those facts, specifically if it turned out that Addison was single and interested in women. After all, Harper wasn't staying in Blueridge permanently. As soon as her dad was well enough to go back to work, she was out of here, back to her clinic and life in Denver. Even if it was currently in a state of shambles.

She hit the call button on her steering wheel and said, "Pete" into the air. The phone connected and began ringing.

Pete answered right away. "Are you here yet?"

"On our way to your store now. Would've been here sooner, but I had to pull over and shut my eyes for a bit."

"The smart thing to do. Pull around back, and I'll open the door."

When she got there, Pete was waiting for her.

She killed the engine and jumped out of the SUV, then rushed to give him a hug. It was amazing how good it was to see him. She released him and stood back. "You look great. Married life agrees with you." He was dressed in boots, jeans, and a navy hoodie with the store logo on the front. His blond hair looked uncombed, but that was his style—one he'd picked up from working the lifts and then giving ski lessons at the resort. If she didn't know better, she'd have thought he grew up on the beach.

"I'm glad to hear someone thinks so." Olive appeared behind him, then pulled her into a hug. "It's so good to see you. It's been far too long." Dressed in boots, skinny jeans, and a red fleece, half-zip pullover, she was just as gorgeous as she'd always been. Long dark hair, blue eyes, and almost as tall as Pete.

"I know. It's not like we live that far apart."

"Come in. Sit for a minute."

"I need to get Daisy out of the car." Just then Eden jumped out of the SUV and headed their way.

"The heck with Daisy. Here's the girl I want to see." Pete locked Eden into a hug and lifted her off the ground.

"Who's Daisy?" Olive pulled her eyebrows together.

"The sweet cocker spaniel I adopted last month."

"Oh. Well, get her and bring her on in." Olive motioned them inside. "We're a pet-friendly store."

She retrieved Daisy and followed them inside into the office of the sporting-goods store. It was larger than she'd expected, tastefully decorated with sports memorabilia and furnished with a desk, couch, and several simple but comfortable chairs.

Olive took the chair behind the desk, and Daisy immediately followed her and jumped onto her lap. Harper hadn't expected that, but Olive didn't seem to mind. As she sank into one of the chairs, Pete sat on the couch, Eden plopped down next to him, and he wrapped his arm around her shoulder and squeezed.

"When did you become such a cute young lady?"

Eden immediately turned red. "Uncle Pete, stop."

"I mean it." He squeezed her shoulder again. "You must be giving your mom all kinds of trouble with boys lining up outside the house."

"Not really. No one's interested in me. There are a whole lot of girls more popular. And they have cars to get places."

"What's that about?"

"You're not getting a car." She veered her stare to Pete. "She's barely sixteen."

"That's the best time."

"Pete." Olive scrunched her eyebrows together.

"Fine." He leaned closer to Eden. "I'll work on them."

Eden's stomach growled and everyone laughed.

"I guess someone's hungry."

"I'm starving. Can we go eat?"

"We'll have to eat outside. After the six-hour drive we made, I don't want to leave Daisy in the car."

"You can leave her with me." Olive continued stroking Daisy as she slept on her lap.

"You're not hungry?"

"I'm fine. I ate before I got here."

Pete stood. "I did not. So, I'm with Eden. Let's eat."

"You're sure you don't mind?"

"Daisy is keeping me warm." She smiled. "Besides, I don't think Daisy would let me get up even if I wanted to."

"Okay, then." She stood. "I can drive."

Pete motioned her and Eden in front of him. "Let's go through the store. It's right down the street."

Harper was impressed once they got into the actual store. They'd increased their inventory a lot since she'd been here last. "The store looks awesome." She glanced around. "You must be doing well."

"We do okay. Olive wants to expand." He rushed in front of them and opened the door that led to the sidewalk. "She's heard a chain store's looking at locating here."

"Really? That's not good."

He nodded. "It would hurt, but I think we can still keep an edge. We know what people want and provide a lot of personalized service."

"Do you still have the contract with the ski resort for rentals?"

"Yeah. And thanks to Gemma, that's not going to change."

The name made her tense. "Gemma." She shook. "I haven't heard that name in a long time." Didn't really ever want to hear it again.

"I know she's not your favorite person, but she cares about the town and the people who own businesses."

"That's good to hear." Hopefully, Gemma had changed over the years since she'd had any contact with her. She'd attended Harper's mom's funeral, but Harper hadn't talked to her. She hadn't interacted much with anyone. After it was over she'd immediately wanted to get the hell out of town.

The diner was, indeed, only a couple of doors down from the store. After they got inside, Pete waved at the waitress and snagged a booth at the side of the restaurant. Eden slid in on one side, and Harper sat across from her. Pete took the menus from the salt-and-pepper rack and handed them each one before he went behind the counter, grabbed a couple of coffee cups, filled them, and came back to the table.

He remained standing and looked at Eden. "You want hot chocolate?"

She nodded and smiled. "Yes, please."

"Where'd she get those manners?" He glanced at Harper. "Not from you."

"Thank you for the coffee, Pete." She rolled her eyes and picked up her menu.

Pete came back with Eden's hot chocolate and slid in next to her. "Everything is good here." It seemed he was a regular.

Eden opened her menu. "Chocolate chip pancakes?"

"Especially those." Pete didn't look at a menu, just stared at Harper.

"What?"

"It's good to see you." He grinned as he bumped Eden. "Both of you."

It had been way too long. "The highway works both ways, you know." She gave him a small jab. Pete never came her way either.

"We really need to take a vacation."

Eden's eyes widened. "All of us?"

"Why not?" He leaned forward and put his arms on the table. "We could go to one of those all-inclusive resorts."

"That would be so cool. Could I bring one of my friends?"

"Of course."

"Hold on, Pete. I think you're getting way ahead of yourself." She shut her menu and slipped it back into the slot by the salt and pepper shakers. "She's still in school, and we both have businesses to run."

"I know. I'm not talking about next week." He raised an eyebrow before he glanced at Eden and then back to Harper. "Maybe in the summer sometime. Olive has hired a couple of pretty competent people at the store, so I think we'll be able to get away for a week."

"Come on, Mom." Eden gave her the sad puppy-dog eyes she always did when she wanted something.

"I'll think about it."

"Yay." Eden bounced in her seat and then gave Pete a high five. "I need to go to the bathroom. Will you get me the chocolate chip pancakes?"

"Sure will." Pete slid out of the booth so Eden could get up.

Eden rushed across the restaurant to the restrooms as the waitress came to the table. Harper didn't recognize her.

"You've got a couple of newcomers with you today, Pete."

"Not really new. Just back for a short time." He glanced at Harper. "This is Dr. Sims's daughter, Dr. Sims." He laughed as the woman pulled her eyebrows together. "That sounded weird."

"It absolutely did." Harper looked up and smiled at the waitress. "I'm Harper. Dr. Sims is my father."

"She's a veterinarian too. She's going to fill in while the doc recovers."

"Oh. Gotcha. I'm glad to hear he's doing better."

"Thanks." Harper picked up the menu to avoid more conversation about her dad.

"The usual for you?" The waitress looked at Pete as she took her pad from her apron pocket.

Pete nodded and hooked his thumb to the empty space next to him. "This one wants the chocolate chip pancakes."

The waitress looked at Harper. "And for you?"

"I'll have the sampler."

"Same as Pete. Chocolate chip pancakes?" The waitress slipped her pad back into her apron.

"Plain for me, thanks."

"You got it."

Harper waited for the waitress to get out of earshot, then focused on Pete. "Why the hell didn't you tell me Addison was back in town?"

He shrugged and moved his eyes back and forth. "Didn't think you'd care."

"I thought she was married and living in God only knows where."

He shook his head. "No. That didn't last long. Logan was an ass."

She leaned in closer. "Did he fuck around on her?"

"I can't say for sure, but it's more than likely. You know how he was in high school—all about himself. He's still single, I think."

"Doesn't she have a child with him? What about that? Does he help her at all?" What a jerk.

"I think so. He's not around much, breezes into town once in a while, but his parents make sure Brook is taken care of." He took a swig of coffee. "They kinda ooze money."

"Well, that's good." That must have been difficult for Addison. At least Harper chose to take on the parenting role, knowing it might be just her alone.

Eden bounced back from the restroom, and Pete stood to let her into the booth.

"Vacation planned?"

"No." Harper rolled her eyes. "See what you've started?"

The waitress delivered their food—a lot of it.

"This is your usual?" Harper would never be able to finish her order. She moved some of the bacon, sausage, and ham to the side of her plate. "You haven't changed at all, have you?"

"Nope." Pete dug into his eggs.

Harper took a bite of her scrambled eggs and swallowed before she pointed her fork at Eden. "You're going to have to help me with this."

"On it." Eden immediately swiped a piece of bacon and ate it.

"How long you here for?" Pete continued to down his food.

"Just until Dad is well enough to get back to work." She sliced a small piece of pancake like it was pie and slid it into her mouth.

"That could be months."

"Could be. Hopefully not." She'd made arrangements to stay as long as she needed, but was hoping to get back to her own clinic in Denver sooner rather than later.

"Cool. That'll give us time to do some snowboarding."

"Skiing for me, thank you." She'd never gotten the hang of using one board with two feet.

"Can we ride the snowmobile?" Eden had almost finished her whole plate of pancakes and was now making her way through Harper's extra breakfast meats.

"You bet." Pete was going to finish his food at a close second. They were so much alike it was ridiculous. "I got a couple of new ones last year."

Eden's eyes lit up, and warmth spread throughout Harper. She wanted more of this—Pete and Eden—but couldn't bring herself to come here more often, to make this town part of her normal routine yet. This visit would play a huge part in whether that would happen in the future.

CHAPTER FIVE

B reakfast with Pete had been fun and comforting. They talked a lot on the phone, sometimes daily, but Harper didn't get the whole Pete experience without seeing him in person, and that was something she dearly missed. Her nerves were calm when she'd left the restaurant and had remained that way while she drove, until she turned into the long gravel driveway that led to the home she grew up in. It wasn't much farther down the road from the main area of town, so she hadn't had near enough time to prepare herself for what she saw before her. The house trim had been painted dark maroon. Quite a difference from the beautiful slate blue her mother had chosen years ago. Also, a new side porch wrapped around from the front, with custom-fashioned rustic spindles and rails. Her mom had always wanted this addition, but they could never afford it before.

She pulled up in front of the house and parked. Eden immediately pushed open the door and went to the porch, where the front door was open with only a screen-door barrier in its place. She followed Eden through the door, and the scent of freshly baked banana bread hit her as she stepped inside. Oddly the smell both comforted and terrified her. She'd given up most baked goods years ago and wasn't used to smelling such wonderful scents or having such mixed feelings about them. She thought she'd left all that behind the last time she'd visited.

The door slapped closed behind her, and immediately her father captured her in a strong yet gentle hug. He wasn't much taller than her, but she felt small in his arms. She had no idea where he'd come from. "There's my girl." He released her. "I'm so glad you're here."

The familiar scent of Old Spice cologne filled her head, and she felt warm all over. How amazing. The comfort and security he gave her never faded.

"It's great to see you, Dad." She examined his face. He looked tired. "Were you napping?"

He shook his head. "Just watching some old westerns on TV."

She glanced around him to peer into the new doorway opposite the kitchen, where he must have appeared from. Her parents' bedroom was on the other side of the wall. "What's with the new doorway to your bedroom?"

"Not the bedroom anymore. We changed it into my office."

She wandered into the room and noticed a small desk, two recliners, and a fifty-inch TV.

Eden flopped into one of the recliners. "This is cool, Grampy."

"Looks like you've got yourself a nice setup." The perfect man cave. "Where's the bedroom now?"

"We built a new one on the back of the house."

She rolled her lips in. "You used the plans you and Mom had drawn up?"

He nodded.

"I need to get our bags." She knew she was being rude, but with the changes to the house igniting a firestorm of anger within her, she couldn't get any other words out.

"Hang on." He pulled open the door, put his hand on her back, and guided her outside. "I'll help you with that."

"Eden and I can handle it. I have to get Daisy as well." She'd decided to leave Daisy in the car until she'd made her entrance.

"We only have one extra bedroom here now."

She pulled her eyebrows together. "What?"

"Your room is still the same, but Patty makes pet toys and clothing to sell at the clinic, so the other one is a sewing room. We've remodeled a little."

"I see that." She didn't know how that was going to work with her, Eden, and Daisy, considering how small her room was. "I guess we can share."

"No need for that. We set up the old cabin for you to stay in. The windows are all new, so they open and close easily now. The heat and air have been checked, and the wood-burning stove should keep you warm in the living room."

"Okay. Eden will probably go stir crazy." She wasn't really okay with it, but this arrangement would give her some distance— time to get used to all the newness of everything. One-on-one with Eden wasn't the easiest thing in the world, and doing it away from civilization was going to be even more difficult.

"The cabin still has the one bedroom, though. We thought Eden could stay here with us, since it's closer to town."

"Oh." She didn't seem to have a choice in the matter.

"Just thought you'd like some privacy."

"That's not necessary. I can stay at the lodge in town. I don't want you to lose out on the rental income."

"Absolutely not. We want you to stay there. Thought it might make you feel more at home since you used to spend so much time there when you were younger. Patty went to the grocery store yesterday. It's stocked with everything you'll need."

The thought of that didn't sound at all appetizing to her right now.

Feeling more at home would never happen here or there. "Okay." She opened the back of the SUV, and Daisy immediately jumped the seat to get to her.

"This must be your new girl." Her dad rubbed Daisy's ears as he leaned in and let her lick his chin. "She's a sweetheart."

"Yep. She is." She still couldn't understand why anyone would want to give her up.

He lifted her from the back and set her on the ground. "We're between fosters right now, so she'll be a treat for Patty."

"Where is Patty?" She plucked Eden's bag from the back of the Ford Explorer. It wasn't nearly heavy enough to have the amount of clothes she would need. She'd probably planned on a little shopping spree at Pete's sporting-goods store.

"She's gone into town to pick up some things for dinner. She's making fried chicken." He walked toward the door. "Are you hungry?"

"Not really. We stopped on the way in and had breakfast with Pete. If you don't mind, I think I'll take a nap when we get inside. I haven't slept since yesterday, and I'm about to pass out." That wasn't completely true, she'd stopped on the drive, but she needed to rest before being confronted with the woman who had taken her mother's place.

"You bet." He held the door while Harper and Daisy entered the house. "Go on into your room. Patty should be home soon. Daisy and I will keep Eden occupied."

She went back inside and down the hallway to what used to be her room, dropped Eden's bag on the floor, and flopped on the bed. She could barely stay awake.

Harper tried to focus as she pried her eyes open. The room was dark, not even a nightlight to cast a glow across the room. How long had she been out? She searched for her phone on the bed. She'd been checking her email when she lay down. Apparently, she hadn't gotten very far into that before she was out. She finally found her phone, pushed the button, and it lit up—almost six o'clock. Wow, right at seven hours, more than she'd been sleeping anywhere lately.

She crept down the hallway and stood at the entrance to the kitchen, watching her father and Patty work the kitchen together, her cooking and him cleaning as each step of the meal progressed. The whole scene was unfamiliar. When she'd lived in this house, her mom did the cooking and Harper did the dishes. Her dad was rarely home before dinner was ready and on the table. Their playful banter was engaging, but also irritating. Were they involved before her mom died? No. She wasn't going there, not now. Not yet, anyway. The delicious scent of fried chicken sent her stomach raging with loud growls of hunger.

She threaded her fingers through her hair and moved to the stove. "Can I help with anything?" It was the polite thing to do, right? The correct thing to do at this moment in time.

Patty glanced up. Her five-foot-four, petite frame seemed inappropriate for such a large personality. "Oh, no, honey. You've had a long day. Grab a beer from the fridge, and sit and relax. We've got this." Patty rubbed Harper's shoulder.

The tenderness in Patty's eyes made it hard not to embrace her. She'd never actually congratulated them—never truly supported the relationship they shared. Somehow, it felt like a betrayal to her mother. She went to the refrigerator, pulled it open, and looked inside, where a six-pack of vanilla porter sat on the top shelf, surrounded by milk, juice, and sodas. She plucked a bottle from the cardboard container and sat at the table. Daisy appeared from the man cave and nudged her for attention. She must've been in there with Eden.

Even now, sitting in her mother's kitchen being welcomed with a perfect meal along with her favorite beer, she couldn't enjoy it. Shouldn't she be happy for them? At least grateful her father had someone to watch out for him?

"Jimmy, can you get me a jar of corn from the shelf in the garage?"

Harper's father headed to the side door, and Harper popped out of her chair, following him out with Daisy right behind her. The familiar nickname had just made it a whole lot easier not to be all in on this pairing. "Since when is it okay to call you Jimmy? You used to hate that." She remembered her mother correcting people when they used the nickname.

"Patty can call me Jimmy if she wants. I've known her since high school, and everybody called me that then." He went down the steps and sped to the detached garage.

She stayed with him increasing her pace. "But Mom couldn't?"

"Your mother had several nicknames for me, but Jimmy wasn't one of them." He gave her a sideways glance. "I didn't hate it. Your mother did. Said it sounded too country."

"So now that she's gone, it's okay?"

"She somehow thought formal names gained more respect. Put me on a higher social plane than others." He stopped, turned, and raised an eyebrow. "Seems you do too."

Her hands went to her hips. "So, now you're calling Mom a snob?"

"Of course not." His shoulders sank as he shook his head. "I'm not going to fight with you about this. I loved your mother very much, but that doesn't change the fact that she's gone." He began walking toward the garage again.

"Do you even miss her?" She couldn't stop the tears from welling in her eyes. "You even added on a new bedroom for Patty. Why didn't you do that for Mom?"

He spun around. "I added the room because I couldn't sleep with another woman in the same one I shared with your mother." He let out a sigh and pulled her into a hug. "Of course I miss her. That's why the old bedroom is *my* room now."

She sobbed into his shoulder. She hadn't thought about that. How hard it must be to live in a home where you'd lost someone you loved. She should have. Even though the furniture had been rearranged and some of the pictures were new, it was still her mother's home.

"Patty's a good woman. She takes care of me, and I like her company." He released her and held her by the shoulders. "You need to give her a chance. Can you do that for me?"

She nodded as she swiped the tears from her eyes.

He took her hand and tugged her toward the garage. "I think we should have some green beans tonight too. They're your favorite, right?"

She nodded. "Did you make them?"

"Yep. Fresh from the garden with your mother's recipe."

"Patty's okay with that?"

He smiled as he pulled open the side door to the garage. "She loved your mother too, you know."

If Patty could embrace her mother's recipes, house, and furniture, Harper would do her best to give her a chance, if only for her father. Even though she missed her mother every moment she spent in this house.

❖

As Addison pulled into the gravel drive, she saw Harper, her hands on her hips, following her father across the yard. She was quite lean and powerful, much more so than she was in high school. Jimmy seemed to be taking her presence in stride as he walked. She sat in the car for a minute watching until they moved out of her line of sight.

"Shit." She grabbed her bag and rushed inside. "What's that about?" She crossed the kitchen and peered out the window to see if she could spot them again.

Her mom turned the chicken pieces in the pan. "What's what about?" She set the tongs on the counter, wiped her hands on her apron, and joined Addison at the window.

"That." She pointed to where Jimmy was standing. He'd taken Harper into his arms and was holding her. She seemed to be crying— no, she was full-on bawling on his shoulder. Addison could see her chest heaving in and out. "What is she so upset about?"

Patty let out a sigh and went back to the stove. "She's not used to all this yet."

"All what?"

"The changes in the house. Me and Jimmy."

"It's been *three years* since you got married, Mom."

"I know, but it's not that long to her. Living in Denver, she doesn't see any of it." Patty shrugged. "Not up close, like you do."

"What happened to make…" she lifted her hands toward the window, "this happen?"

"I called him Jimmy, and she doesn't like that. Faye always called him James."

"Fuck, Mom. You're not Faye."

Patty snapped her head back and raised her eyebrows. "Watch your mouth, young lady."

She rolled her eyes and shook her head. "Sorry—but *come on*. She has to know you two are solid."

"She does, but that doesn't mean she has to like it." Patty took a cutting board from the counter, put it onto the table, and slid a basket of tomatoes next to it. "Now, get away from that window, and make yourself useful." She placed a knife on the board. "I don't want her to catch you watching them." She went back to the chicken. "Is Brook coming for dinner?"

She shook her head. "She's hanging out with Jessie tonight." She washed her hands before she took a plate from the cabinet. "I hope you fried extra drumsticks, 'cause I'm not sharing." The chair screeched across the plaid-patterned, black-and-white tile as she pulled it out and sat.

"I made plenty of everything, and you'll share just the same." Patty glanced over her shoulder. "You look nice tonight."

"Thanks. It was a messy day." Untrue, but a good excuse. She'd stopped at home and changed into some nicer jeans and a brown, cable-knit sweater, combed her hair, and made herself a little more presentable than she was this morning when Harper had arrived at the clinic. Although now, she didn't know why.

She stabbed the knife into a tomato. "You put up with too much crap from her."

"I'd do the same for you." Patty glanced her way. "Don't cut your finger off. I don't need any more stress tonight than I already have."

"You'd better put up with more from me." She continued slicing the tomatoes.

"I think history proves that point."

The side door swung open, and Harper entered carrying a couple of jars of corn. She clearly tried not to make eye contact. Her eyes were red, and Addison could tell she'd been crying.

Jimmy followed her in with two jars of green beans. "Happy likes green beans, so we brought a couple of those too."

Patty smiled. "What a great idea."

Addison raised an eyebrow. "Happy?" She had to hold her laughter as Harper narrowed her eyes and stared at her. She didn't seem very happy now. Addison probably shouldn't have contributed to her mood, but it irritated her how Harper swept in, and instantly everyone catered to her needs.

Her dad must have noticed the exchange. "I mean Harper." He glanced at Harper. "I forget you're all grown up now."

"It's okay, Dad." Harper kissed him on the cheek. "Is there anything I can do to help? Maybe mash the potatoes?" She lifted the lid off the pot of potatoes.

"Jimmy already took care of that." Patty pointed to the refrigerator with the tongs. "There are a few cucumbers in the crisper you can peel." She reached into the drawer next to the stove and took out a peeler.

Harper took the bag of cucumbers from the crisper drawer and dropped it by the sink.

Addison watched her and couldn't stop herself from saying, "You can't run the peels through the garbage disposal. It'll clog." She ignored the well-deserved look from her mom. Why was she being such an ass to the hottest woman she'd seen in a long time?

"Hmm. I would've thought you would've had that fixed with the remodel."

Her dad pulled out a chair and sat. "You can change the sink, but the plumbing still goes the same route to the septic tank."

Patty put a used grocery bag on the counter next to Harper and patted her on the back. "Put the peels in here when you're done. Your dad will put them in the compost bin out back later."

Harper took the bag of cucumbers and moved to the table, taking the seat at the opposite end from Addison. She stared across the table at her as she began to briskly peel the first cucumber. "Am I doing this right?" She raised her eyebrows and held the vegetable up in the air.

Well, this is uncomfortable. She jabbed at another tomato, and seeds spit out the side of it as Harper took rapid, jagged strokes on the cucumber.

"Should we trade?" Harper pointed to the tomato pulp on the table. "You seem to be having trouble with the knife."

"I'm doing fine. I just need a sharper one." She got up and took a larger, sharper knife from the block.

"Oh, no, you don't." Patty took the huge knife from her hand and replaced it with a smaller, serrated one. "This one will work better." She glanced at Harper's cucumber handiwork. "I've never seen two people do such damage to vegetables."

She glanced at the massacred tomatoes on the board in front of her and couldn't contain her laughter. Harper apparently appreciated the sight as much as Addison did, because she began to laugh too. Her eyes met Harper's, and suddenly the kitchen was quiet. She didn't look away—she couldn't. Heat overtook her just as it had this morning when she'd stared into those blue eyes. What was it about Harper that stirred her insides into such a virtual lather?

"Come on, girls. Finish up. The chicken's almost done."

Harper rolled her lips in before she glanced at Patty and then back to the cucumbers on the board. All that came next was silence, except for the sound of knives slicing through vegetables on the cutting boards. Keeping eye contact to a minimum wouldn't guarantee she'd keep all her fingers, but it was certainly a necessary precaution. How was she going to get through dinner avoiding eye contact with Harper?

CHAPTER SIX

As Addison finished drying the dishes, she watched through the kitchen window as Harper hugged her dad, then Eden. "What I want to know is, how did Harper end up with such a sweet daughter?"

"Same way you did, I suppose." Patty stood with her hand on her hip at the screen door as Harper drove away. "Couldn't you have been a little nicer to Harper?"

"Why do I always have to be the nice one?"

"You don't have to be, but you usually are. What's the issue with Harper?"

"I don't know." She tossed the towel onto the counter before she bent to put the last pan in the cabinet. "She just rubs me the wrong way."

"And you don't know why?"

"She's all full of herself and her veterinary practice in Denver."

"Oh, so you're jealous." Patty slid into the chair at the kitchen table and patted the spot adjacent to her. "No one's holding you here, you know."

"I know. It's not that. It's just that everyone is so far ahead of me in every way."

"So it took you a little longer to figure things out in life. You'll get there. You're on your way."

"I want to be there already. Schoolwork was hard in high school, and it's even harder now."

"At least you have Jimmy to guide you."

"A lot of things have changed since he went to school, Mom."

"Well, then maybe Harper can give you some tips while she's here." Patty raised her eyebrows. "I'm sure she would if you'd be a little nicer to her."

Would Harper help her? Would she be able to accept Harper's help? Would she be able to be around her for more than work? Why did she suddenly feel like an awkward teenager? All questions to which she didn't have answers.

She popped out of the chair and headed to the door. "I have to go home and study."

"Okay. I might be a little late in the morning." She glanced toward the chicken coop, where Jim had taken Eden to see the chickens. "Need to make sure Eden is settled in. Do you think Brook can show her around?"

She shrugged. "I don't know, Mom. Brook is almost eighteen and Eden's barely sixteen. I'm not sure they'd have much in common."

Patty raised an eyebrow. "Besides their moms both growing up in this town, you mean?"

She pressed her lips together for a minute. "Okay. I'll ask her, but I can't guarantee she'll want to do it."

"That's all I need. I'm sure I can find a way to persuade Brook if she balks."

"Don't you dare buy her that purse she's been wanting."

"Already bought it—was saving it for her birthday, but might have to give it to her a bit early." Patty winked. "She's just as easy to bribe as you were."

She opened her mouth, intending to dispute the claim, but she couldn't. It was true. If her mom was ever good at one thing, it was persuasion. She knew everyone in town's favorite things and how to get their buy-in on anything she needed or wanted. When Addison was younger, her mom made sure she had all the essentials and sometimes the luxuries too—just like the expensive purse Brook didn't need now. She was the queen of barter, and that hadn't changed. She'd gotten used to some of the finer things in life because of it, and she wasn't sure if that was good or bad. It might have been better if she'd just lived without and never known about them. But then again, she probably wouldn't have ended up with the circle of friends she still maintained. She could probably do without a few of those as well, but that was a whole other story.

Addison threw the car into gear and sped down the gravel road. She didn't live far away, which was nice sometimes and inconvenient at others. She was always fielding questions about who was visiting after her mom or Jimmy drove by and happened to notice a strange car in the driveway. Keeping her personal life private in such a small town was difficult.

When Addison arrived at her house, all the lights inside the house were on. She hadn't expected Brook to be home until later. Since the winter semester began a few weeks ago, Brook hadn't spent a single night at home alone with Addison. She was always at someone else's studying, which had made her realize exactly how alone she was going to be when Brook left for college.

She still had a few months until the end of the school year to get used to the idea, but it seemed to be closing in on her fast. Brook wasn't planning to go that far away, only six and a half hours to Colorado University in Boulder, but she probably wouldn't be close enough to come home every weekend and still keep up with her studies. The only good part about it was that Addison was in her last semester of veterinary studies to get her associate degree, and Brook's absence gave her the peace and quiet she needed to study. Nevertheless, that benefit didn't seem to outweigh the loss she was feeling. She pushed the thought from her mind. No sense stressing over something so far in the future that she had no control over.

Harper had mixed feelings about staying at the cabin. She wasn't worried about being alone. God knows she could use the solitude after the tumultuous past few months she'd been through with V. On one hand, her dad was right. Staying in the cabin would give her more privacy. On the other, she feared Eden wouldn't receive much parenting while she was at the house alone with her dad and Patty. Maybe she was wrong. Her dad hadn't been hard on her, but he'd always pulled the reins back when she needed it. She'd hated that at the time, but once she'd become a parent herself, she'd realized he'd done the right thing.

However, she hadn't been exposed to the city like Eden had been. That introduced a whole new set of problems to wrangle. Eden was a good kid—didn't get into a lot of trouble—but she was easily influenced by others. Harper knew firsthand what kind of trouble bored, small-town kids could get in to, and that's what worried her.

The thousand-square-foot log cabin seemed more rustic and more visible than it used to be, and the drive was shorter than she remembered. Some of the larger trees around the cabin had been removed, which gave the place a much better view of the mountains. A new rustic, split-rail wood fence circled the back, enough of a barrier to keep Daisy contained if she spotted any squirrels. She killed the engine, got out of the car, and helped Daisy to the ground before she took her bag from the back of the Explorer.

Then she punched in the number to the lockbox, retrieved the key, and slid it into the lock. The pungent scent of spruce hit her immediately after she opened the door. It calmed her—all the muscles that had been so tense all evening instantly relaxed. She hadn't realized how much she'd missed this place—couldn't believe how at ease she felt—so much more so than she had at her dad's house. She glanced at the vaulted ceiling and large glass windows and immediately felt like she was home, which was weird, because an hour ago she couldn't wait to get out of this town.

She rolled her bag into the single bedroom, hoisted it onto the bed, and unzipped it before she flopped down next to it and hit the button on her phone for Pete. Daisy immediately jumped up and snuggled in next to her.

"Hey there. How'd it go at dinner tonight?"

"I wasn't as nice as I should've been." She rubbed her hand across Daisy's belly. "Did you know they remodeled the house?"

"I did."

"Why didn't you tell me?"

"I don't know—thought it was something you should see rather than stew about."

"Fuck you, Pete. You should've told me." She rolled from the bed and stood.

"I love you too, Hap."

"And don't call me that. My dad said it in front of Addison, and she had a field day with it."

"Ooh, Addison was there? Did she stay for dinner? Did you talk to her?"

"Yes. She was there, and minimally. Caddy Addie is more of a bitch than she was before." She tossed her socks and underwear into the top drawer. "She's running the fucking clinic."

"Yeah. I knew that too. Doing a pretty good job of it from what I hear."

"Well, that's just peachy. Something to look forward to every day." She filled another drawer with several pairs of jeans and another with her sweaters.

"At least she's nice to look at."

She shoved the drawers closed. "As long as she doesn't open her mouth, we'll be fine."

"Don't bank on that. She's friends with Olive. Once you get to know her, she really is a nice person. Besides, I think you might still like her."

"Nope. Just gonna walk away from that time bomb. I have enough shit going on in my life right now." She strolled through the cabin and took a beer from the six-pack Patty had stocked here as well before she flipped on the outside light, walked out back, and flopped into one of the old chairs on the deck. It creaked and swayed from side to side, ready to collapse at any time.

"What was that?" Pete's voice was loud and concerned. "Make sure you keep an eye out for bears."

"No bears. Not yet anyway." She laughed. "You remember the Adirondack chairs on the deck?" They'd been there since she was a kid.

"Oh, Jesus. Are they still there?"

"Just a couple, and this one's on its death bed." Daisy jumped onto her lap, and the chair creaked even more.

"I'll call the fire department. With the amount of booze we spilled out there, the whole deck is bound to be a fire hazard."

"We did have some good times, didn't we?"

"Absolutely, and I know if Addie had come to only one of those parties without her friends, she would've loosened up. Who knows what might have happened."

"She's not gay, Pete."

"She's not married either." His voice lifted.

"Why are you pushing this?"

"I don't know. Maybe I want you to stay. Plus, you never know about Addie."

"Not staying." And she didn't want to think about Addie—someone she could never have. She flicked a stray pine needle from the arm of the chair. "Sorry. I can't. I have too much to deal with in Denver." And too much hurt to get over in Blueridge.

"Got it, but I'm still going to keep trying."

"Just don't be upset with my answer. Okay?"

"Okay." She heard Olive in the background. "You want me to come out and keep you company? Olive's okay with it."

"Thanks, but I'm going to hit the sack. It's been a long day." Even though she'd taken a seven-hour nap, she was still exhausted. The fried food hadn't helped either.

"Gotcha. We'll talk in the morning."

"Sounds good. Oh, and, thanks for everything, Pete."

"You bet. Love you, girl."

"I love you too." She hit the end button and set her phone on the arm of the chair.

She continued to pet Daisy as she took a few swigs of beer and let the chocolaty flavored porter settle in her mouth before the bubbles tingled as they entered her throat. She hadn't expected to be separated from Eden, but she didn't want to argue at this point, and Eden wanted to stay at the house. It was probably better—closer to town, more company, less solitude. Eden didn't do well with isolation, and her grandfather would keep her busy with chores around the place—something Eden probably hadn't anticipated. She'd learn more about animals and gardening. Now that Patty was there, sewing might come into play as well.

She picked up the phone and hit the number for Eden, who answered on the second ring. "You good there?"

"Def. You didn't tell me you were so cool in high school. Such a rocker."

She'd forgotten about the posters still on the wall. "Believe me, I wasn't." Spending hours in her room with her headphones on listening to music was far from cool.

"Grampy is awesome. He took me out on the Gator and let me drive."

"Not on the roads, right?" He'd taught her to drive that way. Moving hay, transporting seed, doing so many things on the farm.

"No, but I told him I just got my license, and he said I'd come in handy around the place."

"That's great." She wouldn't burst her bubble but knew Eden would get tired of being her grandfather's errand runner soon enough.

"I gotta go, Mom. Someone's calling."

"Okay. Be good, and don't stay on the phone too long. Love you."

"Love you." Eden ended the call, and Harper was left alone. Again. Except for Daisy, who was keeping her lap warm.

She took another pull on her beer before she closed her eyes and took in the silence that came along with mountain living. Today had been long and full of surprises—none of them good. Coming home had been more difficult than she'd anticipated, and if today was any indication, it was only going to get harder. She would have to keep better track of Eden than she did at home, for sure.

Once Harper had finished her beer, she went inside, opened her laptop, and began checking her email, which seemed to be more substantial than usual. She had several messages from her clinic staff, who missed her, which was nice. Working her email at night always helped relieve the stress of her day. She'd become an expert at hiding her emotions from her customers at work, which was a necessity. She had to keep her feelings buried and ignore the pain. Sometimes losing a pet was more difficult than anyone could imagine. Especially when you had to experience it on a regular basis.

Chapter Seven

A ddison's first day working with Harper was going to be challenging. She'd promised her mom that she'd be nice, and she would try her best, but she couldn't make any guarantees. She'd been there since around seven o'clock, checking the schedule for the day and making sure they had all the vaccines and supplies they needed to care for the upcoming patients. Harper had breezed in around eight and gone straight to Jim's office and closed the door. So much for getting along.

It was just before nine when Harper appeared in the lab area of the clinic. "Who's up first?"

"Well, the first patient, Juno, an Australian shepherd, came in for vaccinations at seven thirty. The second, Speckles, a terrier mix, was here at eight. The third, Snowflake, a cat, that came in at eight thirty, just left."

"I see." Harper leaned against the counter. "Usually my staff alerts me when patients are in the clinic and ready to be seen."

"Well, you were late, and I'm not your staff." Who did she think she was?

Harper narrowed her eyes. "I apologize. I wasn't aware the clinic opened that early. Last I knew, Dad didn't open until nine."

"*Last you knew* was a long time ago. We've been opening at seven thirty for years." She checked the schedule on the computer monitor in the corner of the lab. "Next appointment is at nine. Exam-room four. The chart's on the door." She didn't have to check. She'd put the patient in the exam room, but she was so irritated right now, she could battle the fiercest cat in the county in the rain.

"Got it." Harper pressed her lips together before she strolled to the exam room and plucked the chart from the container on the door.

Addison watched her strut into the exam room like she was the smartest person on the planet, but wished she hadn't. Even with Harper's lab coat covering her hips, she could see how they swayed beneath it as Harper walked. The woman was ridiculously sexy, yet infuriating as hell.

"Hi. I'm Dr. H." Before Harper closed the exam-room door, she greeted the customer like they were an old friend she hadn't seen in years. Ugh. The sickeningly sweet voice made her want to vomit. Harper sure put on a good show of being kind and caring for everyone else, but not for Addison. That seemed to be reserved for people who didn't know her very well.

Addison was at the front desk handling calls and checking in customers. She had her book open, yet she hadn't been able to focus enough to get even a few minutes of studying in.

Harper came out of the exam room. "Snowflake needs a distemper vaccination." She set the chart on the counter and made a few notes.

She closed her book. No use trying to study anymore. "If you want me to do it, you'll have to watch the front."

Harper glanced at the book and then around the clinic. "Are you the only one here?"

She nodded. "Jessie won't be in until noon today." She tossed the book into her bag on the floor.

"Okay." Harper slapped the folder closed. "I'll do it."

"Thanks." Why was she thanking her? Harper was acting like the prima donna of all veterinarians. She couldn't even give vaccinations herself now? Wow. Addison watched her walk back through the small hallway to the lab, enjoying the view, then cursed herself for doing it.

After about another fifteen minutes, the door to the exam room opened, and Snowflake and her owner emerged with Harper right behind them. "Thank you so much, Dr. H."

Harper smiled, that fake smile of hers, with her perfectly straight, white teeth emerging from her full, lush lips. "You're very welcome. It was so nice to meet you." She waited for the customer to leave before she turned to Addison, and the smile faded. "The vaccines aren't in any type of order. Do you think you could make time to organize them?"

"Probably not today."

Harper zoomed in closer and scowled. "Why not?"

"Again. I'm watching the front."

"When Jessie gets here, then." Harper spun, took the chart from the next exam room, and went inside.

Addison's temper boiled as she watched Harper walk across the clinic. Now her strut was just damn irritating. She couldn't wait for Jessie to get here, so she could have a break from Harper.

Thankfully, the rest of the morning had gone by quickly. Pretty much every minute was filled with appointments, and she'd kept her interaction with Harper to a minimum. It seemed like the whole population of Blueridge was scheduling now that Harper was here. She guessed they'd heard the clinic had an actual DVM again, which gave her mixed emotions. On one hand she was happy business was good again, and on the other she wondered why some of these customers, who had scheduled visits for routine exams, hadn't made appointments while she was handling them.

Harper came out of one of the exam rooms and handed the file to Addison. "This one's done."

Addison glanced at the filing cabinet. "It goes in there."

"Oh." Harper pulled her eyebrows together and tilted her head. "What an original storage area." She left it on the counter in front of Addison, then entered the next exam room.

Addison popped up to follow her, but the door closed in her face. Who did Harper think she was? Who did Harper think Addison was? Not her staff or her file clerk, that was certain. She picked up the file and went to the cabinet, then spun around and slapped it back on the counter, where it would stay until Harper either asked her nicely to file it or did it herself.

Jessie showed up soon after, at noon, on schedule. First thing she did was reach for the pile of folders that had accumulated on the counter.

"Leave them." Even though it was Jessie's job, and she always took care of the filing for Addison, she was trying to prove a point.

"Okay. What do you want me to do then?"

"Check in patients and get the phone when it rings."

Jessie glanced at the schedule and then looked at the stack of folders. "How many walk-ins have you had today?"

"A few, but most people started scheduling early this morning." Word travels fast in a small town. "I'm going to clean out exam-room one. Don't touch those files."

Once she was finished, she sprayed down the lab area and then went back out front where Jessie was sitting. She totally ignored the vaccines, even though Harper had asked her to organize them.

Harper came out of exam-room two, smiling as she talked to a customer. "We'll see you again next week." She walked with the woman to the counter. "You must be Jessie." She reached out her hand. "It's so nice to meet you. My dad, Dr. Sims, has said plenty of nice things about you." She glanced at Addison and then back at Jessie. "Can you set her up for an appointment next week? After that, would you mind filing these patient records? It seems Addison has been too busy."

"Sure thing, Dr. Sims."

"Harper or Dr. H is fine." Harper smiled. "That'll keep the confusion to a minimum when Dad shows up on occasion during his recovery."

"Cool, Dr. H. I'll get these filed right now."

Addison watched Harper as she went into another exam room. "Way to stand strong with me, Jess."

"What was I supposed to do? She's kinda my boss."

"I hired you, which means I'm your boss. She's just a fill-in for Dr. Sims."

Jessie shrugged. "Same difference to me." She took the folders to the cabinet and began filing them. "She seems nice enough. Why don't you like her?"

"What makes you think I don't like her?"

"Uh, the stack of folders."

"I was trying to prove a point. We all work together here, and no one is above doing any task. We're not going to do anything differently than we do when Dr. Sims is here."

"Gotcha." Jessie continued with filing. "But we don't let Dr. Sims file anymore because he gets them in the wrong place."

She shrugged. "I know, but it's not because he isn't willing to do it." She felt a little childish and was starting to regret even trying to prove her point. It had been a busy day, after all. But if Harper couldn't work with her, soon enough she'd be working against her. She wasn't going to stand for that.

Harper wasn't surprised to see Brook come through the door into the clinic, but she was surprised that Eden was with her. She hadn't met her yet, but Addison had talked about her at dinner the night she arrived. Brook was a couple of years older, and Harper wasn't sure she liked the idea of them hanging out together. Eden was still fairly naive when it came to boys and all the trouble you could get into when you ended up with a not necessarily wrong, but an older crowd. At least she thought she was.

"Hey, Mom. This is Brook." Eden leaned on the counter and grinned like she was about to jump out of her skin.

She glanced up at Brook—fully developed, beautiful Brook. The difference between sixteen and eighteen seemed like light years in their physical appearance. Now she knew she had something to worry about. "Nice to meet you, Brook." She finished the note in the chart she'd been working on. "No school today?"

Brook smiled. "Nice to meet you too. It's flexible Friday."

"Right." She'd forgotten about the days they were given for skiing. "What are you girls up to this afternoon?"

Addison came out of an exam room she'd just finished cleaning. "And why are you together?"

"It's not final yet, but looks like we're going tubing."

Jessie popped out of her chair. "Oh, yeah. I need to call my dad and make sure they don't have the whole place booked."

Addison rifled through a few patient charts on the desk that Jessie was alphabetizing. "Who books the whole place?"

"You'd be surprised. Lately he's had a lot of companies wanting to do team-building outings."

"Maybe we should do one of those." She looked at the ceiling and sighed. "I'd love to push a few people down a slope." Anything to get a rise out of Addison.

Addison glanced at her and raised an eyebrow. "Me too."

"Now that we've got that settled." She pointed at the two girls. "Why are you two together?"

"I went by to see Gran and Grampy, and they suggested I take Eden out with me tonight."

"I'm done with my homework." The what's-it-to-you tone Eden was spewing gave Harper the impression she was looking for opposition, which she was seriously thinking about giving. Then again, maybe she was only trying to assert herself in front of Brook. She flattened her lips and gave Eden a minute to contemplate her actions, which it seemed she did. "Is it okay if I go?" Her tone was much more subdued.

"Sure." She'd let her go out if they were at home, so she would do the same here, for a while. Even if her best instincts told her it was a bad idea. She turned to Jessie. "So if your parents own the ski resort, why don't you work there?"

"Because they already have all the office staff they need, and I don't like working outside in the cold. Plus I love animals."

Harper shrugged and tightened her lips. "That makes sense. I guess."

"Besides, I can only take so much of my mom."

"Oh yeah? Who's your mom? Maybe I know her."

"Gemma Mayfield."

"Oh." She drew the word out but tried not to reveal her dislike for Gemma. The woman had been a pain in Harper's ass all through high school. Always in everyone else's business. She probably hadn't changed much.

Harper scrolled through her social-media feed. Heat burned her neck as she came upon V's feed, and pictures of V and her new girlfriend filled the screen. They were near a hotel or lodge somewhere dressed in long-sleeve T-shirts and jeans. *What the actual fuck?* It definitely didn't look like they were in Denver. Panic shot through her as she continued to scroll and saw more pictures of them—in a hot-springs pool immersed in steam—having a candlelight dinner—cuddling by a firepit. "Damn it."

"What's wrong." Eden came closer and looked at the social-media feed. "Isn't she supposed to be working the clinic while you're gone?"

"Apparently we've had a misunderstanding." Either that or these were old pictures. She hit the clinic's number on her phone and rushed to the lab area. "Hey, Nick. Let me talk to V."

"She's in with a patient."

"You wouldn't be covering for her, would you? I saw her Instagram pictures."

"No. She's back. Took a day trip to The Springs."

"We both know that's more than a day trip." The Springs Resort and Spa was five hours away. No wonder they couldn't reach V the night of the emergency at the clinic. She must have gotten on the road right after she'd left work, which meant V wasn't at the clinic yesterday or this morning.

Totally V's modus operandi. V had a pattern—wine and dine, flirt and flatter, lots of gifts, and finally an all-inclusive getaway to somewhere warm and tropical. Harper had known it was coming soon because V had been with her new girlfriend for a few months. Harper's trip to Blueridge had probably messed up her plans for the all-inclusive. She wasn't sorry about that—at all.

"Who'd she bring in to see patients?"

"She pulled a couple of students from the college."

"Grad students, I hope."

"Definitely, and very smart ones. Everything went fine. We didn't have any major emergencies. Just regular checkups."

"Why didn't you let me know?"

"I didn't know until the other night after you left, and I didn't want you to worry."

"Next time, call me." She'd add it to the list of bad practices she was keeping as ammunition to use if V continued to pull her weight because Harper wouldn't sell to her.

"Will do."

"Is everything else going all right?"

"Pretty much, but everyone misses you already. The customers all ask about you."

"I miss everyone too. Call me if you need me." Before she got choked up, she slid the phone from her ear and hit the end button. She missed her own clinic, her own people, and, ridiculously, she missed V. She remembered their first trip to Cozumel. The villa on the beach, the fishing excursion, fresh seafood, tropical drinks, all the sleepless nights when they couldn't get enough of each other. That was all dead now.

"Is everything okay?" Addison's voice startled Harper out of her thoughts.

"Just some miscommunication in Denver." More like the typical non-communication from V. The usual as of late. She wondered if Eden had filled Addison in about V when she'd left the room. She wasn't in the mood to explain that situation right now.

"Anything I can do to help?"

"Thanks, but no. It's something I have to deal with myself." And she would deal with it soon. One way or another, V would end up being a silent partner in her practice. She should've known better than to mix business with pleasure. She'd made so many mistakes after meeting V, but she was charming and sweet—seemed to anticipate Harper's every need. Sucked her in until Harper had added her to the practice—accepted her money when it was hard to make ends meet. All things she now regretted. The practice she'd worked so hard to rebuild was not only hers anymore. It was partially owned by a narcissist who would never let go.

Addison was deep in her thoughts about what Eden had told her about Harper's phone call, when the door flew open and

Riley swept inside. "Hey, love. I was down this way and thought I'd stop in."

"What are you doing away from the shop?"

"Claire's watching things while I went to get coffee." Riley rushed behind the counter. "I brought you a latte."

"Thanks." She grinned. Riley was her oldest and dearest friend. They'd known each other since elementary school. Had each other's back through thick and thin before their group of friends grew. They were each other's ride or die when things got rough.

Riley glanced at Jessie. "Sorry, sweetheart. I didn't know you were working today, or I would've brought you one too."

"It's okay. We can share." She grabbed an empty Styrofoam cup from the waiting room, poured some into it, and handed it to Jessie.

"Are you wearing eye makeup?" Riley moved closer, pulled her brows together. "I can't remember the last time I've seen you do that."

"I just felt like it today."

The exam room door clicked open. "It's great to see you again too." Harper's voice carried through the clinic as she walked out with a customer and then watched the woman carry her cat out the door. She set the patient chart on the edge of the counter, then smiled. "Riley. Nice to see you again." She turned, went to the next full exam room, took the chart from the door, and went inside.

"Just felt like it, huh?"

She rolled her eyes and shook her head. "Shut up and get out of here."

"Okay." Riley sang the word as she moved toward the door. "But we're going to talk about this later."

Addison turned to Jessie. "Not a word from you about this either." She bopped her on the shoulder and then went into the back room. She had no idea what was going on inside her head. One minute, Harper irritated the fuck out of her, and the next her gentle nature with the animals was making her heart thump.

Addison had managed to stay out of Harper's way for the remainder of the afternoon, taking history and handling lab samples.

She was reluctant to let Jessie go home early, but she'd finished all the filing, and Harper was in exam-room three with the last patient of the day. It seemed that all four exam rooms were full the whole afternoon. She didn't know how they'd managed it and still be able to finish at a decent hour. That never happened when Jim was in the clinic.

After the last patient left the office, Harper dropped the last folder onto the counter. "So, tell me something."

She glanced up to see Harper staring at her. "What?"

"Are we friends?" Harper tilted her head. "Enemies?"

She shrugged. "I don't really know what we are."

"I can accept that. It's an honest answer." Harper put her elbows on the counter, crossed her arms, and leaned closer. "Well, since we both have to work here and will be seeing a lot of each other, how about we start over?"

"You mean pretend you're not a self-absorbed tyrant who thinks scut work is below her?"

Harper raised an eyebrow and gave her a half smile. "I'll do my best to make that untrue. If you agree to meet me halfway." She held out her hand. "Deal?"

"Deal." She reluctantly took Harper's hand—irritated at herself for the jolt that hit her when she felt the softness of Harper's hand in hers. This complication wasn't at all what she needed in her life right now.

CHAPTER EIGHT

Harper took the steaks she'd picked up on her way home from the bag, unwrapped them, and put them on a plate. On her grocery run, she'd also purchased several types of steak seasoning, but she wasn't sure she was in the mood for more than only salt and pepper tonight. She hated to ruin a good piece of meat by adding too many flavors. Steak fries were usually a must, but she didn't have the energy to fry them in a pan the way she liked, so she'd opted for baking potatoes instead.

She washed and dried them thoroughly before she rubbed them with butter, applied a generous amount of kosher salt, and then wrapped them in foil. The oven beeped, preheated to the right temperature, and she put the potatoes on the oven rack. She made a couple of extras in case Olive and Eden decided to join them. If not, she'd use them for breakfast fried potatoes. She washed and chopped the zucchini and yellow squash, along with some white onion and button mushrooms, and dropped them all into a swatch of foil before she sliced a chunk of butter and placed it on top, then sprinkled them with garlic powder, onion powder, salt, and fresh ground pepper. They would go on the grill next to the steaks.

After she plucked a beer from the six-pack in the refrigerator, she glanced around the living room. It looked presentable enough. Pete would be here soon, so maybe she should change out of her jeans and dark-blue, button-down shirt, but she was too tired, and it was still clean. Thankfully, no accidents today, of her own making or by any patients. She flopped into the recliner in the living room.

She had no idea her father's clinic would be so busy, even on the only Saturday of the month they were open. The number of patients she'd seen today was impressive, as was the appointment schedule for the next week. The practice had certainly grown since she'd helped out there as a teenager. She'd thought she was going to get some time to relax while she was here, maybe do some skiing, even hiking if she was still here when the snow melted lower on the mountains some. She could always hike in the snow, but then she couldn't go alone. No serenity in that.

The knock on the door preceded it opening, and she heard Pete's loud bellow. "Honey. I'm home. Where's my beer?"

She chuckled as she got up from the chair. Pete was anything but a chauvinist. "It's in the refrigerator, dear. Where it always is."

He met her halfway across the living room and swept her into a hug. "Did I tell you how glad I am that you're here?"

"You did, and me too. I think." She held onto his shoulders as he kept her feet from the floor. "I'd be happier if you'd put me down." At a little over six feet tall, Pete was lean and fit. Even though she was fairly athletic, Pete never failed to surprise her with his strength.

"Oh, sorry." He dropped her to the floor, took off his black puffer jacket, and tossed it onto the couch before he went to the kitchen. "What's for dinner?"

"What do you think?" She watched him walk around the counter and peruse the food.

"Ooh, steak. My favorite." He opened the foil pouch to check its contents before he stole a piece of squash and popped it into his mouth. "Olive's not going to make it. She's closing tonight."

"She still does that?"

"On occasion, just to let the staff have a break on the weekends." He grabbed another piece of squash and resealed the foil.

"So why tonight? It's not because of me, is it?" Her stomach dropped at the thought that Olive might have issues with her and Pete's friendship after all these years.

He pulled his eyebrows together and shook his head. "Absolutely not. The schedule comes out two weeks in advance. We didn't know you were gonna be here." He circled his finger around the food. "We can do this again next week. Right?"

She grinned, relieved there wasn't an issue. "We can do it every week—every night, if you want."

"That'll last about three days before you're tired of me." He chuckled. "I'll see if I can get Olive on board."

"You know I'll never get tired of you."

"Now you're just blowing sunshine up my ass."

"Oh, my God. *I so am*. You know me too well." She reached into the refrigerator, took out a beer for Pete and another for herself. He grabbed both beers from her, opened them, and handed one back to her. She held hers up and clinked it against Pete's "Whatever works."

"Where's the pup?"

"Out back. She loves the yard." She headed to the back door that she'd left open just enough for Daisy to get in and out. Pete followed her out onto the deck.

"She won't go through the fence?"

"Hasn't yet. The rails are too close for her to get through. She's not really a runner."

"Not like her mama, huh?"

"Fuck you, Pete."

He whistled, and Daisy immediately looked up from where she was sniffing by the fence and trotted across the yard, her ears flopping as she ran. He knelt down to rub them, and she rolled to her side for him to scratch her belly. "She sure is sweet."

"Yeah. I can't imagine why her owner didn't want her. The guy who brought her to the clinic was kind of an ass and seemed to care more about getting rid of her than finding a good home for her."

"Well, she's better off with you anyway." He stood and walked to one of the Adirondack chairs.

"Don't sit in that one." She pulled it to the side of the deck. "It's about to collapse, and I don't want any lawsuits."

"A free ride for the rest of my life. Just what I've been looking for." He raised his eyebrows. "Your dad's homeowners would cover it, right?"

"Not a chance."

"You buy propane?"

She shook her head. "Dad keeps it full for renters."

"Dad's awesome." He turned on the propane and fired up the grill. "I'm cooking, right?"

"Says the Blueridge grill master. I would never presume to take that privilege away from you."

He grinned. "Just checking."

Pete took a seat in one of the folding chairs she'd found in the shed. "I thought Eden was coming."

"She'll probably blow in just in time to eat." She sat in the chair across from him. "Dad's been letting her drive Mom's Ford Escape—using her as his errand girl." She took a pull on her beer. "I'm sure she'll get bored with that soon and want to get to know some of the other kids her age in town."

Pete pulled his lip into a half-cocked smile. "You sure you want to let her do that? I mean, there's only so much to do in this little town." He stood and began cleaning the grill. "Remember all the shit we used to get into up on the mountain?"

"I'm thinking that was more you than me."

He grinned. "Maybe."

"So, tell me what I should be worried about."

"The normal stuff." He hung the grill brush on the hook and closed the lid. "Looking for empty cabins with unlocked doors. Drinking, hanging out, having sex. The normal stuff." He drained the rest of his beer. "You want another?"

"Wait." She put up her hand. "*You* were having sex in high school? With who?"

"Gemma."

She let her mouth drop open. "Gemma Mayfield? Judgiest bitch of all time?"

"The one and only." He headed inside to get another beer.

"You never told me that." She waited patiently for him to return.

"Well, that wouldn't be proper, now would it?" He appeared with two more beers and the steaks.

"But I'm your best friend."

"*You* didn't tell *me* you kissed Addison at your sixteenth birthday party, either." He set one beer on the table and carried the steaks to the grill before he opened the other.

Heat filled her. She hadn't told anyone. "How did you know that. Did she tell you?" She spoke in a rushed whisper, like someone else might hear.

"No. Of course not." He scrunched his lips. "I'm not stupid. I could see it on your face when you came out. No pun intended." He laughed as he put the steaks on the grill.

"I never could get anything past you. Still can't."

He grinned. "I wasn't sure, but now that you've confirmed, why didn't you tell me?"

"You know. The crush thing. I didn't want her to never talk to me again. All of her friends would either hate me—her—or both of us, and then she would hate me for sure."

"Did you guys ever talk about it?"

"No. Never. She acted like it never happened. Pretty much ignored me for the rest of high school anyway."

"Hmm." He raised his eyebrows. "Maybe you're the one that got away."

She hadn't thought of that. She tossed a chair pillow at him. "No fucking way. She fell in love—got married—had a baby."

"I don't think she fell in love. Technically they were together because she got pregnant." He took a pull on his beer and turned the steaks. "And they were never legally married—never got a license or signed anything."

"She had to have felt something for the guy, or she wouldn't have stayed with him, right?"

"That's not what I hear. From what Olive told me, it was rocky from the start."

"So, what happened? I mean, who made the choice to split?"

"He just left."

"Are you fucking serious?" Now she was ready for another beer. She reached for it, but Pete swiped it first, opened it, and handed it to her.

"Yep. So she moved back here with her folks, and that was it."

"What an asshole." The picture of Addison on her own with a baby flashed through her mind, and her stomach clenched. "What about Brook? Does he see her at all?"

"Not really. He stops by when he blows through town every once in a while to see his parents, but that's about it."

"Jesus."

"What are you so upset about? She wasn't any worse off than you were. Except you had me." He grinned.

"Not sure if that was much of a plus." She rolled her eyes at his hurt expression. "Just kidding. I don't think I would've made it without you."

"Ah, you would've been fine, but I'm glad I'm part of Eden's life. Where is the little shit, anyway?"

"Hang on. I'll text her."

Are you coming to dinner? Uncle Pete wants to see you.

She didn't see any bubbles appear, so she set her phone on the table. It chimed almost immediately, and before she could read the text, Eden came through the door.

Pete hauled Eden into a hug. She seemed tiny in his arms. "I knew you wouldn't skip out on dinner."

"Nope. Not on steaks cooked by Blueridge's grill master."

"I see how you are."

Eden chuckled. "Are they ready yet?"

He raised the top of the grill. "You have perfect timing. They're just about to come off."

Harper handed him a plate to put the steaks on and tossed an oven mitt to Eden. "Grab the veggies, and I'll get the potatoes out of the oven."

"What kind?"

"Squash."

"As long as it's not brussels sprouts."

"What do you have against sprouts?" He carried the steaks inside.

"They're icky."

"I've got a recipe to roast them with balsamic vinegar that you'll love. They get all sweet and crunchy." His eyes glazed over as though he could taste them right now. "I'll bring some next time."

Eden shook her head. "Nope. Mom's pulled that on me before."

"Not even a taste? Even with balsamic? When did you get so picky?"

Harper laughed. "Always has been." She carried the potatoes to the table and then went back for the plates. "Eden, can you grab some silverware and napkins?"

"On it." Eden rushed to the kitchen.

Pete set the plate of steaks in the middle of the table. "She's a tough sell."

"You don't even know the half of it." She grinned. "You'd better hurry and get the biggest steak, or she'll take it."

"She's got a little of me in her after all." He snatched up the steak and dropped it onto his plate before he did the same for Harper and Eden.

"She's got a lot of you in her."

Harper took the seat across from Pete so Eden could sit adjacent to each of them. It had been a few months since they'd seen each other, and she knew he'd want to catch up.

"If we had mushrooms, I'd eat them." Eden began slicing a piece of her steak and cut it into smaller bites before she began eating.

"My bad. I forgot." Harper speared a piece of squash and put it into her mouth.

"How about cauliflower?" Pete sliced off a piece of steak and did the exact same thing as Eden. It was uncanny how much of him had come through in her.

Eden grimaced as she chewed. She continued eating like she was in a hot-dog-eating contest at Coney Island.

"Hey. Slow down. There's plenty more. Pete won't eat it all."

She shoved a few more bites into her mouth before she stood. "I gotta get back to Grampy's."

"Eat and run, why don't you?" Pete wasn't one to hold back.

"I told him I'd be back to help feed the chickens. He got a new rooster today. A Sebright. Did you know there's a pecking order with chickens?" Eden's face lit up.

"I did." Harper smiled at Eden's excitement. "Guess who used to help with the chickens before you came along?"

"There's so many fancy ones. They're so cool."

Pete frowned. "Now I'm depressed. I've been placed lower on the cool list than the chickens." He dropped his knife and fork onto his plate.

Eden grinned. "Come on, Uncle Pete. You know you're on the top of my list." She took her plate to the kitchen. "It's just tonight you're behind the chickens…and Grampy."

"Okay. I can move down a slot for him, but no one else."

Harper held up her hand. "Afraid that makes you number four now."

He hit the table lightly with his fist. "Now, that's just not going to fly."

Eden laughed, rushed back to the table, and kissed Harper and then Pete on the cheek. "I'll see you tomorrow, if you're lucky." She turned and rushed out the door.

"I guess Dad has a new helper." Harper laughed. "Wonder where she gets that confidence?" She was so much like Pete it was uncanny.

"She could've picked up some of my bad traits, right?"

"Don't get me wrong. I'm very grateful she seems to have gotten the best of you." She chuckled. "Just remember she got a little of me too. The chickens prove that."

He puffed out his chest. "Chickens, schmickens." He dug into his steak again.

"You are so full of yourself."

"Someone has to be."

"How does Olive like this side of you?"

"She blows me off. We both know who's boss in our relationship."

"I'm glad you ended up with a woman who can take charge of that ego." She took in a deep breath and debated asking the next question. "So why'd you never go public about Gemma?"

He shrugged. "It was only a few times—never permanent. She wanted someone with more potential. Once I blew my shoulder out in baseball, I was never gonna be one of those rich guys."

"Better you found out then, right?"

"Yep. She married some helicopter pilot who owns his own business dropping people skiing on the mountain. He has an interest in the lodge too."

"Wow. She did well for herself."

"Seems that way."

She couldn't help but notice the change in Pete's mood. It seemed maybe he liked Gemma more than he let on, even though he'd found someone so much more suited for himself in Olive. Maybe it was the rejection that got to him. It certainly got to Harper.

"Did anyone at all know?"

"Her close circle of friends. Riley and Addison." He took another pull on his beer. "So how's it working with Addison?"

"Addison." She blew out a breath. "She's a piece of work."

"Oh yeah?" He lifted his eyebrows and shoveled a bite of potato into his mouth.

"Yeah. She's being difficult at the clinic." She gave him a flat smile. "Guess she doesn't like me there."

"Probably doesn't. Your dad sees the patients, but she's been running the place for a long time."

"That explains a lot." She didn't realize her dad had taken such a backseat in the day-to-day operations. "We definitely have different work styles."

"What do you mean by styles?"

"I'm used to being in my own clinic, where the front desk runs smoothly. That's not happening here." She poked around the middle of her potato, swept a nice mixture onto her fork, and then put it into her mouth. They'd turned out really well.

"Ah. She doesn't do everything you say."

"These potatoes are really good." She took another bite.

Pete cut a huge bite of steak and held it in front of his mouth. "Tell me."

"It's not that she doesn't do what I say. It's that she doesn't do anything expected of the office staff." She dropped her fork to the plate. "And I'm pretty sure she does the exact opposite of whatever I ask her just to piss me off."

"You can't blame her. She's not really the office staff. She's a vet tech. Patty usually handles the front office when your dad's there."

She sliced and took a bite of her steak, thinking about his remark while she chewed. "I guess I hadn't thought about that." She set down her fork and grabbed her beer. "So, you think I'm being unreasonable?"

"I think you should look at it from her perspective."

"And that is?"

"She's been working in the clinic for years, and everything's been running smoothly. Then your dad has a heart attack, and she has to run the clinic alone." He took another bite, chewed, and swallowed. "Then you come to town and take over." He poked a couple pieces of squash with his fork. "How would you feel?"

"I'd be pretty fucking pissed off."

He laid his fork on the plate and held up his beer. "There you go. Attitude explained."

"But not excused." She clinked her beer against his.

"Agreed." He relaxed into his chair. "I think it'll change if you take a different approach. Maybe help out with the grunt work some."

"You mean scut work."

He raised his eyebrows. "Semantics. Does it make a difference what it's called?"

She rolled her eyes. "No. I guess not." She drank the rest of her beer and set it on the table. "Okay. I'll try it."

"I can't wait to hear how the honey works versus the vinegar."

"Not sure it will make much difference. Addison doesn't really like me. Never has."

"I'm gonna guess that's probably not true."

"She sure acts like it."

"I refer back to my previous observation. You're the witch who flew in from Denver and dropped a house on her life."

"First off, it was a tornado that dropped the house onto the *wicked witch*, not sweet little Dorothy."

"But it was Dorothy's house."

"Now who's leaning on semantics?"

He let out a loud laugh. "Why don't you be a little nicer? I bet she'll do the same."

"Fine, but if not, she's doing *all* the scut." She relaxed into her chair and crossed her legs.

"If you can get past all the bullshit, who knows? You might end up liking each other." He stood, collected the plates, and took them to the kitchen counter, then headed outside onto the deck, carrying his beer bottle. She followed him out. He checked out one of the Adirondack chairs, wobbling it back and forth. "You gotta stop shopping for oranges at the hardware store."

"What the hell's that supposed to mean?"

"Don't take this personally, but it means stop looking for someone like yourself. You're pretty butch and in control. Keep your eyes, ears, and heart open and find someone different—a woman who challenges and complements you instead. You might find she fills the cracks in your heart like the putty I'm going to use on the arms of this chair."

She dropped into one of the other chairs. "I don't believe in all that *she completes me* crap."

"I didn't say *complete*. I said complements—someone that makes you a better person—makes you want more from life than just work and sleep."

"Where the hell am I going to find someone like that?"

"I'd say there's a beautiful blonde that keeps blocking your path daily that you might want to take a look at."

"Oh, no. That's not gonna happen. I don't care how fucking single she is now. Besides, I don't even know if she's gay."

He shrugged. "That's a whole lot of protesting for someone who doesn't care."

"Just shut it, Pete." She shook her head. "I'll be nicer, but that doesn't mean anything else. Got it?"

"Got it." He seemed to be evaluating the chairs as he drank his beer. "Some of those planks on the back are going to have to be replaced. You can't fix those splits in the wood." She knew that was coming. The seats were good, but several of the backs were bowing at the top.

She'd let the Addison subject rest. Otherwise Pete would start asking questions that she didn't have answers to. Questions about her feelings that she either had to let lie or figure out how she was going to address.

"Maybe replace them with some old skis I've taken out of the rental circulation. I can sand and repaint the rest." He took another pull on his beer. "It's gonna cost you a few more steak dinners, though." He winked.

"I found some stick-on wallpaper in the coat closet. Maybe you can help me liven up the walls in the kitchen too."

"Add a few lunches and I'm in." He drank down the rest of his beer.

"Deal." She knew he'd do it whether she fed him or not, but she loved having him around. Pete was the perfect mate for Olive, whom he adored beyond comprehension. That mate could've been her if she'd been straight. She still got the perks of his friendship, and the arrangement seemed to work out okay for him. Harper was still struggling to find her perfect partner and didn't know if she'd ever find one. Even someone close would work, but she hadn't found that someone either. Maybe she was too picky.

CHAPTER NINE

Harper opened the back door to the clinic quietly because Addison had spent the night to monitor the cat recovering from surgery yesterday. It had been hit by a car and come in late yesterday afternoon. Luckily it had only minor skin lacerations, but since it had arrived late, she'd felt they should keep it. Their usual overnight person wasn't available, Wednesday was his poker night, so Addison had made arrangements for Brook to stay over with Eden and volunteered to be there.

From what Harper's father had told her, Addison spent many hours at the clinic caring for the patients. Seemed her dedication had been the only reason he'd been able to keep the clinic open. When he'd had his heart attack, Addison had jumped in and rescheduled all their current elective procedures and had taken over the day-to-day operation of vaccinations and wellness visits. Addison probably deserved a thank you for all she'd done during their recent struggles with her dad's heart issues, but Harper wasn't ready to give it to her—not with the way Addison had been treating her—not yet, anyway.

She remembered the scut work she'd had to do when she was getting her education. The worst of all the duties was having to restrain animals during exams and take blood. Now, Harper avoided the restraining part as much as possible, but she processed a lot of lab samples and prepared vaccinations and serums herself. She left the kennel cleaning, inventory, and front office stuff to the techs.

She didn't have time to manage any of that at her own clinic and knew she wasn't good at ensuring that the clinic ran smoothly. She hadn't spent eight years in school to do cleaning, filing, and billing. Admittedly, if things were disorganized and something went awry in the clinic because of that fact, she could be a super bitch.

Daisy raced through the door, straight to Addison, who was already up and checking patients.

"Hello, Daisy." Addison squatted and rubbed her ears as Daisy tried to kiss every spot on her face. "I'm happy to see you too."

Harper dropped off her laptop on her dad's desk and then watched Addison interact with Daisy for a minute before she opened the cat's kennel and checked the wound and sutures, which looked good. Sometimes she was more impressed with her surgical skills than she probably should be. The cat seemed responsive and eager to get out.

"How's Max, the lethargic Labrador?" He'd been brought in yesterday with diarrhea and vomiting.

Addison smiled widely, as though Harper had done something extraordinary. "He seems much better today. He pulled the IV out several times during the night, but I finally taped it down securely enough to keep it in." Addison's dedication was admirable.

"Good. Then the treatment worked." They'd given him IV fluids to rehydrate, along with a dose of medication for the symptoms. "You can let the owner know he's ready to go home in a little while…if you agree." Addison had diagnosed him, and Harper had been surprised at the knowledge Addison seemed to possess.

Addison hit her again with the huge smile. "I do. When Jessie gets here, I'll let her know to call."

Harper guessed Addison felt that calling pet owners wasn't part of her job description, which Harper didn't necessarily agree with. She noticed that the male French bulldog named Fizzi, scheduled for a routine teeth cleaning, had already arrived and Addison had already drawn blood samples for pre-surgery blood work. It would give Harper information on how the dog's body was functioning internally, things she couldn't determine from only a physical examination.

"Let me know when the results are ready on Fizzi's bloodwork, and I'll check them so we can get started."

"Here you go." Addison handed her the results.

She scrutinized every detail, not wanting to miss anything. "Looks good."

"Great. I already have the surgical area prepared. I'll get Fizzi." Performing surgery in the mornings was good for both the pet and Harper, because she was at her freshest. Then the pet had time to recover in their care while they monitored it throughout the day.

The procedure went smoothly. Addison anticipated all Harper's needs, and they worked well together—like they'd been doing it for years. After they finished, Harper took off her mask and stretched her back. The surgical table seemed to be set for Addison's height, which made her wonder how much animal care her father had been letting Addison perform.

"Can we raise this table some?" Bending over performing surgery for any amount of time was uncomfortable, and this teeth cleaning had taken longer than expected. It seemed the owner hadn't really kept up oral care on the dog, and several extractions had been involved.

Addison took off her mask. "Sure. I'll get someone in to look at it."

She dropped to a squat. "Can't we do it? Aren't there buttons somewhere under here?" She swiped her fingers under the edge.

"No. It's kind of old and mechanical, not electric. The crank is hard to turn."

She crawled underneath the table and found it.

"Can we do it after we move Fizzi?"

"Got it." She turned the crank and adjusted it up about five inches, which didn't seem that much, but it was a whole lot where your back was concerned. She popped up from the floor.

"Seriously? That couldn't have waited?" Addison stood with brows pulled together and her hands on the dog, like she was holding him steady from falling off the table.

She raised an eyebrow. "I was already down there, and it only took a minute." She didn't know what the big deal was.

"But what if Fizzi had woken up?"

"He didn't. Everything's fine." She checked Fizzi again. Still fast asleep. "Shall we move him to the recovery suite?"

Addison helped her move Fizzi to the large, elevated kennels in the next room, where they would hook him up to the monitors and keep an eye on him.

"Dad has really done some great additions to the clinic." Harper tore off her disposable surgical gown and stuffed it into the trash can. "But not the table." She laughed.

"No. Not the table. Old dog, you know. If it's not broken, why fix it? I created a plan, and we're hoping to make it the premier place in the area to have your pet treated."

Did Addison say *we*? Her stomach twisted. Why did that bother her so much? Maybe because she'd thought if her dad was making plans for the clinic, he would at least run them by her. "Looks like it's getting there."

"We don't have any more appointments scheduled today until one. I'm going to run down the street to the deli and get something for lunch." Addison hung her lab coat on the wall peg, walked toward the door, and then hesitated. "Do you want me to pick something up for you while I'm out?"

She took off her lab coat and hung it next to Addison's. "Mind if I walk with you and pick something up myself?" She had no idea what kind of sandwiches they had at the deli. She glanced at Daisy, who was sleeping in one of the recovery areas. Daisy wouldn't even know she was gone. She grabbed her door key from her bag.

As she stood holding the door, Addison seemed thoughtful, chewing on her lip like she'd regretted asking. "I'm meeting Olive for lunch."

Not an invitation, purely informational. "No worries. I'll just get something and come back here." *Eat by myself in the office while I check email.* That thought actually made her feel a little sad and lonely, but Addison hadn't invited her, and she wouldn't stay if she wasn't wanted. She locked the door and slipped the key into her pocket.

The short walk down the street was awkwardly silent, and Harper regretted asking to come along. She'd thought maybe they could try to get along better, but this situation told her it wasn't going to happen. She pulled the door to the deli open and allowed Addison to enter before her, immediately spotting Olive seated at a table across the room.

Olive stood and came their way. "I was wondering if Addie would bring you along." Olive swept her into a hug. "I'm glad she did. It's so good to see you again."

"It's good to see you too. You look great." And she did, dressed in maroon skinny jeans and a peach, half-zip, fleece pullover. Pete had done well for himself in marrying Olive. "I'm only picking up something to take back to the clinic."

"Why don't you stay and have lunch with us. We can all catch up. Right, Addie?"

"Right." Addison said it, but Harper didn't think she meant it.

"Maybe another time. I've got some email to catch up on, and I need to check in with my clinic in Denver." Both true, but they could've waited. Visiting with Olive would be nice, but it was clear Addison didn't want her there.

"Oh. Okay." Olive seemed confused as she glanced at Addison. "Let's get together for dinner soon. Better yet, you can come over to the house, and Pete can grill."

"Sounds great. Just let me know when." She walked back to the counter and grabbed a pre-made turkey sandwich from the cooler and a bag of chips from the rack. The menu scribbled in chalk on the wall behind the counter had several sandwiches that looked delicious, but this would have to do. She didn't want to hang out here any longer than she had to. She already felt uncomfortable.

Afternoons at her clinic in Denver were typically filled with appointments and discharging surgery patients. Hopefully they wouldn't have much downtime when she had to deal with Addison on subjects other than work.

❖

Addison was deep in thought reading through her textbook in the lab area when she heard the door chime ring, although it had taken her a bit to concentrate after she'd arrived back from lunch. Olive had given her an earful for not inviting Harper to lunch. After all, it was the polite thing to do, and she'd never been a rude person—before now. Now she felt bad about the way she'd acted since Harper had said she'd handle any walk-ins while she studied, even though the afternoon schedule had been light.

"Good afternoon. What can I do for you?" Harper's voice was sweet and strong at the same time. The method seemed to work well with the customers and was one she'd like to learn herself.

"Good afternoon. Is Addison here?"

When she heard Nicki's voice, an alarm in her head went off, yanking her out of studying. She bolted to her feet and rushed to the front. "Hey. What are you doing here?"

"I saw that you'd cancelled your supply pickup, so I thought I'd drop everything off. You know, in case you had an urgent need for something." Nicki grinned as she pushed the box to the side and slid her forearms across the counter to balance herself. "Maybe we could have dinner?"

Harper cleared her throat and held out her hand. "I'm Harper Sims."

"I'm sorry. Where are my manners? This is Nicole Wilson. She owns the vet supply in Ouray." When she'd called this morning to cancel this week's pickup, she hadn't expected Nicki to deliver it. She'd purposely not talked to Nicki or responded to her texts because she didn't want this to happen. She needed time to study and knew exactly what Nicki meant by the need for something urgent. It had nothing to do with supplies.

Nicki shook Harper's hand. "Most people call me Nicki." She glanced to Addison and then back to Harper. "You helping out around here while the doc is recovering?"

Harper smiled. "Something like that."

"Harper is Jim's daughter."

"I gathered there was some relation. With the last name and all." Nicki tilted her head. "You here to stay?"

"No. Just until Dad is well enough to take over again." She smiled and then glanced at Addison. "I have a practice in Denver."

Nicki took out her wallet and slipped a card from one of the slots. "We have customers there as well." She handed the card to Harper. "Let me know if you need anything."

"Thanks." Harper glanced at the card before sliding it into her coat pocket. Then she picked up a pen, flipped it between her fingers, and dropped it to the floor. She picked it up again, tossed it to the desk, and finally put her hands in her coat pockets as she continued surveying Nicki. She'd been fidgeting with everything within arm's reach since Nicki had come in the door. What was that about?

"So what do you say?" Nicki veered her attention to Addison. Apparently she'd noticed Harper's nervousness too.

"Well, I guess I'll get back to work." Harper turned to Addison. "Did you finish studying for your exam?"

"Not yet." She sighed. "I still have another chapter to read."

"I have a quick question about something in the lab." Harper motioned for her to follow her, and she did. "Maybe you should take a break and have dinner with Nicki? I can quiz you in the morning."

She really didn't have time for anything with Nicki tonight. She hesitated, and Harper seemed to notice.

"If you don't want to go, I can make up something to keep you here."

"No. Don't do that. Thanks for the offer, though." Why did she have the urge to let Harper do exactly that? She didn't want to hurt Nicki's feelings, but she really didn't want to go. She was actually a little pissed that Nicki had showed up and expected her to drop everything to go to dinner with her. Her anger had her rethinking what she and Nicki were doing. After all, when someone she loved went out of their way to see her, shouldn't she be happy?

Harper gave her a thumbs-up, and they both went back to the front.

"Just let me finish up a few things."

"Great." Nicki went toward the door. "I'll get the rest of your delivery, and then we can go." She glanced over her shoulder. "There isn't much. I'm sure Harper can take care of putting everything away, right?"

"Right." Addison watched Nicki go through the door. "She's a friend." For some reason she felt the need to update Harper on her status with Nicki but couldn't be truthful.

Harper raised an eyebrow. "I'm sure she is." Harper walked through the hallway toward the office.

"What is that supposed to mean?" She didn't like Harper making assumptions about her life, even if they were accurate.

"She seems nice."

"She is nice." Her voice rose. She had no idea why she was upset.

"Okay. Then I'll close up." Harper smiled slightly. "Have a nice dinner."

Harper didn't seem the slightest bit jealous, which irritated the fuck out of Addison, even though it would be ridiculous for her to be jealous of a connection she knew nothing about.

"Fine." She took off her lab coat and slung it across the chair. "I'll see you tomorrow." She met Nicki at the door, took the box of supplies from her, carried it to the back, and dropped it onto the counter. "Some of these need to be refrigerated, so don't let them sit out."

"Got it." Harper grinned. "Have fun."

"We will." She spun and rushed to meet Nicki at her truck. Harper was pretty irritating for the most part, and she couldn't figure out why she'd rather be at the clinic studying with her than having dinner with Nicki.

Chapter Ten

Nicki started to follow Addison around to get the door of the truck for her.

"I got it," she said as she pulled the door open and slid inside.

Nicki circled the front of the truck and got into the driver's seat. "What was that about?"

She raised her eyebrows. "What was what about?" She played dumb in case Nicki was going to call her on opening her own door. She usually let Nicki do it for her.

"The weirdness with the doc's daughter?" Nicki glanced at her as she pulled out into traffic.

"She just pushes my buttons." She jerked at the seat belt, and it stuck. She growled as she released it, pulled it out slowly, and fastened it. "Sometimes, she's ridiculous."

"Don't you like her?"

"I don't really know her." She sighed. "Since she arrived, it's been like a tornado hit the clinic. We don't do anything the way she does, and apparently it's not up to her standards. She wants to change everything." That was a half-truth, since they'd come to an understanding about some processes.

"Then tell her no. She's not staying permanently, right?"

"No. She's not staying, but she's not wrong about some things."

"So, change those things and keep the rest the same."

"I can't just tell her no. She's Jim's daughter. I'm worried about that too. He wants her to stay."

"Do you think he'll convince her?"

"I don't think she'll leave her practice to come back here."

"What's the name of it?"

"The Total Pet."

Nicki blew out a breath. "Oh. That's her. Let her go back, and steer clear."

"What?" She touched Nicki's arm. "Why?" She needed to know. Harper hadn't told her anything about her life.

"From what I've heard, Harper and her partner used to be together, and now that they aren't, working together has been difficult at best. They both want to buy each other out, but neither will give in and sell."

"If it's a successful practice, I wouldn't either."

"There's more. Harper's partner has a new girlfriend."

"So, the breakup wasn't mutual?" Her stomach knotted at the thought of someone hurting Harper.

"Seems not."

They arrived in front of The Bistro, and Addison hopped out of the car before Nicki had a chance to get around to her side. She didn't like publicizing her personal life in front of everyone in town. Especially when she didn't know exactly what her status was with Nicki.

When they entered the restaurant, Nicki said, "Wow. This place looks fancy."

"It seems that way, but it's very relaxed here." Addison appreciated the crisp, formal look of the place and loved the contrast between the dark hardwood floors and the white table cloths.

They were seated right away. Kevin always made sure to take care of her at the restaurant. All of the staff knew who she was and made sure she always had a table when she dined here.

Once they were seated, the hostess handed them their menus and filled their glasses. Addison set her menu on the table in front of her and took a drink of water.

"You already know what you want?" Nicki flipped through the menu.

She nodded. "I always get the ravioli."

"I don't see ravioli on the menu."

"It's not. The chef makes it special for me."

"They really *do* know you in this town."

"He's a customer at the clinic."

"Gotcha."

Within a matter of minutes, Kevin came out of the kitchen. "Hey, Addison. I didn't know you were coming in tonight, or I would've saved you a better table."

"I didn't know either until about a half hour ago."

Nicki glanced up from the menu. "I kind of showed up and surprised her."

"It was a definite surprise." She raised her eyebrows and looked up at Kevin. "Any chance I can get the ravioli tonight?"

"You, my dear, can have the ravioli any time you want." He glanced at Nicki. "Do you want it as well?"

Nicki shook her head. "No, thanks. I'm not that crazy about it. How about the steak?"

"Medium-rare with linguini on the side?"

"Medium-well with mashed potatoes."

Kevin smiled at Addison. "And how about some wine?"

"Not tonight, thanks. I still have a lot of studying to do, and Nicki has to drive back to Ouray." She didn't catch any reaction from Nicki to her comment. Maybe she'd planned to drive back tonight.

"You work and study too much." He waved the waiter to the table. "Bring them a couple of house salads and a large basket of bread. She loves bread." He grinned at Addison. "I'll have your dinners out for you in just a little while."

"You don't like pasta?" Why was that such a surprise?

Nicki shook her head. "I'm kind of a meat-and-potatoes kind of girl."

How did she not know that? How could she date someone who didn't love her most favorite food in the world? The waiter brought their salads and bread, and Addison watched as Nicki uniformly picked out the cherry tomatoes, cucumbers, and onions and put them on her bread plate. Why had she never noticed this before either?

"When did you start not liking vegetables in your salad?"

"They're okay. I'm just not in the mood for them tonight." Nicki pushed the plate toward her. "You want them?"

"Sure." She picked up the plate and dropped them into her own salad.

They were finishing up when their entrees arrived. Addison's mouth watered as the waiter slid her plate of ravioli in front of her. She never got tired of it.

"Would you like Parmesan cheese?"

She nodded. It was even better with cheese on top.

"Say when."

The waiter grated enough cheese to cover the top of her dish. "That's good."

"How's your steak?"

Nicki cut into her steak and nodded at the waiter. "Looks perfect." She cut off a huge bite and put it into her mouth.

Addison focused on Nicki's mouth and watched her chew, and chew, and chew. Finally, she swallowed. Addison didn't think she was ever going to get that bite down. She watched her cut another piece the same size. Addison reached for the breadbasket, ripped a piece off, and buttered it. She couldn't watch Nicki chew another bite and wondered why it bothered her so much tonight. She took a bite of bread before she cut one of her ravioli into quarters and scooped it into her mouth—enjoying the burst of flavors. She'd never be able to get enough of these, even if she ate them every day for the rest of her life.

Nicki's voice interrupted her enjoyment. "How's the ravioli?"

"It's delicious. Would you like a bite?"

Nicki shook her head. "Nope. I've got all I need right here." She poked at a couple of mushrooms and dragged them through her mashed potatoes before she put them into her mouth.

Was this who she wanted to be with for the rest of her life? "I'll be right back. I need to use the ladies' room." She rushed across the restaurant, pushed through the door, gripped the counter, and stared at herself in the mirror. She didn't know why she was being so nitpicky tonight. She'd never paid that much attention to what

Nicki ate or didn't eat before. Maybe she should have. Is that what people in love did?

Nicki was sweet and took good care of her when they were together. She'd thought that possibly she was the one at times—at others she still wondered. This was one of the other times. Now that Harper had returned to town, she was more confused than ever. The feelings that were hitting her whenever Harper was around were so different from anything she'd felt with Nicki. So much so it scared her. It was weird. They didn't really like each other, plus she knew Harper wasn't staying, and this was Addison's town. She loved it here—had no plans to move. So where did that leave her? In a relationship with Nicki always wanting more? Or alone looking for something better? She splashed water on her face and wiped it dry with one of the fancy towels in the tray in front of her. She had to get through tonight without hurting Nicki's feelings. She'd have time to sort out her feelings after Nicki went back to Ouray.

Addison managed to make it through the rest of their dinner but wasn't sure what came next. When they drove up to the house, she'd expected to see some type of activity through the windows, but there was none. She hoped everything was all right with Brook. She hadn't called or texted during dinner. She unlocked the front door and pushed it open, expecting to find a living room full of teenagers, but was surprised to find the house empty.

"Where's Brook?"

"I don't know. I thought she was going to be here with her friends watching a movie." She took her phone from her bag and typed in a quick text to Brook.

Where are you?

We went to Jessie's. She has Netflix.

Okay. What time will you be home?

Not for a couple more hours.

Okay. Let me know if you're going to be later than that.

A thumbs-up emoji appeared on the screen.

"They decided to go to her friend's instead. Apparently she has more viewing choices." Not wanting Nicki to see the screen, she locked the phone and slipped her phone back into her bag.

"Good. Then we have some time." Nicki closed the front door behind her and then took her into her arms and kissed her.

She kissed her back but didn't go all in. She couldn't with how she was feeling now. She pushed out of Nicki's arms. "Actually, she could be home anytime."

Nicki scrunched her eyebrows. "She's never home before ten."

"She's got a cold, and I told her she should come home early."

Nicki stared at her. "You've been acting strange all night. I'm not sure what's going on here. Is it work? School? Changes at the clinic? Is the new doctor causing problems? Because you haven't been with me all night."

It was definitely Harper, but she shook her head. "I've got a lot on my mind. There's so much to do at the clinic, and I've got a test coming up soon." She didn't want to hurt Nicki. Not here, not now.

"To be clear. I'm not sure what you think we have here, but I don't want a part-time thing. I thought we were working toward something more permanent, but the feeling I'm getting tonight makes me think that's changed."

"We really hadn't discussed that, had we? Something permanent?" She tried to say it gently.

"Okay. I'll admit that we haven't talked about it. So, let's get to it." Nicki went to the couch, sat, and patted the spot next to her. "What do I have to do to make you want that too?"

She reluctantly followed her. "I can't leave Blueridge—my life is here. Brook is in school, and I don't want to leave." That was true to a certain extent. She really liked Nicki a lot, and enjoyed her company, but deep down inside she didn't see her as a partner long-term.

"I'm not asking you to leave. Can't we meet somewhere in the middle? Spend time in both places?"

"I can't be away from Brook. She's in her senior year, and college is coming up soon. I need to be here for her."

Nicki clutched her knees. "I see. You're not willing to commit to anything in the near future, or the far future, it seems."

She didn't respond. She couldn't argue with her, knowing in her heart she might never be able to commit to any permanency with Nicki. The disappointment in Nicki's eyes made her sad in a way, but not sad enough to change her mind. It hurt, but wasn't it the right decision for both of them?

Nicki stood and raked her fingers through her hair. "I guess I'll have to accept that for now, but after Brook is settled in college, we'll need to revisit this. Do you want me to go?"

She nodded. "I think it would be best." She wasn't sure there would be a different outcome after Brook went to college or that it would ever happen with Nicki. She hoped she'd be strong enough not to string her along because she was lonely. She knew in her heart she wasn't all in. Harper's unexpected arrival in town had only added to her uncertainty.

Harper looked at the label on the vaccine vial on the top shelf, then rummaged through the refrigerator to find the older vials. She located several on the right side of the shelf and others on the left, as well as a handful on a whole other shelf. Nothing was in any type of order. How did anyone find anything around here?

Her cell phone buzzed in her pocket, and she looked at the screen and saw it was Eden before she answered. "Hey, love. I thought we could grab some dinner out somewhere tonight." She reached for the rabies vaccine and checked the expiration dates on the bottles, trying to find the oldest vial.

"Can't tonight, Mom."

"Oh. What are you up to?" She put all the vials on one shelf. She would arrange them in order later.

"I'm hanging out with Brook. We're going to see a movie."

"Oh. You two are getting pretty friendly."

She set the vial she'd chosen on the counter, then pulled out a couple of drawers and found a syringe. She set them both together on the counter while she documented the vaccination in the patient chart.

"She comes over a lot to see Gran and Grampy. Gran's been teaching us how to sew."

Great. Eden had a better relationship with Harper's stepmother than she did. "Wait. There isn't a movie theater in town. The closest one is in Telluride, and that's over an hour away." She picked up the vaccine and clenched the vial in her palm.

"We're going to Brook's house. A couple of her friends are coming over."

She relaxed and picked up the syringe from the counter. Eden would be safe there, and she doubted Addison would be out late with all the studying she had to do.

"Okay. Be good and mind your manners."

"Mom," she said with a groan. "You tell me that every time I go somewhere."

"That's my job." She blew out a breath. "I gotta go. Have fun. I love you."

"Love you too."

She slipped her phone into her pocket and bounced back into the exam room where the customer was waiting patiently with her dog. "Sorry. It took me a little longer than I expected to find the syringe. I'm not used to the storage system here yet." She stuck the needle into the vaccine bottle and pulled the syringe plunger, measuring out the proper dose.

"Only you here this evening?" the woman asked. "Addison isn't here?"

"Nope."

"I hope everything is all right."

It was ridiculous how nosy people were here. "She's fine." Probably better than fine by now. Sitting down with her *friend* and eating a nice meal. "She had plans, and this little guy is my last patient." She rubbed the dog's neck and wiped a spot with an alcohol swab as she looked into his eyes. "It's okay, sweetheart. This will be all done in a minute." She pinched a bit of skin at his neck, quickly injected the vaccine, and rubbed the area gently when she was done.

As soon as this last patient was finished, she would reorganize everything. After all, what else did she have to do? Eden was hanging out with Brook and her friends tonight, which was good, she hoped. Olive had the night off, and Pete was staying in with her tonight. It was sweet the way he wanted to be with her every minute of the day.

Working with the person you were living with had its challenges, as she'd found out with V. Work mingled too much with personal things, and soon enough it took over. There was no time to relax at all. After how everything had disintegrated and finally imploded between them, she didn't see how she could be with anyone for a twelve-hour stretch at a time, let alone want to be with them twenty-four seven.

CHAPTER ELEVEN

The phone rang, and it practically scared Harper out of her skin. She'd been in the lab area reorganizing since the clinic had closed over an hour ago. She grabbed the receiver on the wall and checked the caller ID before she answered. It was her dad's number. "Hey. What's up?"

"Hi, honey. I expected Addison to pick up." Patty's voice was cheerful.

"And I expected you to be Eden." She laughed. "Addison's gone to dinner with her friend, Nicki."

"Oh. Nicki's in town?" Patty seemed cautious with her question.

"She delivered supplies, which I'm now trying to put away, but everything is totally disorganized. I've spent the last hour reorganizing everything."

"Well, if you're about done, why don't you come by for dinner?"

She glanced at her watch. It was close to seven, and she had no desire to go home and cook. The whole afternoon had been frustrating, starting with Addison's visitor. "That sounds good. Can I pick up anything on the way?"

"Nope. Just bring yourself and your appetite."

"What are you having?"

"Baked trout, but be warned. Your father's already complaining that it's not fried."

"Sounds good to me." She hadn't had trout in a while, and it was quite tasty. On her way, she'd pick up a bottle of sauvignon blanc to go with the fish. It would be nice to have a good meal and relax. Maybe it would get her mind off Addison.

"Sorry about the supplies. I usually keep them in order. I haven't been up there much since your father's been sick."

"It's fine. Now they're all set up where I can find them."

"I'm sure Addison will love that."

"Will she?" She tilted her head. "She doesn't seem to like much of anything I do."

"That's only because she's used to her own routine, with school and all, and you're kind of right in the middle of it now."

"It shouldn't take me long to get everything cleaned up here. I'll see you soon." She hadn't thought about it that way. Maybe it wasn't personal. Maybe she was upsetting Addison's schedule. She crossed the room to Addison's work area of the lab and put everything she'd moved back in its place. The supply reorganization would be enough to push her to the edge, so no need to shove her off as well. She squatted to pet Daisy. "You want to go have dinner with Patty and Grampy?" Daisy wiggled her butt as always.

People on the street were sparse as she drove through town to the liquor store. Hopefully it was still open. Stores were open until midnight in Denver, but smaller towns pretty much closed at their own discretion. As she pulled up, she noticed the lights were on, so she was in luck. Someone stood at the counter paying, so she weaved through the aisles and found the wine section.

"Harper Sims? Is that you?"

She spun around to find none other than Riley Stone, smiling like she'd just found a long-lost friend. "In the flesh."

"Isn't this a nice coincidence? Running into each other two times within two weeks."

It was a small town, so she didn't find it coincidental at all. "Nice to see you again, Riley." Not completely true. She had no desire to see people from high school and bring up memories she'd rather forget.

"Oh my gosh. It's been so long." Riley rushed toward her, a bottle of wine in each hand, and pulled her into a hug, the bottles clinking as they touched behind her back. "I hear you're doing well in Denver. Have your very own veterinary clinic and all."

"I do okay." She grabbed a bottle of wine from the shelf. "What are you up to these days?"

"I own the boutique a couple of doors down."

"Oh, right. I think Addison told me that." She hadn't, but she didn't want to get into a long discussion about it. As she recalled, Riley could and would talk for hours if you let her.

"Getting some wine to relax with tonight?"

"Actually going to my dad's for dinner."

"Oh, then you'll want to pick up a rosé as well. That's all Patty drinks." Riley plucked a bottle from the shelf and handed it to her. "She likes this one best."

She took it from her. "Thanks for the heads-up." She walked to the counter.

"We should get together sometime for dinner."

"Sure. Give me a ring at the clinic, and we'll set something up." She took out her card and swiped it through the machine, trying to get out of there as quickly as possible. It wasn't really something she wanted to do, but if Riley invited her to dinner, she would go. She said her good-byes and rushed out the door before Riley could protest.

Without knocking, she pulled open the screen door at her dad's home and went inside. "I brought wine." As she entered the house, dinner smelled wonderful, and her stomach immediately growled, letting her know she hadn't eaten since much earlier in the day.

"I hope you brought more than one bottle. Your father's in a mood."

"I brought rosé and white. I'll see what I can do about his mood." She slid them onto the bottom shelf in the refrigerator. "Where is he?"

"Out by the barn with his chickens."

She went out the side door to find her dad. He was right where Patty said he'd be, feeding the chickens.

"Hi, Dad." She kissed him on the cheek.

He grinned. "Well, this is a nice surprise."

"For both of us. The fish Patty's cooking smells wonderful."

"It might smell that way, but it would be better fried." He tossed some seed into the coop.

"I'm sure it will be delicious, and it's better for you baked."

"At least she's making mashed potatoes."

She hadn't seen any potatoes on the stove. "I think she's baking them." She laughed at his obvious dismay.

"I'm going to get healthy whether I want to or not."

"You can slather yours with butter and sour cream. Won't that make you happy?"

"She'll limit that too."

"I'll sneak you some of mine." She had no intention of doing any such thing, but the gesture made him smile. "Eden left you alone tonight, huh?"

"Yeah. She needs to be out with people her own age."

"Not a lot of those here, Dad."

"You got along okay, didn't you?"

"Most of the time." She'd actually hated high school, but she wouldn't burden her father with the details of that now. It was done, and she'd never have to go back again, but she'd make sure Eden wouldn't have the same struggles if she could. Even though hers were different, they were teenage struggles just the same.

He scattered more seed on the ground before he rubbed his hands together, wiping the remaining seed from them. "That should do it." He followed her across the yard.

When they got back inside, Patty had already dished them each up a plate of trout, green beans, and baked potato. Harper's stomach let out a huge growl. "Sorry. I'm starving." She had a habit of skipping lunch most days.

"No need to be starving, honey. Sit down and dig in."

She did just that and inhaled half her fish before having any type of conversation. She looked up from her plate and grinned. "I don't get a lot of home-cooked meals in Denver."

Patty moved the plate of trout over in front of her. "Help yourself. I made plenty."

She took another helping. "So when is Addison finishing school?"

"She's in her last semester and set to finish in May, I think."

"She's doing it all online?" She mixed the butter and sour cream into her potato and took a bite.

Patty nodded. "Jimmy's been helping her with the hands-on things."

She bristled at the nickname for her father but kept her irritation to herself. "What's her plan after that? She'll have to take face-to-face classes if she wants to become a DVM." She continued eating her potato.

"I'm not quite sure she's made up her mind about that." Patty forked the last couple of green beans on her plate. "She'd have to move to Fort Collins, and Brook is planning to go to school in Boulder."

"That's closer than staying here."

"I think she's worried about the cost with them both going at the same time."

"Can't Brook get a student loan?"

Patty shook her head. "Her dad makes too much money."

"He won't pay for it?"

"I think she's too proud to ask him."

"That's ridiculous. Addison should ask him."

"She'll be fine as a tech for now." Jim drank the last of his wine. "Maybe look into it more after Brook graduates from college."

"That's four more years. From what I've seen, she'd make a good vet." She pushed the last of her trout around on her plate. "She's good with the patients and has a soft hand at calming anxious customers."

"She's very good with the animals and their owners. I'm hoping to keep her around as long as I can." He set his fork on the plate and pushed it away.

"That's a little selfish, isn't it?"

"If you'd come back, there wouldn't even be a question."

"I can't do that, Dad. I left this town for a reason, and that reason still stands."

"I think you'll find a lot has changed here, if you'd just give it a chance."

"I know, Dad. Visiting is one thing, but living here is a whole different story."

"Give it some serious consideration. I always thought you and I'd share a practice one day. Maybe not today or even tomorrow, but someday."

"Okay." She got up and carried her plate to the sink. Moving back to Blueridge was not in her plans at all. She was happy in Denver, where people accepted her as she was. There, she didn't have to change or hide anything from anyone. If people didn't like her lifestyle, they went somewhere else for their animal care. In Blueridge there wasn't enough business to lose any of it.

Eden had arrived home before Harper left, so she'd stayed to watch some TV with her in her room. They hadn't spent much time together since they'd arrived, and she'd been feeling guilty about it. She was headed into the bathroom when she heard the doorbell ring. She glanced around the corner and caught a glimpse of Nicki crossing the entry into the kitchen. She waited, expecting to see Addison follow her in, but the door closed, and there was no Addison. Only Patty. Addison had given her the impression they were having dinner, which seemed to be over. Nicki had come all the way here from Ouray to see Addison. Why was Nicki here without her?

She moved quietly down the hallway and leaned against the wall, where she could see their reflections in the glass of the watercolor painting hanging across from her. She knew it was weird, but she needed to find out more details about Nicki and her friendship with Addison. "I'm sorry to stop by like this, Patty. I'm just not sure what to do." Nicki's voice was soft and deflated.

"What's going on? I thought you and Addison were going to dinner. Where is she?"

"We had dinner. Now she's at home with Brook—said she has a cold or something." Nicki let out a sigh.

"Maybe you should've called first. Let her know you were coming."

"I tried. Called and texted her several times. She didn't answer or respond."

"I'm sure she meant to. She's been busy with work and school."

"Tonight, I told her I want something more permanent, and she pretty much said no."

"She did?" Patty's voice rose.

"At least until Brook is out of school."

"That makes sense. Brook has a lot going on in her senior year."

"I totally get that, but I'm not sure she'll be ready when Brook is out of school either. We don't seem to be moving in the same direction. She's been really distant lately."

Harper couldn't help the giddy feeling that came over her. She felt bad for Nicki, but knowing Addison wasn't serious with her made her weirdly happy. But it wasn't like she was staying in Blueridge, and she'd just heard that Addison wasn't leaving any time soon.

Daisy came down the hall, her nails clicking on the hardwood floor, and the conversation stopped for a minute. *Way to blow my cover, girl.* Harper dropped to a crouch and loved on Daisy while she waited until it began again before she rushed down the hall and hopped back on the bed to watch TV with Eden.

Eden stared at the TV. "You were gone long enough. I thought you left."

"No. Just went to the bathroom, and then chatted with your grandpa for a minute."

"Well, you missed the good part."

"Back it up."

Soon Harper heard the front door open and close and then Patty's footsteps as she came down the hallway to her room. "Can you come into the kitchen? I'd like a word." She turned and headed down the hall.

Eden swallowed hard. "Is she talking to me or you?"

"I think me." She sat forward and looked at Eden, steeling herself for a conversation she didn't want to have but was probably totally necessary. She wasn't one to spy on people, but it seemed that she had and had also been found out. "I'll be right back."

Patty was pouring herself a cup of coffee when she got to the kitchen. "You want a cup?" She held up the pot.

"No. Thanks. That would keep me up all night."

"A beer then?" Patty pulled open the refrigerator door.

"No thanks. I'm good."

Patty took a seat at the table and patted the spot in front of the chair adjacent to her. "Come sit down."

"What's up."

"Did you get all of that?"

"What?"

"My conversation with Nicki." She took a sip of coffee and then relaxed into her chair. "You should know that if you can see me in the reflection of the painting, I can also see you."

"I'm sorry. I noticed she came alone and was curious why Addison wasn't with her."

"Well, you heard. She's at home with Brook."

"Have they been dating long? I got the impression this afternoon they were pretty close—figured she spent the night often." A spot-on assumption.

"They've been seeing each other for a while, but Addison usually sees her when she picks up supplies in Ouray—stays over there."

"How often is that? Weekly, monthly?" Jesus. She was asking too many questions. She had to know. This little nugget of information was a game-changer.

Patty scrunched her eyebrows. "Is something going on between you two that I should know about?"

"Me and Addison?" She shook her head. "Absolutely not. She doesn't even like me." *And I'm not too keen on her either. Am I?* She wasn't sure of anything right now.

"I doubt that's true." Patty raised an eyebrow. "Are you two getting along okay at the clinic?"

"Of course. I would never let my personal feelings get in the way of work."

"Feelings?"

She shrugged. "Or lack of feelings." Why did she even care?

"I assume Addison won't either."

"Seems that way so far." She didn't feel it was necessary to tell Patty about their issues.

"If there's tension between you two, maybe I should start spending more time at the clinic to relieve some of it."

"That's not necessary. Dad needs you here. He'll recuperate faster if you stay home. Then he can get back to work, and I can get back to Denver."

"You know he'd love to have you stay—join the practice with him."

"As I said before, I already have a practice in Denver."

"I know. Jimmy told me your partner wants to buy you out."

She hated that her dad told Patty everything. "That's true, but I don't plan on leaving it anytime soon."

Patty reached over and patted her hand. "Do me a favor and don't reject the idea of staying and partnering with your dad right away. He's not going to be able to handle the workload forever, and the town will still need a vet. You'd be a good fit."

"He hadn't even mentioned partnering with him to me until tonight." She'd expected it someday, just not so soon.

"He was waiting for the right time."

"Okay." She stood. "It's getting late. I'd better go home."

"Think about it. There might be more for you here than you realize."

Was Patty talking about more than the practice? Nothing that Harper hadn't had swishing around in her thoughts already. She'd always found Addison attractive. The fact that she and Addison didn't see eye to eye on everything only made her more alluring.

Once she got in the car, all she could think about was Addison. Her thoughts strayed to earlier in the day—Addison's shell-shocked reaction when Nicki showed up at the clinic and the information she'd overheard a little while ago. She hit the button on her steering wheel and called Pete. Once the connection went through, she didn't give him a chance to speak. "Do you know Nicki Wilson? She came into the clinic today."

He hesitated. "Yeah. I know her. She owns a pretty nice vet supply store in Ouray."

"Which also means you know Addison is gay."

"Has been since she came back to town. Doesn't publicize it, though."

"Why didn't you tell me?"

"It's not really my news to tell, and I didn't know it was important to you. Olive told me. They're sorta friends."

"What? You didn't think it was important to tell me that the most popular girl in high school is a lesbian?" She gripped the steering wheel. "It's fucking huge news. Why the hell didn't Olive fill me in on this?" She was acting way more interested than she should for someone who *isn't* interested.

"Why do you care? You don't even like her."

"I don't like her *now*, but you know I had a *huge* crush on her in school."

"So how do you know about Nicki and Addison?"

"Nicki stopped by my dad's tonight to talk to Patty while I was still there. I overheard part of their conversation."

"What'd you hear?"

"Seems like Addison isn't all in on whatever it is they have together. Nicki showed up at the clinic to take her out to dinner. Addison wasn't expecting her and kind of blew her off. I guess Addison usually goes to pick up the supplies. They have dinner and whatever else in Ouray." Her stomach knotted as she spoke. Why did that bother her so?

"Oh. Wow."

"Oh. Wow, what?"

"I wonder what's up with that. They've been seeing each other for a long time."

"Really? How long?"

"At least a couple of years."

"Do you think they're solid?" She still couldn't believe he hadn't told her.

"I have no idea. Olive would know more about that than me."

"Damn it. You need to pay more attention."

He laughed. "Okay. I'll get a full report and let you know."

"No. I don't really want to know."

"Whatever." He laughed. "But it kinda sounds like you do."

"I gotta go." She hit the end button on the phone.

When Harper got to the cabin, she didn't check her email, and she didn't read. She just changed, brushed her teeth, and climbed into bed with Daisy snuggling right beside her. She didn't want to disperse her day and her feelings so easily tonight. Everything about today had been enlightening and exciting in a weird sort of way. So many thoughts swirled through her mind, not the least of which was Addison's availability.

Her phone chimed, and she glanced at the text she'd received from V. Then she quickly typed a response before silencing her phone and veering her thoughts back to the news she'd learned. Addison was, in fact, gay, and she was giving her girlfriend, Nicki, mixed signals. She turned on her side and scrunched the pillow beneath her head. Casual sex with Addison might be exactly what she needed to keep her mind off V. Making her high school crush become a reality she never thought would happen—ever—might be worth the challenge.

CHAPTER TWELVE

Addison sat in her corner of the lab trying to study for her exam tomorrow. She wasn't having much success. She couldn't keep her mind off last night.

She'd woken up this morning feeling guilty. She'd pretty much rejected Nicki, and, other than showing up unexpectedly, she really hadn't done anything wrong. If Nicki had surprised her like that a couple of weeks ago, she would've been thrilled to go to dinner and let her stay over. But it hadn't felt right last night. Her heart just wasn't in it. She was still unsure of what she wanted and was afraid she'd scared her off for good.

So she'd texted Nicki soon after she'd woken this morning to apologize. Nicki had accepted that gesture—told her she'd see her next week. But Addison wasn't sure if she would see her or not. True, she had felt guilty about hurting her, but they'd never made future plans together. With the mixed signals her heart was giving her now, she wasn't sure she ever would.

"How was your dinner last night?" Harper jerked her out of her thoughts.

"It was good. Can't go wrong with pasta." She didn't look up—wasn't sure why Harper wanted to know.

"Right. Italian is one of my favorites."

She swiveled in her stool to find Harper closer than expected and staring at her. "Then you should try The Bistro. It's pretty good, considering it's the only Italian place in town."

"I'll have to do that." Harper smiled as she fidgeted with the pen in her hand. "Maybe you can join me for dinner some night after work?"

Was Harper really asking her out? "Sure."

"We both need to eat, right?" The pen flipped out of Harper's hand, and she caught it before it hit the floor.

"Right. Work, study, eat, sleep. That's pretty much my life." She'd never seen Harper so nervous before...yesterday. It wasn't like her. She was always the coolest.

"Maybe I can help you out with your courses too." She set the pen on the counter, then seemed to fumble, trying to figure out what to do with her hands. Eventually she shoved them into the pockets of her lab coat.

Harper was offering a whole lot of maybes today. "That would be great, if you can spare the time."

"I've got nothing but time while I'm here. I can only take so much of Dad and his chicken stories."

She couldn't help the laugh that escaped her lips. "Thank God he's telling them to you now instead of me."

Harper grinned. "And each egg has a story all its own."

"He does love those chickens, and don't forget those fancy roosters."

"What are they called?"

"I think he has a couple of silkies, a Polish, and that tiny bantam."

"He's got a new one now. Just picked it up this week. A Sebright, maybe?"

"Ooh. He's been waiting on that one. I'll have to go see it. I wonder if he'll advance to top roo." There was always a pecking order when it came to roosters. "He's going to have to separate them at first."

"Top roo? Really." Harper pulled her eyebrows together. "No wonder you get along with him so well. Next time I see him, I'll let him know how much you miss them."

"No. Please don't. I'm begging you. I've heard the stories at least a thousand times. Plus, the eggs." She rolled her eyes. "Don't even get him started on those. Blue, green, orange—so many reasons for so many colors." She swiped the patient chart from Harper's hand. "I'll do all the filing for the rest of the week if you promise not to say a word to him."

Harper gave her a half smile. "I guess I can suffer with his stories for a deal like that." She turned and went to the next full exam room, glanced over her shoulder, and grinned before she entered.

The thrill that coursed through Addison was amazing. What was happening here? Were they actually being nice to each other? Was Harper actually smiling? Yes, she was, and the sight was so beautiful it almost knocked Addison off her feet. She shook her head. *Gotta stop thinking good things can happen from a simple smile.* They never did.

Harper entered her dad's house and hung her jacket on the rack. Patty was already putting dinner on the table and had set only four places, which meant Addison wasn't coming for dinner tonight. She was surprised at how disappointed she was. Her day at the clinic had been unexpectedly pleasant. She and Addison had found a groove and were getting along better than she'd ever thought they would. She'd hoped it might continue tonight at dinner, but apparently Addison had other plans.

She scooped a cup of dog food from the container into the bowl Patty had set out for Daisy. "No Addison and Brook tonight?"

"She's studying for her exam tomorrow, and I'm guessing Brook is either at home with her or already at the basketball game at the high school tonight."

"Oh. They have enough players for a team now?"

Patty nodded. "For the past few years, they have." She slid the roasted chicken she'd cut up into parts onto the table. "They've formed a pretty good coed team."

"That's progress." Not many of the girls, besides her, had wanted to play on sports teams with the boys when she was in high school.

"You have to use what you got, I guess."

Her dad came in through the back door with Eden trailing right behind him.

"Chickens are fed," Eden announced as she went to the sink and washed her hands before she took a seat at the table.

"I guess I could drop by on the way home and see if Addison needs help studying for her exam." She took a hefty bite of chicken.

Her dad glanced up from his food. "She could probably use someone to quiz her."

"Maybe I should go by and check." She ate a few more bites of her chicken.

Patty raised her eyebrows as she glanced at Jim and then back at Harper. "She'd probably be okay with that."

She understood Patty's reaction, considering their snarky interactions when they happened to be at the house at the same time.

Conversation lulled as everyone ate. She didn't really want to talk about the clinic because those conversations always included Addison, and she still wasn't sure exactly how she felt about her. She drove her crazy at the clinic, but Harper was impressed. Addison was about to complete her associate degree in veterinary technology and take the state board exam. She would soon be a certified veterinary-technician specialist. Not everyone was cut out for animal medicine. It looked easy from the outside, but gaining the knowledge and training to be a DVM took as much time and effort as that of a medical doctor. Addison would soon find that out if she chose to continue on the path to become a Doctor of Veterinary Medicine. Harper couldn't help but admire her compassion and dedication.

"There's a basketball game at the high school tonight. Can I borrow the car?" Eden broke through her thoughts.

"I think I'll go by Addison's." Harper carried her plate to the sink and rinsed it before loading it into the dishwasher. "How about I drop you off on my way and pick you up when the game is over."

Eden rolled her eyes. "That's embarrassing. I'm not ten, Mom."

Jim stood. "She's right, you know." He fished a key fob out of his pocket and held it up in the air. "How about you take the Escape? Maybe for good?"

"Dad." She rushed across the kitchen and swiped the keys from his hand. "She just got her license. You can't just give her Mom's car."

He swiped the keys back. "I can, and I did. But like with you, it won't be hers until she proves she can handle the responsibility." He went to the door and motioned for Eden to follow him. "Now let's discuss the rules that go along with the responsibility of owning a car." The car chirped when he clicked the unlock button and then opened the door for Eden. "Go on. Get in." He glanced back at Harper.

Eden climbed into the SUV and moved the seat up. Dressed in jeans and a light-blue sweatshirt, she seemed much too small to be driving. Even though Eden was sixteen, she still thought of Eden as her little girl. She couldn't hang on to that much longer. Eden's petite frame was beginning to develop and reveal her age.

The whole situation was surreal. Her baby girl was growing up, something she hadn't wanted to experience quite so soon. She crossed her arms as her dad recited the same rules he'd given her when she got her first car. One that wasn't nearly as nice as this one.

He flicked the single key attached to the key ring. "There's a house key too." He handed the set to Eden. "It's a school night. Home before eleven." He glanced at Harper and waited for her to agree.

"Ten. Home before ten." She wasn't letting Eden live by the same house rules she grew up under. Too much trouble could happen between the hours of ten and eleven when certain kids were left to their own devices in this town.

Eden nodded before she slid out of the car, threw her arms around his neck, and kissed him on the cheek. "Thanks, Grampy. I'll be home before then. I promise." She slid back into the car and hit the start button.

Harper observed her dad as Eden drove away. The joy she saw on his face was wonderful, something she hadn't seen since before her mom died. She would let him win this battle, if only for that.

"You have no idea what you're unleashing by giving her a car that nice."

"Sure I do. I gave you one, didn't I?"

"Yeah, but I was a good kid."

"And she's not?"

She blew out a breath. "She is, but this town is new to her. The freedom here is different. I knew where not to go and what not to do. She doesn't yet."

"She's got Brook to help her with that."

"That doesn't ease my worries much." Brook seemed like a good kid, but she was older, more developed, and dressed much more provocatively than Harper thought appropriate. If Eden and Brook became better friends, she'd have to take that issue up with Addison at some point.

Addison was deep in thought when the doorbell rang. Who in the world could that be at this time of night? She popped up from the couch and went to the living-room curtain, as she usually did when she wasn't expecting anyone. She slowly pulled it back. It was Harper—on her porch—ringing *her* doorbell. She dropped to the floor, pressed her back against the wall. What the hell was she doing here? She felt her wet hair, glanced at the old sweatpants and hoodie she'd put on after her shower. The bell rang again. She was absolutely not going to answer the door. She would sit here all night if she had to. She heard the door unlock, and her heart raced. Who the hell gave her a key? She raced on all fours across the living room.

"Maybe she's in the shower." Brook's voice became louder as the door opened. "Mom. Are you all right?"

Still on the floor, she cringed. How was she going to explain this? She felt around in the carpet, then reached for her ear. "I'm fine. Just lost an earring."

"But you don't—"

"Usually wear them at night. I know, but I forgot to take them out when I got into the shower."

She got to her feet as Brook stared at her while Harper stood behind her.

"I need money for the game."

"Side pocket." She pointed to her bag sitting on the barstool at the counter. "Take a twenty."

Brook fished the money out of the bag and then rushed to the hall closet. "I forgot my scarf. We're going to hang out after the basketball game."

She cleared her throat and focused on Brook. "Okay. Home before eleven."

"Eden's at the game. Would you mind keeping an eye out for her?"

"On it. She texted me a little bit ago."

"Thanks." Harper seemed genuinely grateful.

"See you later, Mom." Brook rushed by Harper out the door, and suddenly they were left alone.

"Harper...I wasn't expecting you." Her house was a mess, and books were strewn all over the coffee table.

"Sorry. I should've called before stopping by." Harper didn't take her eyes off her. "Your mom said you were studying for your exam tomorrow, and I thought I might be able to help."

"Really?" She raised her eyebrows. "I mean. Yes. I do have an exam." This was not the Harper she'd experienced over the past few days, and she wasn't sure how to respond without sarcasm. Totally foreign to her nature.

"What subject?"

"Anatomy."

"One of my better subjects."

"Oh. Well, I guess I could use the help." She crossed the room and sat on the couch. Harper followed her, sat down next to her. Their thighs grazed as the couch cushion sank. She warmed, Harper's heat seeming to pass directly into her.

She glanced into Harper's eyes and was caught up in the deep blue of them. She immediately gathered up her books. "The kitchen table will probably be better for this."

Harper cleared her throat. "Yeah. I agree."

"You want something to drink?" She took a bottle of water from the refrigerator, screwed off the top, and took a big gulp. She was not going to be able to study at all now. "You know what? I think I'll just go to bed and get some rest." She set the bottle on the counter and rushed to the door. "I appreciate the offer, but my mind will be fresher in the morning."

"Gotcha." Harper went out the door but stopped and turned around. "Why don't you take the morning to study? I can handle the clinic."

"Thanks. I appreciate that." And she did. She was still surprised at this new Harper that seemed to be blooming in front of her. "Good night." She closed the door and pressed her back against it. This was absolutely too much excitement for one night.

CHAPTER THIRTEEN

Harper had been wondering all morning how Addison's exam went. It was going to be a tough one. Vet techs play a crucial role in veterinary clinics by monitoring the health conditions of animal patients—taking X-rays, providing veterinarians with surgical, dental, anesthetic, and other types of assistance.

Patty showed up early. Addison must have told her that Harper had given her the morning off to prepare.

The phone rang as she came out of one of the exam rooms. She stood at the counter making notes in a chart as she half-listened to the phone conversation.

"Why didn't you call her before today?" Patty's voice rose.

"That bad, huh?"

"Calm down, honey. I'll take care of it." Patty hung up the receiver.

"Was that Addison? Did she have trouble with the test?" She was anxious to know how she did.

"Hasn't taken it yet." She straightened a few things on the desk. "She's not real confident at this point that she's going to do well."

"She's been studying a lot. She'll do fine."

Patty blew out a breath. "Tell her that." She gathered up her purse. "She's not going to be able to make the supply run to Ouray today. I'll have to go." She handed Harper a sticky note as she rounded the counter. "Call Jessie to come in early if you need her, or Jimmy if she can't."

"I'll be okay." She watched Patty go out the door, then took out her phone to text Addison.

You're going to do great on your exam.

A minute or two passed before she saw the bubbles appear, and Addison's reply came through. *I'm absolutely going to fail.*

Close your eyes and take a breath. You've got this.

I hope you're right.

Aren't I always? She ended the sentence with a toothed smiley face.

Addison responded with a laugh emoji, and Harper actually laughed out loud. She hoped she'd been able to boost her confidence some, or at least lightened her mood.

Harper left one exam room, scribbled a few notes in the chart, and then immediately took the chart from the next exam room door and entered. Even though they didn't have a lot of scheduled patients, her morning had become super busy with drop-ins. She'd called Jessie, who had come in early, but after Patty left, she'd still been going from one patient to the other.

"So what's going on with Cocoa today?" She held the stethoscope to the terrier's chest. Heart sounded good. She moved it to her stomach and heard it grumble.

"She's not eating well."

"Has she eaten anything out of the ordinary lately?"

"My son's been feeding her from the table a lot."

"What kinds of food is he feeding her?"

"Fast food, chips. She'll eat anything."

She nodded. A hard habit to break. "Okay. Well, get that stopped." She rubbed Cocoa's ears. "It's okay if he's feeding her healthier foods, but those kinds of snacks will only lead to what she's experiencing now."

"Can you give her something to make her feel better?"

She shook her head. "Start her on some steamed rice soaked in chicken broth when you get home, and then later some baked, unseasoned chicken breast." She made a note in the chart. "If she's not better by tomorrow, call me, and we'll take another look at her." She ran her hand down the dog's back. "I think she'll be fine though."

She heard Addison's voice through the door. She seemed either excited or upset. She yanked open the door, not wanting to wait another second to find out.

Addison spun around and pulled her into a hug. "I passed!"

Her stomach jumped, and she held Addison in her arms for a moment longer than necessary, enjoying the feel of her. She was glad Addison had passed, but thrilled to be hugging her.

Addison backed up. "I'm sorry." She looked away and then back again. "I was just so excited."

"And you should be. I knew you could do it."

"Thanks for the pep-text."

"You're so smart…" All of a sudden she was tongue-tied.

"It really helped." Addison smiled softly.

"How about I buy you lunch to celebrate?" She glanced at Jessie. "We're clear for about an hour, aren't we?"

"Yep. Go celebrate. Bring me back a salad, will ya?"

"We will." Addison bounced as she headed for the door, and Harper was truly happy for her.

As they headed down the sidewalk, they saw Olive coming from the other direction. Addison sped toward her and gave her the good news.

"That's awesome!" Olive stood in front of the door to the deli.

"We're having a celebratory lunch. Do you have time to eat with us?"

"Absolutely." She took out her phone. "Let me text Pete and let him know I won't be back with his lunch right away."

"He'll be starving by the time you get back. Why don't you invite him along?"

Olive laughed. "He will be." She typed in the text and then looped her arm in Addison's as they went to the counter. "I'm so proud of you."

After they ordered their food, and Harper paid, insisting it was her way of saying congratulations, they found a table near the window. Addison took a chair on one side, and Olive took one on the other. She opted for the chair next to Addison. Besides, if Pete showed up, he'd want to sit next to Olive.

"Thanks so much for lunch. You really didn't have to."

"Yes, she did." Addison bumped her. "I deserve a prize for all the hours I spent studying."

"You definitely deserve a prize." Harper grinned at Addison's excitement. "Besides, I figured Pete wouldn't complain as much if I did."

Olive smiled, apparently noticing the easy vibe between them. "You two seem to be getting along better."

Addison glanced at Harper. "I think we are."

She nodded. "Definitely." She was trying anyway. "We've come to an agreement."

"Harper's not going to be such a prima donna." Addison grinned.

Harper let her mouth drop open. "And Addison's not going to be such a lazy butt."

Addison giggled. Apparently anything Harper said today was going to slide off Addison's back. She was riding a high that no one could destroy.

Once their lunches were delivered, they discussed everything from the test to sales at the store. Harper was glad for that. She didn't want to focus on what might or might not happen between her and Addison. Today would be about celebrating Addison's victory. It was really good to see her so happy.

Patty came through the door of the clinic and handed Addison a box of supplies before she went back outside to retrieve another. "Nicki asked about you." Patty started unloading the box. "Said you and she hadn't talked since she left last week. Is that true?"

"Yes. I don't know quite how to end it." She'd tried to be gentle with her when she'd come to town. The more she thought about their *arrangement*, the more she realized Nicki wasn't someone she could spend a lifetime with.

"You're going to have to tell her, you know." Patty pursed her lips. "Even if it was casual, it's only fair that you be straight with her. You'd expect the same."

"Got it, Mom."

"Hey. Don't get mad at me because you fell in love with someone else."

"I'm not in love with someone else."

Patty smiled. "You're not?"

"Am I?"

"Oh, honey." Patty laughed. "You curl your hair in the morning, even put on mascara, and you've finally stopped wearing those horrible slippers at work. You've never done that for anyone before." Patty continued to put away the supplies. "I'm sure Brook's happy about your change in habits—having her mother show up in the grocery store in her pajama pants had to be something to live down."

Tears filled her eyes. "Shit."

"Don't worry. Brook got over that a long time ago."

She shook her head. "It's not that." She swiped the tears from her face.

"Then what is it?"

"I can't be in love with Harper. She's going to leave again."

Patty raised her eyebrows. "Again?"

"Yes. Again." She spun around and tossed a few boxes onto a shelf that was too far above her head. "I didn't want her to leave the first time."

"You never told me that."

"Never told her either." She turned around and gripped the counter behind her. "How could I tell you I thought I was in love with Harper when I was pregnant and planning a wedding with Logan?"

Patty took in a breath and smiled softly. "You couldn't, but I wish you had. I don't know how I would've reacted with you being pregnant and all. That was a huge fact for me to deal with at the time. Even so, I think I would've listened. You sure as hell would've been a lot better off now."

"I don't know how Harper did it, Mom." She sank into the chair. "I mean, my friends are so judgmental. I don't know if I can even tell them—I don't know how they'll react."

"About your feelings for Harper?"

She nodded. "And about me in general."

"Well, from what Jim said, Harper didn't tell them. It just happened. In fact, he was the one who outed her to her mother."

"Oh my gosh. How?"

"Someone from the school called to let them know Harper was engaging in lewd behavior on school grounds. Apparently, someone had seen her kissing another girl behind the gym after school one day."

She'd found herself in that very same spot a few times herself with Logan. "Really? Who?"

Patty chuckled. "Riley Stone."

"Riley?" How could she not have known that her best friend had kissed a girl, let alone Harper?

Patty nodded. "He thought it was ridiculous that the school had even called, and he told Faye about it. Of course he had no idea Riley was a girl."

"Wow. Riley never told me that."

"So maybe your friends won't be so judgmental after all. At least the important ones."

"Maybe so." It all made sense now. Riley was the only one of her friends who had never pushed her into a relationship with anyone. Riley, still to this day, in fact only recently, had said for her not to worry, the right person would come along and she'd know immediately they were the one. Could Riley possibly know about her feelings for Harper? Was she that transparent? Would Riley tell the rest of their friends? *Fuck.* She needed to do immediate damage control. She rushed to the door.

"Where are you going?"

"To see Riley."

"Jesus, Addie. I told you that in confidence."

"Don't worry, Mom. This isn't about Riley. It's about me telling her who I am."

❖

The boutique wasn't busy when Addison entered. She spotted Riley behind the counter checking out a customer and rushed to her. She leaned across the counter and whispered in a low growl, "You made out with Harper Sims in high school?"

Riley smiled at the woman she was helping. "I think that will look perfect on you." The woman took the bag from Riley and went to the door. Riley glanced around the small boutique she owned and managed. "Claire, can you take over for a minute?" She narrowed her eyes at Addison. "*You*. Follow me."

She followed Riley into the back room and out the door that led to the paved employee lot behind the various shops that lined Main Street.

"What the hell is wrong with you?" Riley paced. "You can't come into my place of business and spout things like that. Especially when Claire is working. I'm happily married to Bran."

"Is it true?"

"Who told you? Harper?"

She shook her head. "No. Harper would never tell anyone something like that."

"Then who?"

She raised an eyebrow. "So, it's true?"

"You can't tell anyone." Riley kneaded her forehead with her fingers. "It was just something I tried. It didn't work for me."

"What do you mean, *it didn't work*?"

"I mean, I'd close my eyes and try to let it happen, but *nothing* did. It wasn't the same feeling I got when I kissed Bran."

She knew exactly what Riley meant, but the total opposite. "So, you didn't do anything else with Harper?"

"Hell, no. She fucking ignored me after your birthday party. I was an ass, wouldn't go into the closet with her. I chose Bran instead." She raked her fingers through her hair. "You saved me and went in with her. Remember?"

"Yeah. I remember." She stared at the mountains in the distance. "Best fucking kiss of my life."

Riley grabbed her arm. "Seriously?"

She nodded, still uncertain how Riley would take the news.

"You never told anyone either. Did you…with Harper…after that?"

"No. I was too chicken—afraid of what you and everyone else would think."

"Oh my God." Riley's eyes grew wide. "She ignored me because of you?"

She made eye contact. "Maybe…I think so."

"That's fucking fantastic." Riley took her by the shoulders.

"She can be so irritating. Everything has to be done her way." Except for recently, and she didn't know what that was about.

"Does it make you want to send things flying across the room and then crawl across the exam table and drop into her lap?"

"Who are you?" She pulled her eyebrows together as the vision popped into her head.

"I'm your best friend, and I know who's best for you." She giggled. "And now she's back."

"Temporarily."

"We can change that, can't we?" Riley clapped her hands together. "She can take over her dad's practice."

"She already has a practice in Denver."

"She can have both, can't she?"

"I'm not sure. There are strings attached to that one."

"Are they solid?"

She shook her head. "From what I've heard, she's hanging on by a thread."

Riley scrunched her nose. "Which means you'd be the rebound girl. Damn it." She blew out a breath. "What do you have going on after work?"

"Nothing. I think Brook has plans to hang out with her friends."

"Okay, then. Let's meet at the bar. We can eat snacks, drink wine, and flesh out a plan. It'll be fun."

"I'm not sure that's a good idea."

"And I'm not sure I want you to be alone the rest of your life."
She pulled Addison into a hug. "You should shower first. You smell
a little like wet dog." She pushed her out to arm's length and looked
her up and down. "And what the hell are you wearing?"

"Flannel? This is what I wear to work."

"Not anymore you don't." She pulled open the door. "I've got
a few things that will definitely get Harper's interest."

"Uh…thanks. I think."

Riley rushed through the store, pulling several pieces of casual
clothing from the racks, then went behind the counter, folded them
nicely, and put them in a bag. Addison reached for her wallet, but
Riley waved her off.

"Consider it hush money." Riley came around the counter,
handed her the bag, and scooted her out the door. "Meet me at six."

"But."

"Nope. You'd better be there, or I'll find you." She grinned.
"And that might not be pretty." She glanced over her shoulder. "Wear
one of those outfits. You never know who you might run into."

"Fine." She rolled her eyes. "Whatever." She plucked at the
front of her shirt and held it to her nose. *Ugh.* She did smell like
dog. She definitely had to stop using the clinic washer and dryer for
her laundry.

CHAPTER FOURTEEN

B rook took a spot on the couch with her friends. One of them handed her a beer, and she twisted off the top before she relaxed into the cushions and scanned the living room. Johnny's parents were out of town for the weekend, and he'd been planning this party for weeks. Her mom had given her permission to come to the party. Of course, she'd left out the part about no parents, and her mom hadn't asked. She'd been in a great mood and was going out for drinks with Riley.

The place would be packed soon. Well, as packed as it could be for Blueridge. Everyone in their high school was planning to come, plus all the kids who'd graduated within the past couple of years who hadn't left town for college, which added up to about twenty. She was determined that she would not be here for these parties next year.

She saw an unfamiliar girl dressed in black skinny jeans and a tan crop-top sweatshirt, standing in the kitchen doorway alone, fidgeting. Sweatshirt or not, who wore crop-tops in the middle of winter? The girl turned her head, and her long, auburn hair flew as her face came into view. *What the fuck?* She hadn't expected to see Eden at Johnny's party. Which of her friends had invited her? She didn't seem to be hanging out with anyone in particular or any of the groups that had sectioned off into their usual spots. The drinkers were in the living room, the stoners were out back getting high, and the in-betweens were in the kitchen eating whatever they could find to avoid talking to anyone. She was about to get up and go talk to her, when Eden smiled at someone and went farther into the kitchen. Okay. Well, she must know someone here. She relaxed and took a pull on her beer.

She glimpsed Johnny in the kitchen smiling and talking to someone across the room that she couldn't see. Probably his conquest for the night. It still irritated the fuck out of her that he seemed to be able to get any girl he wanted into bed. She'd so wanted to be the last when it had happened to her and felt the urge to warn his newest victim.

She took inventory of her friends. They all seemed to be in the room with her. Maybe she should find Eden and see what she was up to, find out who had invited her. She pushed out of the couch, crossed the living room, and stood at the entrance to the kitchen. Johnny was gone now, and she didn't see Eden. She wandered outside, glanced around—still couldn't find Eden. *Jesus. No.* She ran back inside and up the stairs.

"Eden," she shouted as she took the stairs by twos. She was not letting this happen. "Eden. Where are you? Don't hide from me. I saw you earlier." She turned the knob to Johnny's bedroom and threw open the door, and found them sitting on the side of the bed. "What the fuck are you doing?"

Johnny vaulted to his feet. "Nothing. Just hanging out."

Eden seemed stunned.

"Bullshit." She crossed the room, took Eden's hand, and yanked her from the room. "Stay away from him."

"But he's not lying." Eden yanked her hand free. "We were only talking."

"For now. Eventually, he's all about getting in your pants." She took Eden's hand again and tugged her out of the room and down the stairs.

Eden stopped at the bottom of the steps and glanced up to the top where Johnny was standing, then stopped. "What if that's what I want?"

"Not with him, you don't. Once that happens, he won't even acknowledge you." She didn't break eye contact. "Is *that* what you want?"

Eden pulled her hand free again. "How do you know?" Eden was drunk—she could see it in her eyes.

"Because he's already been in mine." She opened the door. "Now let's go." She hit the clicker on her key fob, and the lights flashed on the small SUV. Before they made it to the car, Eden fell to the grass and started puking. "Jesus." When had she drunk all the alcohol? It was still fairly early. Johnny must've fed her a couple of shots. She knelt next to Eden and gathered her long hair in her hands, waiting while she finished. "Are you okay?"

Eden nodded. "Better now."

"I should've left you up there to puke on that asshole Johnny." She helped Eden to her feet, and Jessie showed up out of nowhere to help put her in the passenger seat.

"What the hell happened?"

"Johnny." She fished Eden's keys out of her pocket and pointed to the Ford Escape. "Can you bring her car to my house?"

"Sure. I'll follow you."

She slid into her car and fired the engine. "If you puke in my car, you're going to clean it. Understand?"

Eden nodded.

"I don't know what I was thinking letting you hang out with my friends. You're still a kid." She stared at the road. "Who invited you?"

"I'm not a kid. I'm full grown."

"Yeah, well, maybe your body is, but your brain isn't." She'd made those mistakes already. Why couldn't she let Eden make her own? Because she wasn't an asshole, that's why. "You can come home with me. Gran and Grampy will flip if they see you like this."

As Harper drove up to her dad's house, she spotted Addison's car but didn't see Eden's. Maybe it was in the garage. The conversation they'd had this morning about going to a party tonight popped into her head. It had better be in the garage, or maybe she was running an errand for Dad or Patty.

She knocked on the front door and waited a minute before she turned the knob and went inside. They'd told her she didn't need to knock, but she felt weird about barging in on them.

Daisy rushed in and jumped on Patty as she stood at the sink washing dishes. Addison dried the pan in her hands and set it on the table before she bent down to pet her. The kitchen smelled wonderful.

"I saved you a plate in case you're hungry." Patty pointed to the plate on the table. "Addison just finished. She had drinks with Riley after work."

She noted Addison's raised eyebrow as she looked at her mother. Possibly a signal to Patty that she'd shared more about Addison's evening than she wanted. Even though she was ridiculously curious, she would leave that one alone. What Addison did with her friends wasn't her business.

"Thanks. I'm starving." She opened up the foil on the plate. *Pork chops, yum.* She plucked the chop from the plate and took a bite. "Didn't get much time for lunch today. Seems like everyone needed something done to their pets before the weekend."

Addison reached in the drawer, took out a fork, and handed it to her. "Oh. Really? I could've come back in." She'd left mid-morning to prep for an online quiz she had scheduled for the afternoon.

She took another bite of the chop and dropped into one of the kitchen chairs. "It was fine. Jessie did really well at spacing out the drop-ins and keeping everyone happy." She swallowed as she forked a generous amount of macaroni and cheese. "How'd your quiz go? I'm assuming well, since you celebrated with Riley." She slipped the pasta into her mouth and silenced a moan as she chewed. Then she immediately took another bite. Patty was an awesome cook.

"I think I did okay. Some of the questions were pretty easy. The essay ones took a little more time, but I think my answers were good."

"Easier than your test yesterday, I hope." She finished what was left of the pork chop before she found the spinach on the plate and ate a bite. She'd never had spinach with macaroni and cheese before. It was a good combination.

"Much easier. Different class."

"Glad to hear that." She pushed away from the table and carried her plate to the sink. Patty immediately took it from her. "I can do that."

"I know, but I'm here, so I'll get it."

"Thanks. Is Eden in her room?"

"She's not here, honey. She's gone to that party Brook went to."

"What?"

"She told me you said it was okay."

"I did not. I specifically told her she couldn't go."

"Oh, my. I didn't know."

She took out her phone and hit Eden's number. "Do you know where it's at?" After four rings the phone went to voice mail.

"I don't, but Addie probably does."

"She's not answering." She hit the button again. A text from Eden came through immediately. She hit the end button and read it.

What's up?

Where are you?

I'm at home watching TV.

Addison put the last of the dishes away and hung the towel on the oven handle. "What did she say?"

She held up the phone for Addison to read. "Oh, no. That's not good."

"You said Brook went too?"

Addison nodded. "I'll call her."

"No. Can you take me to the party?"

"Sure. Let me grab my jacket." She went into the entryway, took a red ski parka from one of the hooks on the wall, and slipped it on. "I'll drive."

Patty stood in the doorway as they left. "I'm sorry, honey."

"Don't worry about it. Not your fault." Her daughter seemed to have picked up a new habit while they'd been there.

She slid into the passenger seat and buckled up. "Do you know the kids that are going to be at the party?" She assumed Addison did, or she wouldn't have let Brook go.

Addison fired up the car and glanced behind them as she backed up. "Yeah. Brook's grown up with them all. You know how it is here. People don't change much." She pulled out of the driveway. "You let Eden go to parties at home, right?"

"Yes, but I usually know the parents, and she doesn't lie to me about it."

"Hmm. Why do you think she lied this time?"

She shrugged. "I don't know. Because I told her no?"

"That would be my guess." Addison kept her eyes on the road. "She probably just wants to get to know some of the kids in town."

The house wasn't far away, and they'd gotten there quickly since the roads were clear. Snow was predicted for later in the night, one of the reasons she'd told Eden she couldn't go. One of the excuses, rather. She wasn't comfortable with her going to a party where she didn't know any of the kids and hadn't had a chance to meet any of the parents yet.

"I don't see her car."

"I don't see Brook's either." She hit the button on her steering wheel and said Brook's name. The ringing came through the speakers, but after a few it went to voice mail, like Eden's had. A text came through next. Kids didn't like to talk on the phone at all these days. Addison pulled to the side of the road, read the text, responded a few times, and showed it to her.

What's up? The standard question.

Where are you?

Home. Where are you?

On my way. Is Eden with you?

Yes. We're hanging out.

She took a breath tried to calm herself. At least she was safe.

Addison dropped her phone into the console slot. "So, not as bad as you thought." Addison raised her eyebrows and smiled.

"No. I guess not." Eden had still lied to her for some reason. "Do you think they were even at the party?"

"I don't know. Brook intended to go. Maybe she ran into Eden there. We'll get the full story out of them when we get there."

Harper's pulse raced when they spotted Eden's car in front of Addison's house. She was so angry, she couldn't even be relieved. She was either going to hug her to death or ground her for life. She didn't know which yet. Eden had gone to a party that she had specifically told her not to attend. Probably the same thing Harper would've done at her age. But that wasn't an excuse.

The relief kicked in when she opened the door and found Eden, Brook, and Jessie sitting at the table eating ice cream. None of them looked drunk or high.

Addison didn't wait for an explanation as she rushed by her and came in hot at Brook. "I can't believe you took her to that party."

Brook narrowed her eyes but didn't speak.

She followed Addison in and did the same with Eden. "And I can't believe you went after I told you not to go." She'd never been so angry with her before.

"Brook made me leave—got me out of there."

"She did?" She couldn't hide the surprise in her voice.

"You did?" Apparently, neither could Addison.

"Of course, I did. I wouldn't let her hook up with any of those jerks."

"Were you going to hook up with someone?"

Eden glanced at Brook. "I hadn't planned on it, but—"

"But anything can happen at those parties. So, as soon as I saw her, I brought her home."

She noticed a shifting of eyes between them and what looked like relief in Eden's. It seemed as though Brook might have saved Eden from a bad choice. "Thank you." She veered her gaze to Eden. "Let's go. You're in big trouble."

"Can I finish my ice cream?"

"Why don't you stay for a few minutes. Have some ice cream yourself." Addison touched her hand. "You girls go into Brook's room and watch some TV." She took off her coat and hung it on the rack by the front door before she headed to the counter. The girls picked up their bowls and left the kitchen. "All I have is vanilla, but I have salted caramel sauce."

"I'm too upset to eat." She shrugged off her coat and hung it on one of the dining-room chairs before she sank into it. "She was going to lose her virginity tonight."

"Maybe." Addison shrugged. "How do you know she hasn't already?" She dipped out two bowls of ice cream and doused them with caramel sauce.

"I don't. I've been ignoring the whole situation." She shook her head. "I should've never left her at Dad and Patty's. They have no idea what to watch out for."

"Maybe not your dad, but my mom knows exactly what happens in this town. She's very plugged into the gossip network." Addison slid one of the bowls in front of her and sat down in the adjacent chair with the other. "She might need a little refresher on teenagers, but I bet we can enlist her to keep you informed when she hears something you need to know about. Especially after tonight. Did you tell her that Eden couldn't go to the party?" She took a bite of ice cream.

"No. I didn't think to, so she probably had no idea. My bad." She swirled her spoon in the caramel sauce.

"So, you let her know in the future, and she can keep an eye out." Addison's spoon clanged against the bowl as she dipped out another bite. "What are you gonna do about it?"

"I don't know." She took a bite of ice cream and gathered her thoughts as the cool creaminess filled her mouth. She wasn't quite sure how she was going to deal with the situation. She'd always trusted Eden in the past. "I've never had to punish her before."

"Seriously?" Addison raised her eyebrows. "Never?"

"No. She's never outright defied me before now."

"At least not that you know of."

"Right. What do you do when Brook gets in trouble?"

"Let's see. The first time, I grounded her from going out for a couple of weeks and took away her phone."

She raised an eyebrow. "The first time?"

"Yeah. She tested me more than once." Addison slipped a small bite into her mouth and swallowed. "It doesn't happen much anymore. We kind of have an understanding now."

"What kind of understanding?"

"I threatened to chaperone her to every party and event she went to if she wasn't straight with me."

"That worked?" She spooned another bite into her mouth.

"She's here with Eden and not at the party, isn't she?"

"That she is." It appeared she was wrong about Brook. She wasn't a bad influence on Eden at all. In fact, she'd been looking after her all along. She finished her ice cream and gathered both their bowls and took them to the sink.

"I can get that." Addison brushed her hand across Harper's back. "Why don't you take Eden home with you tonight? Maybe she needs some mom-time."

"Thanks for talking me down. I probably would've made everything worse if you hadn't."

"Happy to do it. Any time."

She found her way to Brook's room, where the girls were lined up sitting on the bed against the headboard. "Come on. Take your bowl into the kitchen, and put on your coat. You're spending the night with me tonight."

"Am I in trouble?"

"We'll talk about it later." She glanced at Addison, who had followed her, and found herself on the receiving end of a soft smile. Everything she'd said made sense, and Harper was grateful for her advice. "I'll see you tomorrow?"

"I'll open up in the morning. That'll give you time to get Eden settled back at the house."

The woman was a saint, helping her out in so many ways. Boy, had she been wrong about her.

❖

Harper stopped briefly at her dad's house to let him and Patty know she was taking Eden home with her tonight. She picked up Daisy and grabbed her laptop from her SUV. Maybe she did need some time with her. She'd been a little focused on herself lately and didn't want that to be the reason Eden was acting out. A heart-to-heart would be good for both of them.

Eden rounded the car to the driver's side.

"Uh-uh. I'm driving." She put out her hand, and Eden slapped the key fob into her palm as she passed her, heading back around to the passenger side. She slid into the driver's seat and adjusted the seat farther back. Eden was still an inch or two shorter than her.

The fifteen-minute ride was quiet. Not a peep from Eden.

"This rides pretty good." She moved the wheel back and forth, making the car swerve, trying to get a reaction from Eden. "Maybe I should ask Dad to let me drive it."

"You wouldn't."

"Oh yes, I would." She watched the road. "But I already have the Explorer. This would probably be a bit too small for work, don't you think?"

"Way too small. Besides, Grampy gave it to me."

"I guess he did."

When they arrived at the cabin, Eden jumped out of the car and waited at the front door for Harper to unlock it. Daisy lined up right behind her. She'd barely turned the knob before they both bolted inside.

"Hold on, young lady. We have something to discuss." She couldn't believe that she sounded exactly like her mother. A good thing at this point. She dropped the keys on the coffee table next to her laptop and sat on the couch. Eden stood by the counter with her arms across her chest. Harper patted the spot next to her. "Come sit down."

Eden crossed the room and flopped onto the couch. "I didn't do anything wrong." Daisy jumped up next to her, circled a few times until she was satisfied with her spot, and lay down.

"I think you did. You went to a party when I told you not to, and you lied to me about it."

"I didn't drink anything."

"Another lie. You smell like a brewery. You're lucky Brook saved your ass." She relaxed into the couch. "What do you think your punishment should be?"

"No parties for a week."

She laughed. "That's a little light, don't you think?"

"Okay, then what?" Eden seemed nervous.

"I was thinking of locking you in your room and nailing the windows shut, but they might haul me off to jail for that." She smiled. "No driving the car except to and from the clinic, and trips to the store for Dad or Patty."

Eden's eyebrows pulled together, and her mouth dropped open. Harper had to hold in her laugh. "How am I supposed to get around?"

"That's the point. You're not going anywhere for two weeks."

"Two weeks? That's crazy."

"Want to shoot for three? You're lucky it's not a month."

"Fine. I'm going to bed." She popped off the couch. "Can you move, so I can pull out the couch?"

"Nope. You're sleeping with me." She picked up her laptop from the coffee table. "I'm not about to let you have access to an escape route tonight."

"You have got to calm down. I'm not going anywhere."

"You're damn right you're not, and don't tell me to calm down. You're the one who's broken the trust here, not me."

"Fine." She turned and walked toward the bedroom.

"Don't take my spot. I'm on the right."

"I'm *so* taking it."

"You can wear one of my T-shirts in the drawer, and there's an extra toothbrush in the bathroom." Daisy snuggled up against her as she opened her laptop and logged in. "I'll be in shortly."

"No hurry," Eden shouted. "The TV better work in here."

"What do you think, Daisy?" She scratched her back. "Maybe I should take that away too."

"Stop," Eden shouted, and she heard the sound of the TV click on before the door closed.

She logged into her email to see if anything urgent was going on that she needed to address at the clinic in Denver. She couldn't trust that V would be handling everything. She'd already proved herself to be unreliable.

Yet she didn't have that problem at all with Addison. In fact, Addison seemed to be there for everything she needed—work and personal. It was nice to have someone take some of the responsibility off her shoulders for a change.

CHAPTER FIFTEEN

There hadn't been much more discussion about Eden's punishment or why she'd gone to the party without permission. Harper thought a boy must be involved, but Eden wasn't talking. Harper knew she was being naive about teenagers having sex. She'd convinced herself that Eden wasn't even thinking about it, but now she was sure that wasn't true. So many nights she'd gone to bed at home in Denver while Eden had a friend over, some of whom were boys. She couldn't help but wonder if she'd been experimenting. Had she truly been that blind?

She'd dropped Eden off at her dad's and sent her to her room before she had a very frank discussion with her dad and Patty. They completely understood her concerns and agreed to be more vigilant about checking with Harper before letting Eden go out. She hated to turn them into watchdogs, but besides chaining Eden to her side, she had no other way to keep tabs on her.

When she arrived at the clinic, Addison had everything running smoothly, just as she'd promised she would when Harper and Eden left her house last night.

"Hey. I didn't expect you in this early. How was your night?" Addison smiled as she reached down to pet Daisy. "You get everything straightened out with Eden?"

"I think so. She wasn't thrilled with her punishment."

"Oh, yeah? What did you decide on?"

"No parties or going out for a couple of weeks, and I took the car away."

"Good play. I bet she didn't like that at all."

"Nope. It isn't too much, is it? For a first-time offender?"

"I think it fits the crime. I'm seriously surprised she's never done anything wrong."

"Yeah, well. I've always trusted her. That might not have been wise. She could've been getting away with murder right under my nose in Denver."

"I doubt it. Everything is new to her here. She's testing the waters."

"I sure hope so, or I'm a much worse mother than I thought."

"Don't beat yourself up about it. You're not a bad mom. It happens to all of us."

"I appreciate that. Thanks for helping me out last night."

"I was happy to do it. I'm glad it all turned out okay." Addison plucked a patient chart from the counter. "It could've been so much worse."

Addison was right about that, and Harper was very thankful she was. "Who's up next?"

"A golden retriever who seems to have a ball stuck on his tongue." Addison handed her the chart.

"Oh. That should be interesting." She took the chart from Addison and read through the notes. "No other major health concerns for Tuck, though." She didn't know how this would play out. It could be as easy as easing the ball from the dog's tongue or as difficult as having to anesthetize him to remove the ball and part of his tongue. It might be a longer morning than she anticipated. "I might need your help on this one. Plus, if we can't get the ball free, it could be a good case for your internship." She pushed open the door slightly, giving the dog a moment to move if it happened to be lying next to the door. She didn't make a practice of knocking. That just got the animals riled up.

"Good morning, Mr. Jones. I'm Dr. H." She glanced down at Tuck. "I hear Tuck had a tangle with a rubber ball and can't seem to shake it." She kneeled, and the dog squealed and nipped at Harper as she tried to assess the ball on his tongue. "How long has it been like this?"

"I'm not sure. About thirty minutes ago I noticed he hadn't put the ball down in a while. He kept bumping me in the leg with it, and I thought he wanted to play. When I tried to get it from him, he squealed." His eyes widened. "That's when I called."

"It looks like the tip of his tongue is stuck." She grasped his jaw, prompting the dog to open his mouth. "Hopefully it hasn't been like this for long. If it has, we'll have to do surgery to remove the part of his tongue that lost blood flow."

"Oh my gosh. I should've been paying more attention. I didn't even know the ball was there. The neighbor kids lose things across the fence all the time, and he gets into all kinds of stuff around the yard."

Addison touched his arm. "It's not your fault. Dogs eat things."

She glanced at Addison. "I need you to hold his jaw open while I examine him." She directed her attention to Mr. Jones. "Can you keep him calm while I gauge how much of his tongue is in there?"

"Sure." He rubbed the dog's shoulders and tried to maintain eye contact with him.

The dog tried to pull out of Addison's grasp, but she held him steady, giving Harper a chance to assess the situation. "Looks like it's just the tip. Hold him tight while I squeeze the sides of the ball. Hopefully it will loosen. I'm going to try to remove it really quickly, so he might yelp." She did exactly as she said, squeezed the ball close to where it was attached, and between the dog moving his tongue and her pulling the ball, his tongue slipped out. "Success." She held up the ball. "Now let's give him a minute to calm down without us in the room, and then I'll come back and take a look at him." She went to the door.

"We'll be back in a few minutes." Addison followed her out and into the lab area. "That was awesome. He wouldn't even let me touch it."

"Well, that wasn't all me. You two kept him still and calm while I examined him. Otherwise we would've had to sedate him. Still might have to do something else."

"Still. Great job in there."

She smiled, and for some reason that compliment meant something. She knew how to do her job, had for many years, but to know Addison was impressed—even proud of her—felt good.

The next patient was a calico cat named Hashbrown, whose owner was a woman in her mid-thirties. Harper never had the best relationships with cats, and most didn't take well to her. Not the best reputation for a vet.

The woman held the cat close to her chest as she stroked his head. "I think he has a bladder infection. He's peeing all over the house."

"Did you bring a urine sample?"

"Nope. Doesn't pee on demand." The woman shook her head. "Sorry. I'm not trying to be rude. I've only had him a couple of months, and this is the first time I've ever had a cat. I've always had dogs."

"Why did you decide to get one instead of a dog?"

"I work a lot, and one of my friends told me they don't require as much maintenance."

Not the best reason to get a cat, but understandable. "They definitely have different behaviors."

"I'm finding that out. He climbs on *everything* and doesn't listen to me at all. Not sure I made the right decision."

She glanced at his chart. "You think he's about a year old?"

"Yes. My friend's cat had a litter, and she convinced me to take one."

"The same friend who told you cats were easy?"

The woman nodded. "The only thing that really bothers me is the peeing."

"Okay. We'll have to take him to the back to get a urine sample."

Once they got him to the lab area, he squirmed and wiggled as Harper tried to hold him close to her chest, but then he suddenly went wild like he knew what was coming.

The first scratch wasn't too bad, but the second tore a couple of gashes in her forearm. A risk that came with the job.

"Oh my gosh. He got you good."

"I'm fine. Let's just finish this."

Addison stopped, backed up, and grinned.

She pressed her lips together and looked at the ceiling. "He's peeing on me, isn't he?" He'd gotten so stressed he peed all down her coat.

"Yep." Addison chuckled. "Got a big sample now."

She shoved the cat into Addison's arms. "I'll be right back." Thank God it hadn't soaked through and they had more in the back. She could hear Addison laughing as she went to the office and took a clean coat from the rack. Normally being laughed at would have irritated her, but Addison seemed to be laughing with her at the situation more than at her.

Addison had taken the huge handful of fur back to the exam room, so she went directly there to gather more information. "What kind of litter box do you use?" It was clear she wasn't going to get a sample today. She had no desire to add more scratches to her already shredded arms.

"I don't have a litter box. I let him out twice a day."

Mystery solved and it cost her only five scratches and a clean coat. "Get a litter box—one with a hood. He's not a dog. Won't go to the door when he has to go to the bathroom. He'll find a place and do his business." Harper opened the door to the waiting area for her.

"Okay. I'll do that." The woman grabbed up her cat and went through the door.

Addison followed her. "We have training classes for cats." She went behind the counter and said something to Jessie, then slid a piece of paper, presumably a schedule, on the counter for the woman to read.

She went to the lab area, rolled up her sleeves, and found an alcohol swab to clean her wounds. The first one was deep and stung like the dickens when she dabbed it with the alcohol.

"I told Jessie to give her the visit for free, but charge her five hundred dollars for the cleaning bill. She did sign her up for training classes." Addison's eyes widened as she came into the room. "Oh my gosh. He really got you." She took another alcohol pad from the box and started cleaning the wounds for Harper.

She found herself staring at the blondness of Addison's hair, how it met in the middle of her head perfectly and the ends were captured loosely into a ponytail. No highlights, no lowlights, only pure, natural blond. She found herself following the blond strands to the creamy skin just behind her ear and then to her neck, where it met the collar of her jacket. *Jesus. She's beautiful.* She moved closer, took in a breath, and caught the subtle scent of cucumber—fresh, light, and a tad citrusy. Addison glanced up and smiled—she'd been caught.

She cleared her throat. "I should get back to work. Which room next?"

"Relax. You're free for an hour." Addison continued cleaning the wounds, then took out some antibiotic ointment and bandages. "Let's get these wrapped up."

She forced herself to settle against the counter and let Addison take care of her as she applied the ointment and wrapped each wound gently.

"The small ones should be okay for now. I think Band-Aids would only get in your way."

"Thanks. I…" She didn't know what to say, how to express her gratitude. V had never once bandaged a wound for her with such care.

"You're welcome. You might need to start wearing Kevlar-reinforced sleeves." She chuckled.

"Have Jessie add some to the supply order."

"Done."

Addison grinned, and the pain in her arms vanished. All she felt was the tingle in her belly. What was this woman doing to her?

Addison entered her mother's house and hung her coat on the wall peg. Harper had beaten her there and was already sitting at the table. "Something smells really good."

"Where's Brook tonight?"

"At home studying."

"She's gonna miss her granny's spaghetti?" Jimmy said from the doorway as he entered the room. "Must be a big test."

"She's taking the ACTs soon. I told her I'd bring her some, and lots of garlic bread."

"I'll fix her a bowl now before it all gets eaten."

"Thanks. I know she'll appreciate it."

Eden appeared from the hallway. "Brook gets all the special stuff."

Harper raised an eyebrow. "I'd keep your comments to yourself. She saved your ass last night."

Eden gave Harper a sheepish look and sank into one of the kitchen chairs.

Seemed she was a bit jealous of Brook. Not unusual for a sixteen-year-old to envy the freedom of an almost eighteen-year-old. Addison had similar feelings when she was younger. She glanced at Harper. Still did sometimes. Eden didn't realize that sometimes those freedoms came with consequences—sometimes temporary, sometimes permanent. She had to admit that Brook was a permanent consequence she was happy to have even if her goals had changed—been put off longer than she'd anticipated.

"There's plenty for everyone." Patty rubbed Eden's shoulder. "I bought that kind of popcorn you like. You can have some later." She handed her a stack of napkins. "Now be a dear and set the table."

Eden seemed to perk up a bit. She popped out of her chair, headed for the silverware drawer, and gathered up a bunch of forks.

"Set a spoon out for your Grampy and one for you and your mom if you want one."

"Nah. We don't use spoons." Eden grabbed one from the drawer and placed it next to the fork at her grandfather's place. Then she went to the cabinet and took down the salad bowls and plates. Seemed Eden was trying to get on her grandparents' good side early. They'd be an easier sell than Harper when it came to getting her freedom.

"Why don't you let me help you with those." Addison took the plates from Eden and set them next to the stove. "Anyone want wine?" She crossed the room and took a bottle of red from the wine rack on the buffet.

"I'm in for a glass, maybe two." Harper got up, found the glasses in the cabinet, and set them on the table.

Eden picked up a glass. "Can I have some?"

"No." Addison and Harper spoke at the same time.

"You can grab the salad out of the refrigerator, though." Addison opened the bottle and set it next to the glasses, then put a container of Parmesan cheese on the table before she took each bowl from Patty as she filled them with pasta and sauce.

"It's so nice to have both of you for dinner tonight." Patty put the basket of garlic bread in the middle of the table and sat. "How was your day?"

"More eventful than usual." Harper pulled up her sleeves, dipped out some salad, and passed the bowl to Addison.

"Oh, my. What happened to your arms?"

"Ornery cat."

"That looks more like an angry cat."

"Was not happy about giving a urine sample."

"Sometimes you have to diagnose without." Jim poured a large amount of Italian dressing on his salad.

"Oh, she got one." She laughed and grinned at Harper. "All down her lab coat."

"Nothing was wrong with the cat. Seemed the woman had never had one before, didn't know about litter boxes."

They all laughed. That one even got Eden to smile.

"And don't forget the dog that got the ball stuck on his tongue."

"Whose dog was that?" Jim asked as he forked a bite of salad. "Russ Jones?"

"How'd you know?"

"He's in all the time. I've told him a thousand times to clean up his yard. Tuck gets into everything."

"That's totally right." She shook her head.

"Thankfully, the tongue came back to life, or our day would've been even longer." Harper smiled at Addison as she twirled a forkful of spaghetti and stuffed it into her mouth.

"How are the chickens, Eden? I hear you're taking care of them now." Addison had heard from Patty how excited Eden got whenever it was time to feed them or check for eggs.

Eden looked up from her plate and took a drink to wash down her last bite. "The chickens are great. We got the chick brooder set up yesterday."

"Ooh, do we have chicks already?" Chick hatching was one of Addison's favorite times of year.

"No. Not yet. We were making sure everything works. Grampy says we have to set it up before they hatch."

"Right, and you did that?" Harper raised her eyebrows.

"She did." Jim grinned at Eden as though she'd just received a blue ribbon at the state fair. "The heat lamp is all set, and she's checked the temperature for several days. I think it's ready to go."

"All the bedding and chick starter are ready for hatch day." Eden took a bite of garlic bread.

"Wow. You're really on top of it." Addison was impressed.

Jimmy nodded. "She is, and she's been very patient." He picked up his wine and held it in the air, toasting her. "The chicks should hatch soon."

"Isn't it kind of early to hatch chickens?"

"Maybe, but I thought she'd like to see it, so I set the eggs early."

It seemed Eden had never experienced chickens before and found the entire process of fertilizing and laying eggs fascinating. Would Eden follow in Harper's footsteps and become a veterinarian? Brook had no interest whatsoever. Her first choice for a career was in computer science, website development in particular. She liked the idea of building virtual worlds on the internet that anyone could visit from anywhere in the world, even if they couldn't afford it. Addison guessed she'd had enough of the outdoors growing up in Blueridge.

Eden finished what was left on her plate before she got up, took her plate to the sink, rinsed it, and put it in the dishwasher.

"Where are you off to?" Patty asked. "Why don't you sit down and visit with us? Have some cake."

"I'm finished. I'd like to go to my room now."

"I wonder how long she's going to hold on to that anger?" Patty watched Eden walk down the hallway to her room.

"Probably about a week. Then she'll start trying to get me to give her the car back."

They all chuckled.

"It's not funny." The comment came from the hallway, just before Eden slammed her door.

Jim lifted an eyebrow and grinned. "Seems she's got a little of her mother in her."

"Harper was like that as a teenager?" Addison's interest was piqued.

He nodded. "Had to take that door off more than once."

She tilted her head and stared at Harper. "I would've never guessed that. You were so quiet in school."

"Was I?" Harper carried her plate to the sink. "I'm up for cake. Anyone else?"

"She definitely thought she ran the house. Still does." He winked as Harper collected his dinner plate, and then Patty's, and then Addison's as she stood to help.

"I got it." Harper rinsed and loaded the rest of the plates before she lifted the foil from the top of the rectangular cake pan. She looked at Patty and widened her eyes. "Chocolate?"

"With buttercream frosting."

"My favorite." She took four cake plates from the cabinet.

Addison rolled her eyes playfully. "Harper gets all the special stuff."

Harper laughed loudly. "Well, we have to have some sort of balance here, don't we?"

Addison's belly tingled as she watched Harper cut the cake and place a slice on each of the plates on the counter. The somersaults began when Harper reached over her shoulder and set one of the plates in front of her. Jesus, she smelled good. Like raspberries and cream, and she wanted nothing more than to drown herself in that smell and taste right now.

"You girls want coffee?" Patty went to the pot and poured a couple of mugs.

She raised her hand. "I'll have some. I have more homework to do."

"None for me, thanks." Harper dug into her cake and moaned as she chewed, sending Addison's belly into full-on gymnastics.

"Did you get much rest last night?" Patty glanced down the hall as she handed Jim his cup of coffee. "Eden didn't come out of her room much at all today."

"Only to feed the chickens and check for eggs." Jim took a swig of his coffee. "She loves those chickens."

"It took me a while to fall asleep, but once I did, I slept fine." Harper cut another bite of her cake and scooped it onto her fork. "She wanted to sleep on the couch, but I made her come in with me. That might've been a little drastic, but I was angry at the whole situation. I think she got the message."

"I hope so. I'd hate to be taking the door off for her too." Jim grinned as he forked a chunk of cake.

"I still can't believe that." Addison touched Harper's hand, then drew back when she saw Harper's eyes and realized what she'd done. Way too much familiarity going on today. She glanced at her mother, who seemed to notice the exchange.

Patty glanced at her watch. "Finish your cake, Jimmy. That sitcom you like is coming on in a few minutes. After that I want to see the rest of that show from last night. I think we both fell asleep." Patty glanced at Addison and Harper. "You two can clean up, can't you?"

This was her mom's totally obvious way of leaving them alone together. "Sure. We got it." She glanced at Harper.

"On it." Harper smiled. "Do you want some help with your homework?"

"Sure." She didn't know what this new thing between her and Harper was, but she liked it a whole lot better than what it had been before.

CHAPTER SIXTEEN

Lunch bag in hand, Harper knocked on the door but had no answer. She couldn't believe how quickly Friday had arrived. Working with Addison instead of against each other at the clinic made everything run a whole lot smoother. Addison should be there since she'd left early to study. She moved closer and heard music through the door. It was faint, but definitely music. She went to the garage and looked through the window. Her car was there. She went to her SUV, opened the door, and stared back at the house. What if something was wrong? What if Addison was hurt? Panic rushed through her, and she slammed the Explorer door shut and ran to the door, rang the doorbell several times, then knocked again, only louder this time. Still no answer. She turned the doorknob—unlocked—pushed open the door, and ventured inside.

Something smelled wonderful, chicken maybe. She checked the kitchen first. Addison's keys were on the counter, so she had to be there somewhere. She set the lunchbox on the counter next to the crockpot, which had to be the source of the delicious aroma filling the house. She lifted the cover, and the scent of Italian herbs wafted into her nose. She was tempted to find a spoon and take a taste, but Addison's safety was her first priority.

"Addison?" The music became louder as she ventured through the living room into the hallway that led to the bedrooms. "You here?" When she caught sight of movement in the master bedroom she stopped and inched her way toward the door. Addison was alone and dancing; she could see her in the mirror. Dressed in black yoga pants and a royal-blue athletic bra, she held small weights in each hand. She'd never seen her so free and loose. The tingle in her belly resurfaced, the pure joy she felt watching happy Addison unexpected. Propping her shoulder against the wall, she watched Addison dance, which made her realize what she'd been missing and question her current path with V in the city. She didn't want to lose this feeling right here—ever.

Addison made eye contact in the mirror and spun to the door. "How did you get in here?"

"I rang the bell and knocked several times." She pushed away from the wall. "I got worried, and the door was open."

Addison narrowed her eyes. "The bell is broken, and the door was not open."

"It was unlocked."

Addison raised her eyebrows. "You got worried?"

"Well, yes. If you were dead on the bathroom floor, who would run the clinic?" She tried to blow off the situation as though it meant nothing. Revealing her feelings had never been easy for her.

Addison tilted her head. "You were worried about the clinic." Her voice was low, tinged with skepticism.

"Of course." She cleared her throat. "Whatever you have cooking in that crockpot smells delicious."

"Italian chicken soup." Addison moved toward her and stopped just short of the doorway. "You're welcome to stay and have a bowl."

"Thanks. I'd love that." She wanted to stay and have a whole lot more than a bowl of soup, but that would do for now. "I don't know if I could eat anything else after smelling it."

Addison smiled and then seemed to stop herself from enjoying the moment. "Exactly why are you here?"

"Your mom asked me to drop off your lunch bag. She said you have only the one and will need it Monday."

Addison scrunched her eyebrows. "My mom said that?"

She nodded. "I put it on the counter."

"And you were willing to drop it off?"

"Sure. Why wouldn't I be?"

"No reason." She clutched the door. "I need to take a quick shower. There's beer and wine in the fridge. Help yourself."

"Do you mind if I bring Daisy inside?"

"Of course not." She closed the door quickly.

Harper ventured back down the hallway and outside to get Daisy. She filled the travel bowl with kibble she kept in a container in the back of her SUV and set it just inside the entry to the kitchen. Then she pulled out several drawers to find a spoon before she took the top off the crockpot and snagged a bite. It tasted as wonderful as it smelled. Just like heaven. She didn't cook much for herself, so a home-cooked meal was always welcome. She'd been getting a lot of those lately.

She set the lid back on top and pulled open the refrigerator, where she found a bottle of chardonnay and a few craft beers. Addison had good taste in liquor. She grabbed a bottle of ale and popped off the top, then settled in on the couch and took a sip. She glanced around the place. Simple yet elegant, like Addison. She shook her head at herself. Addison was proving to be so much different than she'd thought in the past.

Addison leaned against the door and took a deep breath. She couldn't believe Harper was here, in her house again—just on the other side of the door. She wanted, more than anything, to open the door, pull her into the bedroom, and ravish her for hours. She needed to slow those thoughts way down—to a crawl even. A few minor connections here and there meant nothing. Harper was not staying. She was going back to her practice in the city at some point. It would be bad to let her heart lead her down that path of destruction—again. But Jesus—Harper was like a sparkler that burned hot and bright. She clouded Addison's vision from everything else around her, and God knew, she loved fireworks.

Why hadn't she told Harper how she'd felt before? Why couldn't she have been stronger? Why couldn't she have told her friends to butt the hell out of her love life? So many questions without answers. Maybe this was a new beginning with a different ending. Could it be? Possibly, if she'd relax and let it happen.

She pushed away from the door and headed to the shower. She hadn't seen that lunch bag in years. She didn't know whether to kill or thank her mother when she saw her tomorrow. She'd know for sure in the next few hours.

She took a quick shower, then washed her hair and dried it partially before she put on a small amount of mascara and eyeliner. Makeup was not in her normal routine, and why did she feel the need to put it on for Harper? If Harper was going to like her, it would need to be for exactly who she was, not a character she would play. She scrubbed it off and then applied moisturizer to her face. After slipping on a pair of comfortable gray, fleece leggings and a red sweatshirt, she headed into the living room. The scent of chicken soup instantly had her stomach screaming to be fed.

Harper was sitting on the couch with Daisy at her feet and seemed to choke on the swig of beer she was taking when Addison walked into the room. She immediately set it down and stood.

"Wow. You're glowing." Harper swept her hands down her jeans as though wiping them clean of something. Harper seemed just as nervous as she was.

"The hot shower." She smiled—her cheeks heating. The makeup hadn't been necessary at all.

Harper cleared her throat but didn't lose eye contact. "You look really good. I probably haven't said that before, or said it correctly, even if I tried. I've been kind of an ass since I came to town."

Harper stared, and she felt a little uncomfortable, as though she were standing naked in front of her—no clothes—no walls—no preconceptions. She felt totally seen. "Thank you." She gave her a sideways smile. "You have been an ass, but then again so have I."

"So we're done with that now?" Harper raised her eyebrows.

"I think we've been over this before, but I'll put away the daggers if you will."

Harper grinned. "Several times. Maybe this time for real?"

"Yes. For real this time." As she turned and walked into the kitchen, she hoped this was truly the end of their hostilities.

Harper followed her into the kitchen. "I went ahead and got some bowls out and silverware ready for the soup. I hope you don't mind."

"No. Not at all." And she didn't. "You found the beer as well."

"Yeah." Harper pulled open the refrigerator. "Can I get you one?"

"Water for me. I have to study tonight."

Harper reached into the refrigerator, took out a bottle of water, twisted the cap off, and handed it to her. "Maybe I can stay and help you with that?"

"I don't want to hold you up if you have something to do."

"I'm totally free. Since Eden can't go out, Brook is hanging out with her tonight at the house. It seems Brook has taken Eden under her wing."

"Seems that way. Brook is very good at making new kids feel comfortable."

"Kind of like her mother was in high school." Harper grinned. "But more of a hard sell now."

"I thought we were putting the daggers away?"

"Sorry. Just my inept attempt at flirting, I guess."

A zing shot through her as the words resonated. She continued dipping out the soup and let it settle, and it did—deep in her belly. "Would you mind grabbing the bread from the oven?" She'd almost forgotten about it. She'd put it in to warm earlier and left it in the oven before she'd started exercising. Thankfully, she'd wrapped it in foil and set the oven on a low temperature.

She reached into the cabinet and slid out a small breadbasket. Harper took the hot pad from the counter and retrieved the bread from the oven. She dropped the whole package into the breadbasket and carried it to the table. Addison couldn't help but notice how polite, even helpful Harper was being. She'd just finished sprinkling a small amount of Parmesan cheese on the top of the soup when she felt Harper close behind her—almost too close.

She took in a deep breath and pushed one of the mugs farther to the side counter. "Can you grab the mugs and meet me at the table?"

"You bet." Harper looped the forefinger of each hand in each of the bowl handles and carried them to the table.

She poured a small amount of olive oil into a bowl and doused it with dried basil, thyme, and rosemary. She also grabbed the bowl of Parmesan and met Harper at the table, where she still stood, waiting for her.

Harper had her hands clasped around the top of one of the chairs. "Is this where you sit?"

"Actually, I usually sit so I can see out the front window."

Harper rushed around the table to that chair and pulled it out for her. Wow. Who was this Harper, and where had she hidden the arrogant, selfish Harper that Addison knew and disliked?

"Thank you." Her hands shook as she set the bowls of herbs and cheese in the middle of the table. She knew how to manage the old Harper, but this new, nice Harper was making her unsettlingly nervous. Even though she'd already had a peek of nice Harper this week and had to admit she was a pleasure to work with.

Once seated, Harper picked up the breadbasket, opened the foil, and offered a piece to her. "What's on your agenda for studying tonight?"

Again with the niceness. "Veterinary critical care. I have another test coming up soon."

"Ooh, that one's exciting. I think they leave that class until last so you don't get freaked out."

"Yeah. It definitely would've scared me if I'd taken it earlier."

"But now you've had practice and know what you're doing."

"I wouldn't say I know what I'm doing, but I have had a lot of practice." She laughed. "Your dad's good about letting me do the procedures."

"I'm glad to hear that. I plan to make sure you get as much practice as possible while I'm here."

"I really appreciate that." She stirred her spoon in her soup. "Can I be honest with you?"

"Of course. I expect nothing less." Harper dipped a piece of bread into the herb mixture and took a bite.

"When you got here, I was worried you might not let me do anything." She looked down at her bowl and scooped out a spoonful of soup. "I mean, I just didn't know."

"I might be a stickler for the rules, but that doesn't mean I want you to fail. You're in the middle of your internship semester, right?"

She nodded. "I am. Your dad's been pretty generous with his reports."

"I don't see any reason why I won't be as well. As long as you perform the procedures correctly."

A weight immediately lifted from her shoulders. She'd been worried for nothing. She was good at her job, and Harper didn't have any reason to think anything less. Jim would probably still send the reports, with Harper's input. She hadn't let her instructor know he was off on medical leave.

"This soup is fantastic." Harper spooned another bite into her mouth. "And this bread is delicious." She snagged another piece. "Did you make it too?"

She shook her head. "No. The bakery did that."

"Bravo to you and the bakery."

"Thanks. This meal is one of my favorites, and it's easy. I just throw all the ingredients into the pot, set it on low, and let it cook all day." She took a swig of water. "I can give you the recipe if you'd like."

"I'd love that. It'll come in handy when I get back to Denver. I spend a lot of long days in the clinic there."

"Tell me about your clinic."

"It's not huge, but we're in a great location. It's not as profitable as I'd like yet. I still owe a fair amount of money, because buying a clinic is expensive." She took another bite and swallowed. "But it's worth every penny."

"Your dad said you've had it for a few years now."

"Close to five."

"He's very proud of you, you know." She stuffed a piece of bread into her mouth and swallowed. "Tells everyone who will listen about you and your practice."

Harper smiled. "So that's why everyone who comes into the clinic seems to know me."

"I'm pretty sure he'd have a shrine erected in the lobby if Patty would let him."

Harper laughed that hearty laugh of hers. "I'm sure you'd all love that." She finished the last of the soup in her bowl. "Do you mind if I have a little more?"

"No. Not at all." She pushed out of her chair. "I'll have another ladle full as well."

"I'll get it." Harper took both their bowls to the kitchen and dipped more into each, then came back to the table. "If you don't watch out, I might end up here for dinner every night."

"I'll be sure to make plenty then." She still wasn't sure what was happening between them, but if she didn't know better, she'd think Harper was nervous. Maybe she should stop wondering and enjoy what was happening.

Brook rushed through the front door just before eleven. "Hey, Mom." She stopped and seemed to assess them at the table. "I'm going to bed." She headed down the hallway, and they heard a door close.

It seemed as though they'd been studying for hours, but Harper wasn't ready to leave yet. She hoped Addison wasn't ready to let her either. "Can we take a break? Maybe watch some TV?" She pushed away from the table. "I've found it's always best to study in spurts so my mind doesn't get fuzzy."

"You still study?"

Harper nodded. "I have to keep up on new research, techniques, and procedures."

Addison groaned. "So the studying never ends."

She laughed. "Afraid not."

Addison stood and stretched her arms above her head. The sliver of flesh peeking out between Addison's sweatshirt and sweats immediately caught Harper's attention. She glanced up to see she'd been busted, her cheeks warming. "I could use something cool to drink, if you have anything."

Addison went to the kitchen and opened the refrigerator. "I have water and soda." She plucked a soda from the shelf for herself. "Want some popcorn?"

"If we're having popcorn, then I'll need a soda."

Addison handed her the one in her hand and grabbed another.

She popped open her can. "When you continue with your bachelor's degree, you should find yourself a study group. It will help you a lot, and then you'll already have resources when you move on to veterinary school."

Addison hesitated. "I'm not sure when that's going to happen."

"Oh. I thought you'd want to do it right away."

"I haven't figured out the finances yet. With Brook going to college and all."

"Gotcha. You shouldn't wait too long, though. Veterinary school is very competitive, so you'll want to continue while everything's still fresh in your mind." She took a sip of her soda. "For what it's worth, I think you'll make a great doctor."

"Really?" Addison took a packet of popcorn from the cabinet and kneaded it with her fingers, then put it in the microwave and hit the popcorn button.

"Sure. You're great with people, you make sound decisions, and you ask questions when you don't know something. Most of the time." She grinned because it hadn't been easy for Addison to ask Harper questions at first. "Plus, you seem to handle the stress well. Most people don't realize the physical and emotional stress that comes with the job."

"It's hard sometimes." Addison stared at the timer on the microwave as it counted down the seconds.

"Yep. Very hard, and heartbreaking at times, but we continue because we love animals."

"Being a mother hasn't hurt. It's given me more compassion, I think."

"I agree. It changed me."

The microwave buzzer rang, and Addison retrieved the popcorn, opened the bag, and spilled it out into a large wooden salad bowl. She gathered the bowl and her soda. "What do you want to watch?"

She noticed the Apple TV device on the shelf below the TV. "I have Netflix on my phone, if you want to stream something." She'd heard from Eden that Addison didn't have Netflix. "Or we can watch a DVD if you'd rather."

"Netflix is fine. There are a couple of shows I want to watch, but I haven't subscribed yet."

She felt giddy about watching a show with Addison. Choosing a show versus a movie meant the possibility of nights like tonight happening again, and Harper was more than okay with that.

When Harper woke, the show they'd been watching was on episode seven, and she was pinned to the couch. She lifted her head and found Addison's head on her shoulder, the rest of her twisted on top of her like a cat in what looked like the most uncomfortable position. Daisy lay on the couch at her feet. No wonder she couldn't feel her arm. She shifted slightly to free it and held it up in the air, deciding where to put it. It tingled as the blood flow returned. Addison was still sound asleep, and she really didn't want to wake her. She'd want to study more, and Harper felt she needed the rest. They could catch up on studying in the morning, but she could never really catch up on sleep.

She gently laid her arm across Addison and stroked her hair lightly. She should've resisted the urge but couldn't. Addison shifted, and she thought she was going to wake. Instead, she settled into the crook of Harper's arm. Soon she heard soft breathing, accompanied by tiny snores, and knew Addison was fast asleep again. She found her phone with her other hand, scrolled through Netflix, and clicked on a movie to put on in the background until she fell back to sleep herself. She had to admit, having Addison curled up beside her didn't feel odd at all. On the contrary, it felt absolutely wonderful—more comfortable than she'd felt with anyone in a long time.

CHAPTER SEVENTEEN

Addison curled into the warm body beneath her, wrapped her arm around her waist, and snuggled her face into the soft pillow under her head. Such a wonderful dream she'd been having. She took in a deep breath and caught the spicy scent of black orchid, pomegranate, and mahogany—felt the rapid heartbeat beneath her cheek. Her eyes flew open, and she realized she was wrapped up with Harper on the couch. She didn't dare move. Harper's hand was tangled in her hair. How had they ended up this way? The last she remembered, they were watching a Netflix show and eating popcorn. The TV screen was dark. Had Harper woken during the night and turned it off? She moved slightly to glance up to see if Harper was still asleep.

"You're awake." Harper sounded groggy.

"Well, this is awkward." She pushed out of Harper's arms and sat. "I'm so sorry. I don't know what happened last night."

Harper smiled. "Don't apologize. You were tired."

"I guess so. What time is it?"

"It's still early. A little after seven."

"Oh, my." She pushed her hair out of her face. "How long have you been awake?"

"Not long. You were sleeping so well, I didn't want to wake you."

"I guess I needed the rest." She hadn't slept so long and so good in weeks. "I need to get changed and go to the clinic."

"Tell you what." Harper stood. "Why don't you take the morning off? We don't have a lot of appointments this morning since it's Saturday. I can take care of them." She walked to the dining-room table and took her coat from the back of the chair.

She stood and followed her to the door. "Are you sure?"

"I'm sure." She slipped on her coat. "You can come over to my place this afternoon, and I'll help you study more." She laughed. "Only this time you won't be so tired, and we'll actually get more studying in."

"That sounds great." She couldn't believe how happy planning to see Harper again made her.

Harper opened the door and went out, Daisy trailing behind.

"Harper."

Harper turned around. "Yeah?"

"Thank you again for helping me." She followed her out.

Harper smiled softly. "It really is my pleasure."

She was wrong about that. Last night had been completely Addison's pleasure. She only hoped she hadn't snored or, worse yet, drooled on her.

Harper shifted from one foot to the other and backed up slightly. "You're probably going to think this is weird, but when you stand this close to me, it makes me nervous. I feel like I'm sixteen again and going to throw up."

She knew exactly how Harper felt. Her stomach rattled every time she came near. "Well, don't do that." She laughed. "That would be a memory I don't think I could erase."

Harper chewed on her bottom lip. "So, here's the deal. I think I've been in love with you since we first met—even more so after you kissed me that night in the closet." Harper glanced around the porch, the yard, the street—looked everywhere before she settled her gaze back on Addison. "I know you have someone in your life." She shrugged. "And I still have a mess to take care of in Denver, but I have never felt with anyone like I do when I'm with you."

She was stunned—didn't know how to respond—didn't know if she could find the words for what she wanted to say. Before she could get them out, Harper turned around and headed to her

Explorer. *What the hell?* This was too much. She'd just convinced herself to let something happen with Harper—to take it seriously—and now Harper had spilled her guts and was leaving.

She followed Harper to her SUV. "What *is wrong* with you?" She planted her hands on her hips. "You can't just show up at my house all full of your feelings and then just leave. That is ridiculously unfair."

Harper stopped. Turned around. "Technically, I didn't just show up. I've been here all night." She tilted her head. "I didn't think you wanted me in that way."

"You need to stop thinking for me and start asking me." She rushed to her, took her face in her hands, and kissed her. Every one of her nerve endings fired. When Harper's tongue dipped into her mouth, she knew she wasn't alone in this attraction. The kiss was every bit as good as she'd anticipated—soft, slow, and seeking. How had she never done this before?

"Mom?" She heard Brook's voice come through the fog in her head and broke the kiss. "Mom. Why is the front door open? What are you doing out here? It's cold."

She glanced over her shoulder. "Just thanking Harper for her help studying." She returned her gaze to Harper, locked eyes with her. "Thank you."

Harper bit her bottom lip as she grinned. "Again. My pleasure." She spun and bounced to her SUV.

Addison waited until she loaded Daisy, backed out, and drove away before she turned and went inside. She needed to wait until the fire burning within every one of her limbs died down a bit.

Harper climbed down from the ladder when she heard the knock on the door. After she'd left the clinic this morning, she'd decided the cabin needed a bit of a makeover. She remembered the rolls of stick-on wallpaper she found in the closet when she arrived. Even though there were plenty of windows, the darkness of the kitchen above the cabinets was getting to her. They'd changed it out multiple times over the years when she was younger, so she was experienced at how to do it. At least in the cabin.

She opened the door to find Addison looking gorgeous in black skinny jeans, snow boots, and a long, charcoal down coat with a fleece-lined hood that her blond hair draped across. She couldn't wait to see what she was wearing underneath. "Hey."

Addison smiled. "Hey."

She took in the vision before she waved her inside. "Come on in."

Addison set her books on the table and unzipped her jacket. Harper helped her take it off and hung it in the closet by the front door.

Addison seemed to notice her handiwork. "What's going on here?"

"There was wallpaper in the closet, so I thought I'd lighten the place up a bit."

"Yeah. Mom and I picked it out a few months ago. We hadn't had a chance to schedule someone to put it up."

"Well, here I am. Wallpaper applier extraordinaire."

"Looks like you're living up to that title."

She laughed "I wouldn't say that, but I've done it once or twice. This kind is pretty easy." She was almost halfway done. "I'll finish after we're done studying." She picked a roll up off the counter and waved it in the air. "Unless you want to help?"

"Sure. I can try."

"Have you done it before?"

"No, but how hard can it be? Besides, you've helped me so much this past week, I feel I should pay you back somehow."

"Okay." Harper smiled. "What's on the study log for today?"

"Let's do this now." Addison took the roll of wallpaper from her. "I don't need to study any more today. I put some time in this morning after you left."

She pulled her eyebrows together. "You were supposed to rest. Have some *me* time."

"I did that last night." Addison's cheeks reddened. "I'm so sorry I fell asleep on you."

"Don't worry about it." She could see the sincerity in Addison's eyes. "Really. It was kind of nice actually." She probably shouldn't have said that—didn't know exactly what to do or say after this morning's kiss. She was trying to be more honest about her feelings when it came to Addison. Otherwise the wisecracking asshole in her would rear its ugly head again.

"Where do we start?"

"You handle the wallpaper down here, and I'll get on the ladder." She climbed up to the third rung. "Hand me the end of the roll, and I'll peel the backing from it." Addison gave her the roll. "I'm going to need quite a bit at first. After that, you can handle the prep while I smooth it on the wall. Okay?"

"That sounds easy enough." Addison took the roll from her.

They'd done two sections without any problems, but when they got farther into the kitchen corner, the ladder placement couldn't get Harper quite as close. "I need more paper." She pulled at the wallpaper, but there was no leeway. She pulled again and then glanced over her shoulder when it didn't budge. "What's going on?"

"I'm stuck."

She twisted on the ladder and caught a glimpse of Addison standing below her wrapped up in the wallpaper. "You took that much backing off already?" She sat on the top of the ladder and took in the panicked look in Addison's eyes—bit her lip to stop herself from laughing.

"I didn't mean to. I tried to put it back, but I couldn't. You're too fast." One of Addison's hands worked furiously trying to free her other arm from the bond. A perfect mummy in the making.

Harper could keep her captured like this for hours if she felt the need. She held her laughter as she climbed down the ladder and tugged at the wallpaper that had somehow wrapped itself like a blanket around Addison. The unintentional consequences of the tug were alarming. Now Addison was in her arms—close enough to breathe in the same air—close enough to kiss if she moved a mere inch forward. Addison wet her lips with her tongue before she caught the bottom one between her teeth. Sweet Lord, she was beautiful—enticing—fucking gorgeous in every way.

She raked her fingers through her hair. What was happening to her? The high school crush she'd had so many years ago was hitting her hormones hard. She took in a breath before she twirled her out away from her, ripping the wallpaper from Addison as she spun.

Addison wasn't at all the girl—woman—she'd imagined so many years ago. She wasn't perfect, sweet, and kind. She was hot, sexy, and desirable. So many things were coming to light about Addison that she'd never imagined before, and they were stirring so many emotions in Harper that she hadn't felt before. She never in a million years had expected Addison to be here, at the cabin, helping her with anything, let alone this close, wrapped up in wallpaper and looking so ridiculously hot.

"Are you okay?" She rushed toward her. "I didn't pull your hair, did I?" She instinctively wrapped her arms around Addison's waist to steady her. The zap that shot through her was unreal—a serious wake-up call.

"No. I thought maybe you were going to…It just startled me."

"I was going to—I mean, I had to do it fast, or I was afraid you'd panic."

"I think I'm already panicked." She picked remnants of wallpaper from her clothes and then glanced at the wall. "We're definitely going to need more wallpaper." She laughed.

When Addison caught Harper's eyes again, the look of pure innocence came through, and she couldn't stop herself. She moved quickly, took Addison's face in her hands, and kissed her with all she had. She let her hands roam to her waist and felt herself being pushed against the wall, reveling in the excitement of being kissed. Everything felt amazing—Addison's hands, Addison's body, Addison's hands up her shirt, running across her spine, squeezing, tugging, pinching. She had to cool this connection somehow, or they were going to end up doing a whole lot more than kissing. She tore her lips away, put her hands on Addison's arms, and pushed her away.

"We need to stop. Eden might be here soon. She's staying the night." That was a lousy excuse, but it was all she had.

"Now who's panicking?" The glimmer in Addison's eyes had her wanting to tug her right back to where she was and finish what they'd started.

"I'm sorry. This is all new to me." She took in a breath, blew it out, and released Addison.

Addison reached up and moved a stray strand of hair from Harper's forehead. "I haven't kissed a lot of women."

She grinned as she settled the thrill coursing through her. It was ridiculously powerful. "I have to admit that I've kissed plenty of them." The disappointed look in Addison's eyes gave her the need to explain more. "But I've never kissed a woman that I've been this attracted to before."

Addison's eyes brightened, and she chewed on her bottom lip. "Same."

"Damn it." She did exactly what she was afraid of, closed the distance between them and kissed Addison again. She was so caught up in the sensations Addison was bringing out that she didn't hear the car drive up, almost didn't hear the door open. *Fuck.* She pushed Addison away and darted across the kitchen.

"Hey, Mom. Can I borrow your maroon sweater? It goes with my pink shirt." Eden stopped before she got to the hallway and glanced at Addison and then back at her. "Jesus, Mom. Can you stop embarrassing me?" Eden rushed down the hallway.

"Are you okay?" Addison looked down the hallway and then back at Harper. "Why is she upset?"

"It's weird for her to see me kissing women." She put her hands in her back pockets like a fifteen-year-old and spun to find Addison propped up against the counter, eyes wide, watching her. What had she done? She'd made the woman she both loved and hated know exactly what she wanted, and it felt spectacular. But she'd also pissed off Eden.

"Did she see us?" Addison raised her eyebrows.

She tilted her head. "Let's just say you look pretty hot, and I certainly feel that way."

Addison grinned.

Brook came in the door next. "What's going on?" Double whammy.

"We had a little snafu with the wallpaper." She gathered the trail of wallpaper that had been wrapped around Addison, wadded it up, and tossed it into the trash.

"I kind of messed it up." Addison chimed in. "Took the backing off too soon." She shook her head and averted her eyes as the blush came over her face.

"Could've happened to anyone." She was so glad it happened to Addison, and that they were alone when it had.

Brook laughed. "Yeah. Mom's not very good with the do-it-yourself stuff."

She grinned at Addison, taking in her sweet, self-deprecating smile. "We all have our weaknesses." And now she knew that kissing wasn't one of Addison's.

"Hey. I was doing okay until the wallpaper took on a life of its own."

"Yes, you certainly were." She couldn't take her eyes off Addison. Then she heard someone clear their throat.

"You two are acting strange." Brook was standing in the doorway watching them.

"Sorry. Probably just need some food." She opened the refrigerator, grabbed a couple of bottles of water, and handed one to Addison. "What are you girls up to tonight?" She'd let Eden off restriction early, as long as she hung out with Brook.

"I'm going with Brook to her friend's house." Eden appeared from the hallway.

"Probably a whole lot less than you are." Brook leaned against the counter and picked up one of the wallpaper rolls. "Should I take Eden home with me, so you two can finish *wallpapering*?" She raised her eyebrows.

"I'm not sure how much more wallpapering we're going to get done, but she can spend the night with you if you want."

"Whatever." Brook shook her head. "We'll see you tomorrow."

"Be good." She and Addison spoke in unison and then laughed at each other as she closed the door. Now if they can just manage to be good themselves. Walking back, she tried not to move too fast or too slow, getting her thoughts and words straight in her head.

"What are you going to do about that?"

"What? Eden? She'll get over it."

"Not that." Addison took Harper's face in her hands. "This."

Before she knew it she was being kissed with such force and skill, she had to wrap her hands around Addison for balance. Once they broke the kiss, Harper struggled for breath. "Maybe you and I should quit for now?"

Addison grinned. "Get away from here and let the wallpaper settle for a bit."

"I think that would be a good idea." She was on fire, and the last thing she wanted to do was stop, but she needed to figure out her feelings before she went any further with Addison.

"You up for some pasta?"

"Sounds great. I'm always up for pasta." Honestly, she wasn't a bit hungry for food at that very moment.

CHAPTER EIGHTEEN

Addison watched Harper say something to Daisy as she rubbed her head, then pull the door to the cabin shut and head to her car. "Why don't I drive?" She waved Harper over. "I know where it is and the best place to park." She didn't want to have a discussion on whether to take separate cars. That would put more distance between them than she wanted right now. Especially after those two mind-blowing kisses. The vibe she got from Harper was unreal—was this what everyone talked about? The feeling you get when you find your other half? The one who makes the world make sense? The egg to her nog?

A tingle rushed through her as Harper gave her a sideways glance. She'd never experienced that feeling before Harper, at least not to this degree. She wanted to explore it—see where it took her. She reached across the console and held Harper's hand. The smile she received was exciting—scary as hell—but exciting just the same.

"We don't have a whole lot of choice locally when it comes to Italian food." She kept her eyes on the road as she spoke. She was attempting to not get distracted by Harper, which did no good at all, considering the scent of her spiced perfume wafting through the car. "The place opened a couple of years ago. The chef used to take ski holidays here when he lived in Denver. He wanted to have his own place and found that having it in Denver would be pretty costly."

"Denver is pretty expensive compared to here, I guess."

After she found a parking space from the angled spots already filled on the street, they slowly walked side by side along the sidewalk to the restaurant. It was amazing how busy a ski town can be when the slopes were open.

She spotted and waved at one of the clinic customers, who was sitting on one of the many benches in front of the small shops that lined the street. His dog, Tuffy, was lying on the sidewalk by his feet. He was a cute little black-and-white cocker spaniel and dachshund mix, who stood up and wagged his tail as they approached.

The man spoke as they got closer. "You have any open appointments later this week?" He stood as a woman came out of the butcher shop, whom she recognized as his wife.

"I think so. What's going on with Tuffy?" She reached down and rubbed his ear.

"He hasn't been eating right. Won't even touch his food the last few days." The woman held up the bag in her hand. "Just picking up some chicken breast to cook for him."

"Has he gotten into anything in the yard?"

"He likes to chase the critters out there, so I never know what he might've gotten into." He rubbed Tuffy's chin. "I did notice he's been eating grass lately."

"How old is he?" Harper held the back of her hand in front of Tuffy's nose, and he sniffed it.

"Eight, close to being nine."

Harper gently scratched his cheek. "Try mixing a little pumpkin or sweet potatoes with some of the roasted chicken. If that doesn't work, try some plain oatmeal with a little bit of banana. Either one of those should help settle his stomach."

The couple glanced at Addison, then back at Harper, who was now kneeling next to Tuffy, having her cheek bathed while she examined his belly. "His belly feels a little swollen." Harper glanced up at them while she continued to examine Tuffy.

"This is Harper Sims. She's taking patients at the clinic while Dr. Sims is recuperating."

"Oh. You're the daughter he's always bragging about."

Harper smiled but didn't respond, which was a plus in Addison's book. How could she respond other than to agree, and that would be arrogant.

"If he doesn't start eating better in the next couple of days, bring him in, and we'll see him." Harper glanced at Addison. "We can do that, right?"

"Of course."

"Thanks. We will." He nodded. "Thanks for the advice on the food. We'd better get to the market to pick up some sweet potatoes." He guided his wife in front of him, and the three of them strolled down the sidewalk.

Addison got all warm inside watching them walk away. She hoped to have someone to grow old with someday like that.

"Nice people."

"Yeah. They've been coming into the clinic since as long as I can remember. They used to have three dogs. Now they've only got Tuffy."

"I'm sorry to hear that."

"They've adjusted, and Tuffy's not too active for them anymore."

They arrived in front of the restaurant. "I hope you like this place."

Harper rushed in front of her and pulled open the door. "I'm sure I will. Pete mentioned it the other night."

"Right. I forgot you're good friends with him."

"You could say that."

"You make it sound like there's more."

"There is. He's Eden's father."

"Oh. Wow. I didn't know that." She was surprised at how matter-of-factly Harper had announced that fact.

The hostess asked if they had a reservation, and Addison nodded. "Two for Foster." She'd booked a table on her phone reservation app before they'd left the cabin.

"Right this way." The hostess led them to a small table in the back of the restaurant.

"Thanks." She took her seat and had to know more. "Is he involved in her life? I mean, does she know?" She pulled her eyebrows together.

Harper nodded casually as the hostess handed them their menus and said, "Your waiter will be right with you."

The waiter immediately brought a basket of bread and the wine list.

Harper took the list from him and scanned it. "You want to get a bottle of wine?"

"Sure."

"Merlot okay with you?"

"That sounds good." It felt like Harper was intentionally holding back to keep her in suspense.

Harper waited until the waiter was out of earshot. "Yes. She knows, but Pete doesn't take an active role in parenting. He's Uncle Pete to her."

"I guess he'd make a pretty good uncle."

Harper nodded as she snagged a piece of bread. "He told me you're good friends with Olive."

She nodded, unsure why he'd told Harper about the friendship. "Yeah. She's really sweet."

"How did you two meet?"

"It's kind of weird. I actually met her through Logan's family. Olive's family bought the sporting-goods store because Logan's dad gave them the lead on it. They lived in Denver and wanted to get away from the city." She broke off a piece of bread and chewed while she contemplated her next words. "Olive made me realize Logan was never going to be the father I needed for Brook."

"How so?"

"Apparently he'd been friendly with her in Denver before they moved here." She swallowed hard, not wanting to go into how *friendly*. "Outside of that, she helped me more than he did—was around more than he ever was." She grabbed the napkin in her lap, wiped the sweat from her palms. "Don't get me wrong. Nothing romantic or sexual ever happened between us. It was purely platonic. Still is. She's totally in love with Pete. She showed me what a good partner does."

"Was the divorce difficult?"

She shook her head. "No. We were never legally married. We kept up appearances, let everyone think we were. His family pushed for it, but my dad wouldn't have any part of it."

"Smart guy, your dad."

She nodded. "Definitely saved me from a lot of anger and money spent on divorce."

"Does he pay child support?"

"Yep. Brook gets a check every month. It goes straight into her college fund."

"At least there's that." Harper fiddled with the fork in front of her. "Do you ever wonder what might have happened if you'd married him?"

"Not really." She wondered more about Harper than she did anyone else. "I've been fine on my own. With Dad and Mom's help, then just Mom's after Dad passed."

"Right. I was so sorry to hear about that."

"Dad was a big social drinker, smoked way too much. Congestive heart failure. It was only a matter of time before his heart gave out." She pushed the sadness from her mind. "It's good that you're here with your dad, spending time with him. You never know when that time might end. I'm glad Jim's doing better now."

"Me too. He still needs to take it easy until the doctor gives him the okay to come back to work."

The waiter returned to the table in the nick of time. She didn't want to go into that phase of her life any more than she had to. "Are you two ready to order?"

She picked up the menu and pretended to read it. "I'll have the chef's ravioli."

Harper scrunched her eyebrows. "I don't see that on the menu."

"It's not. He makes it for the special once in a while, but he'll make it if you ask."

"I think I might like to try it but want the pappardelle too."

"Order it. We'll share."

Harper smiled and bit on her bottom lip before she glanced up at the waiter. "We'll do that. She'll have the ravioli and I'll have the pappardelle."

For some reason, listening to Harper order food for them both made her all warm inside. She'd been on her own for so long, it was a gesture she'd totally forgotten about but, oddly, was perfectly fine with.

The complete eye contact paired with the silence between them was nothing less than intimate. Her comfort level wasn't being tasked at all. This was the type of intrinsic familiarity she craved and hadn't shared with anyone else.

It seemed like the waiter had just left when Kevin, the chef and owner of the restaurant, came out of the kitchen and walked straight to their table. "It's good to see you, Addie."

"I can't stay away from your wonderful food."

Harper glanced at the chef and flashed that beautiful smile of hers. "I hear you came from Denver? That's where I live."

A reminder that Harper wasn't here to stay. She couldn't help the sinking feeling that came over her. "This is Harper, Dr. Sims's daughter."

"Kevin Ryan." He held out his hand and Harper shook it.

"Not a name I would expect for the chef of an Italian restaurant in a ridiculously small ski town in Colorado."

"There's only so much you can do with Irish food."

"He has a spectacular Irish menu that he runs the whole week of St Patrick's Day." One of Addison's favorite dishes was bangers and mash. She inevitably was left to come alone because Brook wasn't a fan of anything Irish, except red hair.

Harper glanced at Addison. "I'll have to plan on being in town for that."

The thought sent a thrill through Addison, and her stomach bounced.

"What brings you here? Skiing?"

"I'm hoping to do some of that, but I'm here to see patients at my dad's veterinary clinic while he recuperates from a heart attack." She glanced at Addison. "To help Addison, that is."

"Right." He glanced at Addison. "She takes good care of my boy, Munch."

"Munch. That's a cute name. What breed?"

"He's a boxer that eats everything in sight." He laughed. "The reason for the name."

"Even a few things he shouldn't." Addison laughed. "Your dad had to surgically remove a squeaky toy from his belly once."

"He loves string, and don't even get me started on my wife's jewelry."

"Ah, a dog with style. I'd like to meet Munch someday."

"I'll bring him by the clinic." He grinned as though Harper had given him an invitation to a Rockies baseball game. "How long are you here for?"

"I'm not exactly sure." Harper glanced across the table at her. "At least a few more weeks. I want to make sure Dad is fully recovered, and I need to finish a few other things."

Was that regret she saw in Harper's eyes or just a warning that she wouldn't be around for long? She couldn't maintain the eye contact. "I ordered your special ravioli Bolognese. I hope you don't mind."

He grinned. "Nope. Not at all. That's how I knew you were here." He glanced at Harper. "Orders it every time."

Harper laughed loudly. "I'll try to get her out of that box she's stuck in. I ordered the pappardelle, and we're going to share."

"Good choice." He winked. "If you two will excuse me, I'll start working on your dinner."

Soon after the chef left, the waiter showed up at the table with a bottle of merlot that they hadn't ordered. "Chef's compliments."

"He must really like you." Harper's lips pulled into a half-smile. "Seems you're popular in this little town."

She shrugged as she tried to suppress the giddy feeling that recognition from Harper gave her. "I do okay."

The waiter poured a small amount into the glass between the two of them. Harper reached for it but then pushed it to Addison to taste. "Merlot it is." The laugh burst out of Harper's mouth like a Jell-O shot squeezed from a vise, which made her like her even more.

Addison took a sip and nodded before she relaxed into her chair and enjoyed the moment. Harper had such a great laugh, the kind that didn't hold back—no restraint, no caution, just outright unfiltered joy. She wished she could be so free—be less worried about what others thought of her.

❖

Without them having to ask, the waiter brought two additional plates along with the main dishes. Harper was disappointed because she would've enjoyed snagging bites from Addison's plate much more than eating from her own. The intimacy of sharing meals excited her in a weird sort of way.

"Parmesan cheese?" The waiter held up the wedge.

"Of course," they both said and then grinned at each other.

The pasta was completely covered when Addison held up her hand. "That's good."

"You like a little ravioli with your cheese, eh?"

"It's the perfect balance."

"I'll trust you on that." She picked up one of the plates and spun several forks of pappardelle on it, then passed it across the table to Addison.

Addison spooned several ravioli onto the other plate and handed it to her before spooning the same amount onto her own plate and then waited for Harper to take a bite of the ravioli.

"Well?"

"You're right. It's perfect." Everything seemed perfect tonight.

She picked up the bottle of wine and refilled their glasses. She was thoroughly enjoying Addison's company. Either the atmosphere or the wine seemed to be loosening Addison up, which was a fresh sight she hadn't seen much of since she'd arrived in town. Well, except for earlier, when she'd been on the receiving end of a skillfully maneuvered kiss—twice. She tingled at the thought of doing it again and found herself staring at Addison's lips as she talked. Maybe she was the one who was actually loosening up. She hadn't enjoyed a night out and a good meal with another woman in forever. Especially a beautiful woman whom she wanted to spend the rest of the evening with. This was certainly a surprise and had her thinking of things she hadn't in quite some time.

"Whatcha thinking about?" Addison set her fork on the plate and wiped her mouth. "You're awfully quiet."

"I was…It was nothing, really."

"Tell me." Addison raised her eyebrows as she reached for her glass of wine. "Please?"

"I wasn't expecting this. The dinner—the wine—you." She shifted in her chair. "You're so different than you were when I first arrived in town." She took in a breath and shook her head. "I think I'm different too. I don't know what's happened, but I really like you, and I honestly never thought that would happen."

Addison covered her mouth, almost spitting wine everywhere as she laughed. "I think that's the sweetest thing you've ever said to me, in a weird sort of way."

"Oh my God. I'm sorry. That sounded awful."

"It did, but I know exactly what you mean." Addison reached across the table and took her hand. "I haven't felt this comfortable with you since middle school."

"Before you ditched me for the popular girls."

"Yeah. I guess so." She released her hand, attempted to pull it back across the table, but Harper grasped it by her fingers and held on.

"I'm not mad about that. Not any of it. We went in different directions, that's all."

"So what do we do now?"

"I don't really know." She blew out a breath because she had no clue. "Maybe take it slow? See if it sticks?"

"You mean see if we can still be nice to each other after working together for a couple of weeks?"

"Something like that." She smiled. "I have to say you surprised the shit out of me with that kiss this morning."

"I surprised you?" She raised her eyebrows. "Your declaration of love was…" Addison's cheeks reddened, and she took in a deep breath. "I'm not usually that aggressive."

"You should be more often." Her own cheeks heated. Was she really flirting like a teenager? She poured them each more wine and took a big gulp.

"Noted. Forewarning. I'm not going home with you tonight."
Addison picked up her fork, jabbed a ravioli, and stuffed it into her
mouth.

"Then how am I getting there? You drove, remember?"

She grinned. "You know what I mean. I'll get you home safely,
but that's it."

"Damn. I was hoping for a different kind of ride." She winked,
and Addison turned even redder. This particular shade of red looked
beautiful on her.

"I'm thinking that will come soon enough."

She raised her wineglass. "One can only hope."

Addison picked up hers and held it in the air as well. "To hope."
She lifted an eyebrow as she brought the glass to her lips.

Holy shit. This was going to be a wild ride. She was already
feeling the dip in her stomach like she was cresting the top of a
thousand-mile-high roller coaster. The thrill coursing through her at
this moment was phenomenal. It would also be one she knew she
wouldn't be able to resist. Not after all the fantasies she'd had about
Addison as a teenager.

Chapter Nineteen

Harper's phone rang, jogging her out of her dreams. Addison hadn't stayed over, but that didn't mean she couldn't dream about it. She recognized the number right away. It was the clinic in Denver. Why were they calling so early? Why were they calling her on Sunday? "This is Harper."

"Good morning, Dr. H. How are you?"

Jeremy was being very polite this morning. Something was up. "I'm good, Jeremy. How are you? How's everything going there?"

"The clinic's running smoothly. Dr. V's been here a lot since you've been gone. I have some bad news, though."

"Is everyone okay?"

"Yes. Sorry. Didn't mean to scare you." He hesitated. "I'm calling about the dog you adopted."

"Daisy? What about her?" She reached over and petted her. "She's thriving here." Daisy loved the freedom of the land around her. She had so much to explore.

"The owner showed up, wanting her back. I meant to call you yesterday but got busy."

"But he gave her up because he didn't have time for her."

"He did give her up, but apparently Daisy belongs to his girlfriend, Peyton, and she wasn't aware he'd dropped her off here."

"What? She's been with me for months."

"Yeah. He told her that Daisy had jumped out of the car somewhere and he couldn't find her."

"Oh my God." She rubbed Daisy's ear. "And she wants her back." Her stomach dropped like she'd been punched. She couldn't help the sadness in her voice along with the sigh that escaped her lungs. She'd grown to love Daisy as her own.

"Yeah. Apparently, they had a fight, and her boyfriend told her what he'd done."

"Are they still together? I'm not putting her back into that household."

"No. They broke up, and she's moved in with her parents, who love the dog as much as she does. Her mom came in with her."

Sadness bubbled in her throat. "When?" She settled her voice. "When do they want her back?"

"As soon as possible, but I told them you were out of town, and I'd have to contact you."

"I think I have a couple of procedures scheduled over the next few days. I'll have to check." Her mind was so scattered she couldn't recall what appointments were scheduled this week.

"I got Peyton's number, sending it now. Thought you'd probably want to talk to her." Her phone buzzed against her ear when the text came through. "Let me know when you're certain, and we'll arrange a time to meet the owner. I suppose you can set that up yourself if you want. Whatever works for you." The line was silent for a moment. "If it makes you feel any better, she's really nice and seems to care a lot about Daisy—both her and her mom."

"Thanks, Jeremy, but it doesn't. I'll talk to you tomorrow." She couldn't stay on the call any longer or she'd start blubbering into the phone. She hit the end button and dropped her phone to the night table before she leaned forward and held her head in her hands. The tears streaming from her eyes blurred her vision. Daisy had been the only thing that had gotten her through the lonely nights at home. V had moved out without warning, and Eden was always doing her own thing, like teenagers do. Daisy had been the one constant and was there no matter what. Now she would be alone again, which was proof that this kind of pain wasn't worth getting attached to anyone or any place.

Oddly enough, the first person she wanted to call wasn't V or even Pete. It was Addison, but she wouldn't call her. She couldn't share this loss with anyone right now.

❖

Addison had called Harper several times, and sent a few texts as well, but hadn't received a response. Was she really ghosting her after what happened yesterday—after what happened last night? After several mind-blowing kisses, an absolutely wonderful dinner, and another mind-blowing kiss? Was Harper angry that she hadn't stayed over with her last night? Was sex all Harper wanted from her? Her stomach churned.

She couldn't believe this was happening after the night had gone so well. She'd walked Harper to the door, and as she'd stood in the doorway contemplating her next steps, Harper had swept her into her arms and kissed her with such passion, she'd let go—given her everything she had—was torn as to whether she should stay or go when Harper had opened the door and invited her inside. It had taken all her willpower to leave Harper standing there looking so beautiful. She'd thought Harper understood they needed to take things slow, but maybe she was wrong.

She swiped her keys from the counter, put on her jacket, and rushed out the door. She had to get this straight between them. Thankfully the drive was short, and she didn't have a lot of time to imagine horrible scenarios in her head—the fault of her own insecurities. More time meant more anxiety.

She saw Harper's SUV in the driveway and smoke coming from the chimney as she pulled up. She bolted from the car and rushed to the porch, but stopped herself from pounding on the door. She took in a breath and calmed her nerves before she knocked gently. She was about to knock louder when the door swung open.

Harper stood before her, eyes swollen and red. *What the hell was going on?* Then the tears began to flow, and Harper mumbled something about Daisy that she couldn't quite make out. Her stomach dropped. "Is Daisy okay? Did she get out? Has she been hurt?"

Harper shook her head and fell into her arms. "I have to give her back." She let out a sob.

She held Harper tightly. "Oh my gosh. Why? What happened?"

"Her owner." She let out another sob. "Wants her back."

"We'll just tell them no." She guided her toward the couch to sit and sat next to her. "They gave her up. They can't have her back." *Who in the world would do something like that?*

Harper took in a deep breath and swiped the tears from her face. "It's more complicated than that." She looked away, anywhere but at her. "You must think I'm an idiot."

"Don't do that." She touched Harper's cheek with her fingers and wiped the remaining tears from it. "I don't think that at all. Tell me what happened." She knew it was selfish, but she was relieved that the crisis wasn't about them.

Harper explained how the man who'd brought Daisy in and surrendered her wasn't actually her owner and that her owner, his ex-girlfriend, hadn't known what he'd done. She couldn't believe someone could be so cruel. Her heart ached for Harper, but also for Daisy's owner. She didn't like it, but she understood why Harper had to return Daisy.

She took off her jacket and dropped it to the floor. "I'm so sorry, honey." She moved closer and urged Harper to lean on her. "We'll make sure it's a good home."

"We have to. I'm not leaving her with someone who doesn't take good care of her." Harper bolted away from her. "And the boyfriend had better be gone." She leaned against her again. "Jackass."

"You're being too kind. I was thinking of much stronger words." That got a laugh from Harper, and she was grateful for it.

"I don't think I've ever heard you swear."

"I try to keep it to the voices in my head."

Another chuckle from Harper. "Should I be worried about those?"

She grinned. "Not as long as you stay on my good side."

Harper became serious as she gazed up at her. "Thank you for checking on me...for this." Tears began to well in her eyes.

She kissed her on the forehead and held her closer. "I'm here for you." *Always*.

At this moment she felt she would be there for Harper through awful moments like this and much happier ones in the future. As long as Harper would let her.

❖

"Mom." The screen door slapped shut. "Are you all right? Why aren't you answering my texts?" Eden circled around the chairs and stood in front of her. "Why are you crying?"

She quickly swiped at her eyes as Daisy got up from her lap and greeted Eden. She hadn't heard her drive up. "I'm fine."

"No. You're not. You weren't talking to V again, were you?"

"No. I wasn't talking to V." She glanced at Daisy, who was still soaking up the attention from Eden. "Apparently Daisy has another owner who wants her back."

"You're not going to give her back, though, right?"

She shrugged. "I kinda have to."

"What the hell, Mom. Why?" Eden seemed as upset as she was.

She took in a deep breath. "The girlfriend didn't know the boyfriend had left her. Seems he lied to her."

"So, just screw us?" Eden dropped to the deck and hugged Daisy.

She nodded. "I know, honey. But put yourself in the girlfriend's place. Wouldn't you want her back? It's just one of those weird situations. We have to let her go."

"What if she doesn't love her like we do?"

"I'll make sure before I give her back. Believe me."

Addison reached across and held her hand. "We'll do a home visit first. Check it out before we leave her."

Addison had called several times earlier, sent a few texts as well, then appeared at her door soon after because she hadn't answered. Harper was an absolute mess—had been crying since she received the news. Addison had consoled her—held her in her arms, and helped her think the situation through. To realize what was the right thing to do. Addison seemed to get why she had agreed to let Daisy go.

She nodded. "Yeah." She'd never been more grateful for anyone's support—never really felt comfortable accepting anyone else's support except Pete's when she was pregnant with Eden. This was so different than that.

"Make sure it's a suitable place." Addison squeezed her hand.

"Mom." Eden's eyes were wet with tears. "I want to stay here tonight with you and Daisy."

"Okay. We talked to the owner a little while ago. I'm going to take her tomorrow." The sooner the break the better.

"I'll go with you." Addison squeezed her hand. "Jim can fill in for us. The schedule's light. I'll have Mom reschedule anything we can."

She looked up at Addison and couldn't help but feel grateful to her for helping her through this. She'd always done everything like this alone before.

❖

In most cases when they did home visits, they weren't there to judge home decor, furniture, or housekeeping skills. But Harper was going to make sure everything was perfect. The home had to be dog friendly, and she wouldn't stand for it if they indicated in any way that Daisy would be an outside dog. The houses in the country neighborhood were spaced apart nicely, and it looked like they had a fair amount of acreage behind each one. She could see when they drove up that the yard was fenced. That only meant Daisy would be contained, though. The condition of the yard was yet to be determined.

A tall brunette and a buff cocker spaniel greeted them at the door. It was almost the same color as Daisy, only a little lighter. The dog stood at the woman's feet and didn't dart out the door.

"Hi. I'm Dr. Sims." She wasn't being nice or giving up the formal title for this one. Not yet anyway.

Addison reached out her hand. "I'm Addison."

The woman took her hand and shook it. "June Fairchild. Nice to meet you."

"Nice to meet you too." Addison poked Harper in the side with her elbow.

"Yes. Nice to meet you." She smiled slightly and shifted to have a better line of sight into the house.

Addison squatted to let the cocker spaniel sniff her hand before gently petting her head. "This one's a sweetheart. What's her name?"

"Goldie. Short for Marigold."

"Well, hello there, Goldie. You are so sweet." She let her hand drop, and Goldie immediately nuzzled her nose under it, wanting more attention.

Harper smiled. She enjoyed watching Addison interact with animals. She really had a way with them.

"I was under the impression you were bringing Daisy."

"We are. I mean, we did." She glanced at the Explorer, where Daisy had taken over the driver's seat. "She's in the SUV."

"I'd like to see your home first. May we come in?"

The door opened farther, and a younger woman came out, forcing Addison to fall back on her butt. "Where is she? Can I see her now?" She spotted Daisy in the Explorer and took off toward it. The other cocker spaniel ran after her.

"I'm sorry. That's my daughter, Peyton." June frowned as she watched her race across the yard. "You spoke to her on the phone."

"Right. For some reason, I thought she was a little older."

Addison stood and swiped the dirt from her butt with her hand. "I'll get her." She rushed to follow Peyton, backed her up from the SUV, and motioned for her to sit on the grass and wait. Then she opened the door, leashed Daisy, and lifted her to the ground. Daisy ran straight to Peyton waiting on the lawn. She could see that the dog was super excited to see Peyton, and the other dog was yipping and playing with Daisy. Harper's heart cracked a tiny bit more. She was hoping she could ignore the joy in the girl's eyes, but she couldn't. She shrugged it off. That didn't mean Peyton was a good mom to Daisy. She didn't seem to have very good judgment when it came to boyfriends.

"She's twenty-two but sounds very mature on the phone." June smiled as she watched her play with Daisy. "She loves Daisy. We were heartbroken when we thought she'd been lost."

"Is the other dog related?"

"Yes. They're sisters."

"Would you like to come in and see the house while the dogs play in the yard together?"

She nodded. "They're both very well behaved."

"All it takes is a little training."

After being given a tour of the kitchen and dining room, they ended up in the living room, where Addison and Peyton had come inside with the dogs.

Harper started in with the questions. "Do you have a vet you're using?" She continued scrutinizing the house. "It's best to have a vet set up before you bring your dog home, rather than rushing to find one in the case of an emergency."

The mother spoke up. "We do. And we're not new at this."

Harper lifted an eyebrow. The mother was a saucy one.

Addison interrupted. "We know that. It's just that we've gotten attached, and you know how that is, right?"

The mother took in a breath. "I can understand. When Peyton took Daisy to live with her and that horrible boyfriend of hers, it was awful." She knelt and rubbed Daisy's ears, and the dog buzzed up against her. "I missed this little one following me around everywhere."

"Will Daisy be living here or with Peyton when she moves out again?"

Peyton said, "With me."

June said, "Here."

They spoke simultaneously.

"Honestly, I don't have plans to move out anytime soon." Peyton rolled in her lips. "I don't have the money to replace all the stuff I left at my boyfriend's house."

"They'll both be living with us. I'm not letting Daisy go again." June seemed to understand Harper's reluctance. "Would you like to stay for some coffee on the back patio?"

"Coffee would be wonderful." Addison quickly moved between them and opened the sliding-glass door. The dogs ran out and played together in the yard.

June clicked on the outside propane heater lamp before she went back inside to get the drinks. Soon she brought a tray of coffee, sugar, and cream to the table on the back patio, where they all sat and watched the dogs play together. Harper could see Daisy got along with Goldie and seemed happy to be home. *Home.* The word stuck in her head. Not Harper's home, Daisy's home. She was happy here with Goldie. She had to let her go.

After they finished their coffee, Harper set her cup on the tray and stood. "We'd better be going." She didn't think she could take much more of watching Daisy play. It would only draw the pain out.

June led them back through the living room to the front door and picked up a brightly colored collar from the entryway table. "I still have her collar from before Peyton moved out." June removed the collar around Daisy's neck and handed it to Harper, then replaced it with one that matched Goldie's.

She rubbed the silver name tag she'd had made for Daisy between her finger and her thumb. This was getting very real, very fast. She removed the name tag from the collar and handed it to June. "That has my personal cell on it if you need to contact me for anything." She'd had the name of her clinic printed on the back as well.

"Our veterinarian is close to retirement, and I believe your clinic is closer. I'd like to bring the dogs to you in the future. If that's okay?"

A slight surge of happiness swelled inside her. It didn't outweigh the loss, but it lessened it a little. "I'd like that." She gave Daisy one last back scratch before she spun and rushed to the SUV. She needed some distance now, or she wouldn't be able to leave her.

"It was nice meeting you." Addison's voice carried loudly as she turned and waved before she rounded the car, opened the door, and slid into the passenger seat. "Do you want me to drive?"

She swiped the tears from her face. "No. I've got it." She threw the car into gear and sped down the road. "Why couldn't they have been horrible people?"

Addison clutched Harper's hand. "She'll be fine with them, and there will be other dogs who need a loving mom like you."

CHAPTER TWENTY

Addison thought Harper had finally relaxed, but she seemed to stiffen when they drove into the clinic parking lot. The place looked busy, with almost every space in the parking lot occupied. Harper pulled around to the back, where there were several more cars and a few empty spaces. Harper put the car into park and took in a deep breath. Was she nervous about showing Addison her clinic—her success? She'd hoped they'd gotten past that by now—that it wasn't important to her.

"Are you okay?"

"Yeah. Just readying myself to see V."

"Is she running the clinic while you're gone?" She already knew who Vanessa was from what Nicki had told her, but she wanted to hear the specifics from Harper.

"V is my partner."

"Is she more than your partner in the business?"

"She was." Harper stared at the building. "We haven't been together personally for close to a year." She tightened her grip on the steering wheel. "She's been trying to force me out of the practice."

"Maybe we should come back tomorrow."

"No. I need to make an appearance today and tomorrow. Make sure everything's running smoothly. V isn't very good at the details."

Just then the back door flew open, and a man and woman rushed out. Harper threw open the door of the SUV, hopped out, and was pulled into a group hug.

Was one of them V? Addison got out of the car and moved around to where they were.

When she caught Harper's glance, her smile was broad and genuine. "Hey, guys. This is Addison. She's the tech who's been running the show at my dad's clinic." She motioned back to them. "This is Jeremy and Kathy. They're the best techs in Denver. Been with me since I bought the clinic."

She smiled. "Nice to meet you."

"You too," Jeremy said. "Dr. H says you're pretty awesome too."

She grinned as pride hit her hard. "She did, did she?" She glanced at Harper.

Harper smiled. "I did." She shrugged. "Because you are… sometimes." She winked.

The tingle was back, and she couldn't seem to look away from Harper. Then someone at the back door caught Harper's eye, and she stiffened again. Addison followed her line of sight to find a tall brunette in a lab coat leaning against the doorjamb with her arms crossed. *V.* She had short hair, narrow eyes, and a somewhat prominent nose. Her olive skin was beautifully tanned, like she'd been born in the sun. She was striking, to say the least.

"V." Harper walked toward the doorway. "You're looking good."

Neither one of them smiled.

V pushed off the doorway and stood blocking the door. "You look tired."

Addison watched the exchange and couldn't believe the woman couldn't even be civil in her greeting to Harper. What a fucking bitch. No wonder Harper was stressed.

"Well, I've been working rather than vacationing at The Springs. Haven't been getting much sleep lately—spending a lot of time after hours at my dad's clinic. It's been a little busier than I expected."

She could see V's mood change at the comment. She flattened her lips in before she spoke. "How's your dad?"

It hadn't been that busy. Harper had been spending the extra hours helping her study in the evenings. Maybe it was too much for her—maybe Addison should refuse her help.

Once they moved inside, Harper seemed to spot someone she knew and went straight to the waiting room. Addison watched her as she squatted in front of the woman and petted her puppy.

"That woman has recently adopted another dog." Jeremy stood next to her. "Harper helped her through the loss of her older dog. She's been wanting to introduce her to the new pup."

"That's very sweet of her."

V crossed her arms and leaned against the counter. "Is Harper going to stay in Blueridge?"

"I wouldn't know."

"Oh. I thought maybe you and she were involved."

"No. Just friends." She wasn't about to tell V anything about what had been happening between them. She'd only use it against her.

Harper came back their way with a huge smile on her face. "She's been a customer for a long time, lost her dog last year, and just got a new puppy."

"Oh. I'm so sorry to hear she lost her dog." Her heart tugged. "I'm happy she's found a new one."

"Me too." Harper turned and looked at them again. "She's very sweet. Would you mind if I do her wellness check really quickly?"

"Of course not. I'm sure she'd appreciate that."

Harper grabbed the chart and waved them into an empty exam room.

"You sure you're not involved?"

"Absolutely sure."

V brushed past her. "That's too bad. It would get her out of my hair. Maybe she'd finally sell me the practice."

"I wouldn't count on it." She held her tongue, even though Addison would like nothing better than for Harper to sell and move to Blueridge. There were so many things she wanted to spew at V right now, but this wasn't the time. Harper was in a good mood, and that would spoil it. Plus, she didn't really have the right. Did she?

Probably, but then she would blow everything she'd just told V, and she would probably use it against Harper. She refused to have any part in that.

❖

Addison was surprised at how small Harper's house was compared to the yard. It seemed she was more concerned about having space outdoors for whatever animals she brought home rather than space inside. It was a simple ranch house painted sage green, Addison's favorite color, with dark-green trim that accented it nicely, set on what looked to be close to three acres. Had Harper picked out the colors herself, or had it been painted before she moved in?

Harper unlocked the door and pushed it open, then waved Addison inside before her. Her bedside manner wasn't the best, but her manners were always impeccable.

She dropped their take-out Chinese food on the counter and went looking for plates.

"Cabinet to the left of the sink. Bottom shelf." Harper went down the hallway out of sight.

She took a couple of plates from the cabinet before she pulled a few drawers open and found the silverware. There weren't a lot of kitchen utensils in this kitchen. She opened several containers and put spoons in them and dropped an eggroll onto each plate from the waxed bag. She waited a few minutes for Harper to reappear, but she didn't, so she loaded each plate with a spoonful of broccoli beef, chicken fried rice, and vegetable lo mien. If that wasn't enough for Harper, she could help herself to more. After taking both plates and silverware to the dining-room table, she went in search of drinks. She found a couple of vanilla porters in the refrigerator and brought them to the table as well.

Harper emerged from the hallway and seemed to look different. Had she washed her face? She couldn't really tell, because Harper didn't wear much makeup—didn't have to. She had beautiful long, dark lashes and perfect eyebrows that hung symmetrically above her blue eyes. They seemed more vivid now, so she must've been crying.

"I took the liberty of making your plate." She glanced at the food in the place adjacent from her. "I hope you don't mind."

"No. Not at all. Thanks." Harper plucked the bottle opener from the side of the refrigerator. "I see you found the good stuff."

"That's all the beer you had."

Harper popped the top from each of the bottles. "It's all the beer you need."

"If we were having tacos, I would have to disagree."

"Then we would've stopped at the liquor store on the way home." Harper smiled, and Addison was surprised at how grateful she was for her expression. They hadn't conversed much on the way home, and she'd been worried about her. Clearly she wasn't over V.

She picked up an eggroll, took a bite, and moaned. "These are delicious."

"If I lived in Denver, I think I would have Chinese food every day."

Harper grinned. "Every Thursday—but never on Sunday. The substitute cook works Sunday, and it's not as good."

"I can't imagine it not being good, even with a different cook."

"Yeah. You don't get this kind of food in Blueridge." She took another bite and savored the taste. "So, tacos on Sunday?"

"That can be arranged, if you ever end up here on a Sunday." Harper made eye contact and held it for a few minutes.

"Noted." She broke contact and took another bite, which felt stuck in her throat after she swallowed. What was happening here? Was that an invitation? Were they having a moment—flirting again?

They ate the rest of the meal in silence. It seemed neither one of them knew where to go from here. Were they becoming friends— more than friends? Did Harper want that? Did Addison want that? *Slow down, girl. You helped a friend out today. That's all she is.* She glanced up from her plate and caught Harper gazing at her. *Oh, boy. That's much more than a friend look.*

"Thank you for coming with me today."

"Of course. I know how hard it was for you."

"It was very hard. I'm not sure how or why I got so attached to Daisy. I guess she came into my life at the right time." She took a pull on her beer. "V and I had been having lots of issues. Daisy was a good distraction."

"You still have feelings for V?"

"Feelings? Maybe. I'm not sure what to call them." She pushed the food around on her plate. "There are so many reasons for us not to be together. We're not really compatible at all. I guess it's just hard to let go of someone you thought was your future."

"I get that. I had a hard time realizing I would never be happy with Logan. Let alone any other man."

"When did you realize that about yourself?"

"I think I knew it all along, but was afraid to admit it." She finished the last bit on her plate and stood. "I wasn't as strong as you."

"I wasn't strong. I just wasn't going to put myself in any sexual situation with a man."

"I was confused, and then I got pregnant. If I had married Logan, that would've been a lie I couldn't get myself out of. I couldn't do that to myself or to him." She loaded her plate into the dishwasher. "Before you left, I thought we were friends."

"Did you?" Harper shrugged. "Didn't seem like it—especially around *your* friends." She shoveled the last bit of food into her mouth.

"I'm sorry. I'm not a rule-breaker. Never have been."

"Was there a rule involved in being my friend?" She carried her plate to the kitchen.

"No. I mean, yes. My friends had them, and I was a follower."

"And now?" She dropped her plate into the dishwasher and closed it before she took another swig of her beer.

"Let's just say I've learned from my mistakes. I was so confused back then. I didn't know if I was gay or just exploring the unknown. I liked the attention I got from boys."

Harper moved closer. "And now?"

Addison closed the distance between them, let her mouth cover Harper's. When Harper let her lips open slightly, she slipped her tongue between them—took in the sweet taste of vanilla porter as she deepened the kiss. She was on fire and didn't know how to douse the flames. Harper stoked it with each stroke of her tongue. She took Harper into her arms, and each part of them touched—soft breasts, pelvis, and thighs—so much contact.

Suddenly Harper broke away, put some distance between them. Gripped the counter to steady herself as she leaned against it. "Definitely gay."

She licked her lips. "I haven't felt like this since you left."

"You ignored me for *months*."

"Not ignored—avoided because I didn't want to acknowledge my feelings—that I actually might be gay and someone would find out. I was so jealous of you—that you could be who you wanted to be."

"You could've done that too. We could have done it *together*."

She shook her head. "No. I could've never withstood the ridicule of the popular girls. I was too weak for that then, and possibly still am now." Why else would she leave town every time she needed to seek comfort in a woman's arms—a woman's bed—and not ever invite her to come to her home. The whole situation was fucked up, and Nicki didn't deserve the *half-out* life she was living. She was ashamed of herself for not having the strength to tell her friends who she really was.

"I finally got over that teenage crush, or whatever it was I had for you. It took months, maybe even years, but I did it." Harper rubbed her forehead. "At least I thought I had until I woke up with you in my arms, and now you're here telling me you had feelings for me too? You can't ignore me for twenty years, show up in my life, and start to care about me."

"Technically, you showed up in mine." Addison moved closer, took Harper's hands. "And I never stopped caring. I always thought you'd stay."

"You were with Logan." Harper yanked her hands from Addison. "I couldn't stay and watch you be all in love with someone else."

"I couldn't be all in love with someone else because I wanted it to be you. I would've…"

Harper's eyes widened. "You would've what?"

"I would've gone with you if you'd asked."

Harper moved closer, hovered her lips close to hers. "If you'd asked, I would've stayed."

That was a fact Addison hadn't known. This issue wasn't going to stay unresolved. She crushed Harper's lips with her own again, wrapped her arms around her, slipped her hands up the back of her shirt. Sweet Lord, she wanted to do so much more.

"Stop." Harper pushed her away. "Just stop." She paced the small space of the kitchen. "You should've contacted me and told me you didn't get married."

"I always thought you'd come back, and when that never happened, I thought you'd moved on—were happy in Denver. Seems you were." Addison brushed a strand of hair from Harper's forehead.

"And what about now? This…us? Are you ready to come out to the world? Because I don't live in the closet. I won't."

Was she in a place back then where she could've had a full-blown out relationship with Harper? Would she have disappointed her if she had left town with her and couldn't? Was she there now? "I don't know."

"I need more than that." Harper rolled her lips in and backed up, putting more distance between them. "You have a child—Logan's child. One who doesn't know the history behind who you are. Who you want to be."

"I realize that, and you have Eden." She would've given that all to Harper if she'd only asked, but not in Blueridge.

"There aren't any parental strings attached to Eden. Pete was the donor, and I carried her." She sucked in a deep breath. "That was the breaking point of the relationship I had at the time."

"Really? She didn't want children?" She moved closer.

"No. She wanted freedom to do what she wanted when she wanted." The sadness in Harper's eyes was heartbreaking. "So I left her to that."

"Oh my gosh. That must have been hard on Eden."

"She doesn't know—never will. It wasn't about her. It was about me."

"So you went through everything alone?" The thought of that type of isolation crushed Addison, and she wanted to take Harper into her arms and hold her.

"Not completely. Pete has been involved in her life, and I have a good circle of friends. I stayed in Fort Collins for a few months after graduation from vet school, then found a clinic that needed someone with my skills and dove in to work. Those people became my family and helped me with Eden. When the owner decided to retire, I bought the practice. Then V came into the picture and provided money to keep it afloat until it became successful."

"That's good. I'm glad everything worked out for you." She bit her bottom lip, holding back what she really wanted to say. That she'd have been there for her if she'd known. They could've raised their girls together. Could they have? Maybe that wouldn't have worked. Addison hadn't been very strong then at all. Would Harper have made her stronger, or would they have only fought more?

"But now, V and I are no longer together, and we both want the practice."

"So, no chance of you taking over your dad's clinic?" She blew the words out softly, the disappointment in her voice plain.

"He'll be back on his feet and back to work soon. I can't take that from him."

"I'm sure he'd love to have you back in Blueridge working with him."

"I'm not so sure about that. We have different ideas about treatment. He's pretty old school."

"True, but at least he listens."

"Does he? I haven't found that to be true."

"It might take him some time to come around, but if you're subtle about it, he does."

Harper laughed. "I've never been one for subtle."

"You and he are so much alike it's ridiculous."

"You think so?"

"I know so." She couldn't prevent the laugh that flew from her lips or the giddy feeling in her stomach when Harper tilted her head and grinned. "Just the other day when you insisted on taking blood instead of letting me do it. You don't trust anyone else to do things right. He used to be that way too."

"That was a special case."

She widened her eyes. "Every case that's come into the clinic has been special so far."

Harper took in a deep breath. "I'll try to be better about that. Otherwise you're never going to learn."

She couldn't stop the smile that spread across her face. "I feel like we're having a breakthrough moment here."

"Yeah. I think we are." Harper smiled softly as she stared into her eyes. "You brought your textbook, didn't you?" She reached into the refrigerator and took out a couple bottles of water.

"I can look at that tomorrow." She followed her into the living room. "You've had a tough day. You should rest."

Harper shook her head. "Get your book. Let's do it now." She brushed past her, went into the small living room, and flopped onto the couch. "We need to review that chapter one more time before we move on to the next."

"I don't want to interfere with your sleep."

She scrunched her eyebrows together. "What?"

"You told V that you hadn't been getting much sleep. That you'd been working after hours. I know that's because of me. I don't want you to feel obligated to help me."

"I want to help you."

"But—"

"No buts." She shifted to face Addison. "I tell V a lot of things that aren't necessarily true. She'll use anything she can to take the clinic from me, so I don't trust her with the details of my life anymore."

"Am I a detail of your life?"

"Sort of." Harper looked away, blew out a breath.

"What does that mean?"

Harper regained eye contact. "It means that I'm not sure when or how, but you've become an important detail in my life that I haven't quite figured out yet. Can we leave it at that for now?"

The warmth that spread through her was unreal. How could so little make her feel so good? She wanted to toss everything she'd thought about Harper out the window—ignore all the warning signs and spend the rest of the night wrapped up in her arms kissing her.

"Okay." She crossed the room and picked up her backpack from where she'd dropped it by the door when they'd arrived. She would do her best to concentrate on school, but the elephant with the unresolved feelings in the room was going to make it mighty difficult.

CHAPTER TWENTY-ONE

Harper was comfy and warm, but her arm felt like it had been cut from her shoulder as she adjusted it on the couch. The heaviness on her chest wouldn't let her shift. She opened her eyes to see strands of blond hair under her chin and Addison's arm wrapped around her waist. She couldn't move without dumping her to the floor. They'd fallen asleep again while studying. The last she remembered, they were going over cat anatomy. In fact, she'd performed a whole surgery in her dreams. Her mind never seemed to stop.

She shifted again, hoping to nudge Addison into waking. No luck. Addison tightened her grip around her waist and snuggled in closer. The expanse from Harper's waist to her neck seemed to be a perfect fit for Addison, and she had to admit it felt really nice having her there—sharing her warmth. This was getting to be a habit she didn't want to break, but her arm felt dead and had to be moved. She slowly pulled her hand out from under Addison and maneuvered her into the crook of her shoulder. She bit her lip as her whole arm tingled and the blood began to flow through it. Addison still didn't wake up.

She'd let her sleep, Addison had been working and studying nonstop since Harper arrived in Blueridge. It had been so sweet of her to volunteer to come with her to Denver, and she didn't know if she could've left Daisy if she hadn't. Besides, there were worse places she could be. The comfort Addison provided soothed her—made her feel safe somehow. She tugged the throw from the back of the couch and draped it across them as best she could. She closed her eyes and took in the scent of Addison's citrus shampoo. She could stand to remain in this position for a couple more hours. It was still dark outside, and she had no place else to be—no place she'd rather be, honestly.

When Harper woke again, she was alone on the couch. The blanket she'd pulled over them earlier was now the only thing keeping her warm, and it wasn't doing a very good job. She turned onto her side, and the scent of fresh brewed coffee wafted into her nose. She lifted her head to peer into the kitchen, and caught the sight of Addison doing something there. Even first thing in the morning, Addison was gorgeous. She took in a deep breath and enjoyed the feeling of comfort she brought.

Addison smiled as she made eye contact. "Hey. You're up."

"Why didn't you wake me?"

"You were sleeping so well. I thought you needed the rest." She glanced at the counter. "I didn't mean to crowd you last night. You're probably going to be sore today."

She sat up, scratched her head, made an attempt at smoothing her hair. "You didn't. I slept well."

The grin on Addison's face was beautiful. "I thought I'd make breakfast. You don't have much in the fridge besides eggs and American cheese, but I found some spinach in the freezer and a can of mushrooms in the pantry. I hope you like omelets."

Addison seemed to fit right into place in Harper's kitchen, a place Harper had never felt comfortable. She wasn't much of a cook. She'd tried more when Eden was a child, but it didn't always work out for the best. Thankfully her friends were good about sharing simple, kid-friendly recipes, which helped immensely. As Eden had gotten older, she'd relied on pre-made dinners and takeout. It was best for the both of them, so they didn't starve.

"Sounds great." She got up and headed to the bathroom. Since she'd been unable to move earlier, her need to pee was outweighing the desire to eat right now. "I'll be back. I gotta…" She pointed down the hallway.

"Take your time, and I'll start on breakfast."

The reflection she saw in the mirror wasn't very forgiving. Her dark hair was matted to one side, but the circles under her eyes didn't seem quite as dark as they had been in the past. Her eyes weren't lying. Last night she'd slept better than, well, the last time she'd woken up with Addison in her arms.

She ran a brush through her hair and pulled it back into a ponytail. She wasn't one for makeup. She had nothing to cover her dark circles or brighten her eyes, so she splashed her face with water and washed it, and then brushed her teeth.

When she walked into the kitchen, Addison had already set the table and was well on her way to cooking a couple of delicious-looking omelets. "Can I help?"

"Nope." Addison handed her a cup of freshly poured, steaming coffee and pointed to the counter. "But you can keep me company."

She would do that with pleasure. Harper took the coffee from her and settled in at the counter where she was directed. She sipped her coffee while she watched Addison squeeze the water from the thawed spinach and drain the mushrooms before she set them aside and poured the eggs she'd beaten into the saucepan. She hadn't had anyone cook for her in years, and definitely not anyone who was good at it.

At first glance it looked like Addison had put on some mascara, maybe a bit of eyeliner too. Or maybe she was beautiful without it. Warmth rushed her as she remembered the feeling of waking with Addison lying against her during the night. Soft, warm, and secure—all feelings she was unaccustomed to experiencing. At least not in quite some time.

Addison added all the remaining ingredients and then glanced up at Harper. A sweet smile spread slowly across Addison's face, and her cheeks seemed to redden. She was staring—admiring Addison's beauty—and couldn't seem to look away. Addison blinked slowly, and Harper was taken by her long, lush lashes. She seemed to be saying something. What that was, Harper had no clue. "I'm sorry?"

Addison's smile widened, and now Harper was the one blushing. "Salt and pepper?" She held up a shaker.

She thrust the intimate thoughts from her mind and cleared her throat. "Absolutely."

Last night was a close call. She didn't know what she'd been thinking kissing Addison like that. She couldn't seem to keep it casual, and they clearly had no future together. She was coming back here, and Addison was going to remain in Blueridge. Long-distance relationships were hard and rarely worked in the long run.

"You slept really good last night." Addison slid a plate in front of her and sat down on the barstool next to her.

"Yeah. I usually sleep like a rock." Not true, but she wouldn't tell Addison that. She shoveled a bite of omelet into her mouth. "This is delicious."

Addison chewed and swallowed. "Thank you. It's something you can never really get wrong as long as you have eggs and cheese." She sipped her coffee.

"I might have gotten it wrong once or twice." She took another bite. "But you seem to know the trick." She cut another chunk and held it on the end of her fork. "It's kind of funny that you've fixed me two meals now, and I've done nothing in return."

"I wouldn't say that. You've never cooked for me, but you've done plenty of other things." Addison ate a couple more bites. "I don't think I'd have been able to keep up with school if you hadn't helped me."

"You had a lot on your plate with work, school, and Brook." She took a drink of coffee and then laughed. "I'm glad we're not still enemies."

"We were never really enemies. Were we?" Addison peered over her coffee cup at her.

"Maybe not."

"Such a shame. So much time lost." Addison bit her bottom lip as she stared into her eyes, then looked at her plate, finished eating the last of her omelet, and took her dishes to the sink.

It seemed like she couldn't get out of her seat fast enough. "Too much time." She carried her plate to the sink where Addison was standing, took Addison's plate from her, and slid it into the dishwasher. "I'll run this before we leave." She spun to face Addison after she finished loading it. "Thank you for breakfast."

Suddenly they were very close again—too close—and she couldn't resist the ruby lips in front of her. The kiss was soft and sweet at first, but then it morphed into a deep, intimate one that stirred her deep inside. She found herself pushed up against the counter, felt hands roaming her back, sides, now her breasts. Sweet Lord, Addison could kiss. Every pulse point was throbbing, and all the right spots were tingling. She wanted to let go—let whatever this magic was between them happen. Maybe if she gave in to it, the desire would lessen. When the kiss ended, Addison was pressed up against her with her arms wrapped around her.

"Wow." She had no other words.

"Yeah, wow." It didn't seem Addison had any either.

"We should get to the clinic." Against every will she had she wanted Addison to disagree.

Addison took in a deep breath. "Yeah. We should, but I don't want to. Not yet anyway."

She felt the pure need when Addison crushed her lips with her own, thrust her tongue into her mouth. This was not how this was going to go down. She maneuvered Addison around—lifted her onto the counter, let her wrap her legs around her waist. The buttons on Addison's shirt were no match for the lightning speed at which her fingers were moving. She needed to touch every part of Addison that was hidden behind them. Soft, milky-white breasts tumbled into her hands when she finally found the clasp to her bra and set them free. Hard, pink nipples stared at her waiting to be consumed. The moan that escaped Addison's lips when Harper took one into her mouth sent a gush of liquid to her panties.

"Take me to bed." The low growl the words were delivered with took the choice from her.

So much for knowing this was a bad idea. It felt way too good not to explore it more. She pulled Addison off the counter, let her slide down her until her feet hit the floor. The friction was almost unbearable. She took Addison's hand and led her to the bedroom. She suddenly began to falter, felt unsure about what was about to happen. Addison, obviously determined, took the lead and pushed her to the bed.

"Are you okay?" Addison's voice was soft and sweet.

She nodded, trying to form the words she wanted to say. So much of what she'd thought about Addison had proved to be untrue, and her willpower had been completely decimated by the desire in her eyes. "You are so beautiful. I never thought anything like this would happen between us." She was unsuccessful at spilling her feelings fully. That was only a small part of what she was feeling. All her hopes and fears would remain locked away deep in her heart for the time being.

Addison kissed her again before she got to her knees, unbuttoned Harper's pants, and then stood as she tugged them off. Harper sat up, pulled the shirt from her head as Addison shed her pants, then climbed onto her lap, straddling her. She kissed her again as she popped the clasp on Harper's bra. A thrill went through her, and her wetness increased as they melded skin to skin. This was unbelievable. It was incredible to feel alive again. She'd felt dead inside for so long.

Addison urged her to lie back on the bed and kissed her deeply one more time before she trailed her tongue down her neck, across her collarbone, and down to her breasts. She took one into her mouth, twirled her tongue around her nipple, producing a jolt in Harper she never wanted to stop. Addison took over with her hand when she switched her mouth to the other and did the same. Harper squirmed beneath her, and she felt Addison smile against her breast.

Addison crawled her way down farther, tugged off Harper's briefs. "I've waited so long for this." Words Harper thought she'd never hear.

She placed soft kisses on her belly, increasing Harper's anticipation to a level she almost couldn't control. When she dipped her head lower and kissed all around her center, she let out a growl. Addison laughed and took a quick swipe before she made eye contact and pushed her tongue deeper, stroking her softly, then gradually adding more pressure.

Harper wanted to hold out, savor the moment, but she began spiraling to the crest until the orgasm hit her with such immediacy, such power, that she had to let go. The orgasm climbed higher, felt deeper, than any she remembered. She trembled and screamed, and Addison eased up, but after a moment she buried herself between Harper's legs farther and immediately sent Harper spiraling into another intense orgasm. It was clear who was behind the wheel in this journey to pleasure, and Harper was happy to let Addison drive.

When Addison finally released Harper from the pleasure plane she'd taken her to, she crawled up her body and kissed her sweetly. "That...you...were wonderful."

"I think you have that reversed."

Addison shook her head. "No. You let me do what I wanted, and it was perfect."

"You're perfect." She wanted to tell Addison so much but swallowed her words—the emotion bubbling inside. She captured her mouth again, tasted herself on her lips as she rolled to her side and slipped her hand between them. As she slid a finger easily between Addison's folds she felt the wetness there—felt her harden against the pressure. Addison pulled her on top, grabbed her ass, tugged her closer for more friction. No. This was not going to happen this way. She wanted much more out of this encounter. Harper slid her hand from between them, continued the friction as she explored Addison's breast with her tongue, then the other. So sweet—soft— so responsive. She could spend the whole morning right here with Addison's nipples in her mouth, swirling her tongue around them.

"Harper, please." The words came from Addison's mouth in an urgent whisper, and she knew it was time to move on.

She trailed her tongue down Addison's side, across her hip, and then into the valley where her thigh met her stomach and slowly made it between her legs to paradise. She was on fire, but Harper wanted to savor everything about Addison for as long as she could— her sweet, tangy taste—the softness of her skin—her strength as she lifted her hips into her.

Addison grabbed hold of her head as she raised her hips again, urging her closer. She wouldn't make her wait. She pushed Addison's legs farther apart and dove in—took her into her mouth, swirled her tongue around. Addison moaned, and she slipped a finger inside, dragged it across the sweet spot she knew would push her over the edge, and it did. Addison writhed beneath her as her rhythm and pressure increased. She tugged at Harper's hair as she cried out with pleasure—the most beautiful sound in the world. Harper didn't let up, removed her finger, replaced it with her tongue as she swept up and down, circling her with each pass.

Addison released Harper's hair and searched for her hand, led it back to her center. Harper obliged, slipping her finger back inside, finding the magic spot as she continued to suck, lick, and swirl until Addison stiffened and grabbed the bedsheets as she tumbled into orgasm again. Such a beautiful sight—head back, neck strained, diving all in to the mystical pleasure she was feeling. It was cold in the house, but with the fire racing through her veins, she barely noticed. She would remember this sight—this morning, forever.

Addison squeezed her legs together, pushing her out from the delicious spot where she'd been. She'd been so focused on Addison's belly as it tightened, bounced, and released over and over again, she hadn't realized it might have been too much.

She crawled up next to Addison and took her into her arms. "I'm sorry."

Addison gave her a lazy smile. "Never be sorry for something as awesome as that." She kissed her softly. "I just can't anymore."

She reached between Addison's legs, stroked a finger through her folds, and felt her twitch.

"Stop. If you keep that up, I won't ever want to get out of this bed."

"Would that be so bad?"

"No. It wouldn't be bad at all, but people might miss us—send out a search party. They'd find us here wrapped in each other's arms, completely exhausted."

"I like the idea of that."

"I bet you do." Addison brushed a strand of hair from Harper's eyes. "I never thought I'd end up in bed with the hot, sulky girl from high school."

"No? Really? You never thought about it?"

"I did think about it once or twice."

She raised an eyebrow.

"Okay. I thought about it a lot."

"I'm glad to hear I wasn't the only one dreaming about it." She grinned. "I lied earlier."

Addison pulled her brows together. "About what?"

"I never sleep well."

"So you didn't last night?"

"No. I did. Just don't usually."

"Well, maybe I can help you sleep better in the future." Addison grinned. "Or not sleep at all."

"I think I'd like both of those options."

"What time are we heading back today?"

"I need to stop by the clinic and check on a few more things this morning before we head out."

"Good. I'd like to see how everything is going."

"You know you have a gift with animals, right?"

"I don't know if it's a gift, but I do what I can."

"It's definitely a gift. Don't let anyone tell you otherwise."

"Okay." Addison blushed, and Harper wanted to make love to her all over again—not leave this bed for days. She would if they didn't have to drive back to Blueridge today. "I need to take a shower before we head out."

"Mind if I join you?" Addison's voice was soft, and her cheeks reddened as though she was embarrassed she'd asked.

"I'd be very happy if you did." She kissed her softly, tried to calm any insecurities she might be having.

Addison cupped her hand behind her neck and gave her another long lingering kiss. More than washing was about to happen in the shower. She was so thankful it was big enough for two.

CHAPTER TWENTY-TWO

When Harper entered the clinic, the waiting room was full, as were all the exam rooms. She waved Jeremy to the back from the front counter. "Where is V?"

"Went to lunch. Been gone for a couple of hours. The customers are getting irritated."

"I can see that. How far behind is she?"

"Three, maybe four patients."

She turned to Addison. "Do you mind if I take care of the patients already in the exam rooms?"

"No. Not at all. Can I help?"

"That'd be great." She went to the laundry area, grabbed a couple of lab coats that were hanging on the rod, handed one to Addison, and slipped the other one on herself. "I'll start in exam one. If you'll go to exam two and see what's needed, I'll be there next."

"On it." Addison smiled and went down the hall.

"Thanks." Her stomach swirled like a tornado had just touched down inside her as she watched Addison's hips sway. The woman was a hell of a partner in bed—wild, generous, and tender. She was currently adding saint to the list, which was the perfect combination for a storm Harper wasn't sure she was ready for. Why couldn't she already live in Denver? Life would be much simpler then. Wouldn't it?

They were halfway through the backed-up appointments when V finally showed up.

"Where the hell have you been?"

"That's not your business."

"The hell it isn't. This is my practice too." She took her by the arm. "You can't keep draining money from it unless you're willing to put some effort into making money too. At least take care of the patients while I'm away." V glanced at her arm and she released it. "I'm not working here right now, so there's no reason to avoid coming in."

"If I start taking care of business, will you sell your half to me?"

"I'll consider it." She bit her bottom lip, holding back everything she wanted to say. "But if you don't start working at it, there won't be anything left to sell." She raised her eyebrows. "Got it?"

"Got it." V took off her jacket, hung it on the coat rack, and put on her lab coat. "Don't you need to be on the road?"

"Yeah." She tugged off her own lab coat and jammed it into the hamper. When she spun around, she almost knocked Addison over. "Fuck." She grabbed her by the shoulders. "Sorry." She softened her voice. "Are you ready to go?"

"Let me hand this chart over to Jeremy." Addison brushed past her, found Jeremy out front, and handed him the file before she followed Harper outside and settled into the passenger seat. "We accomplished a lot today."

"We did. We're a good team."

"So why don't you let V have the clinic? Start a new one without her? Or come to Blueridge and partner with your dad?"

"I rebuilt that clinic, put my heart and sweat into it." Harper gripped the steering wheel. "I'm afraid she'll ruin it. All my customers will be disappointed, and my reputation will be decimated."

"Surely she wouldn't let that happen. She's not that evil, is she?"

"I don't know. V can be ruthless when she wants to." She drew in a breath. "She's already taken more than she's put in, and the clinic can't function much longer like that."

She found a playlist on her phone and hit play, then reached across the console and took Addison's hand. She wanted to relax and get back to Blueridge. Right now it seemed like she was being tugged in a hundred different directions. She didn't know how she was going to resolve this situation before she came back to Denver again.

❖

When they arrived at Addison's house, she grabbed her bag from the backseat. Harper rushed to the front of the SUV and took it from her. "Let me help you with that."

She could get it perfectly well herself, but she let Harper take it just the same.

Once they were inside, her cell phone rang. She saw it was her mom and put it on speaker while she snagged a couple of beers from the fridge. "Hey, Mom. We just made it in." She held the beer up in the air as Harper came into the room after dropping the bag in the bedroom.

Harper nodded, took them from her, and searched for the bottle opener in the drawer.

"You must be tired. You two want to come to the house for dinner tonight? I'm making one of Jimmy's favorites—baked chicken and rice."

One of Harper's mom's specialties. "What time?" She opened another drawer and rummaged through it.

"Seven. I need to stop at the store on my way home and pick up some cheese for it."

"Mom never made it like that." Harper finally found the bottle opener and popped the lid off one of the bottles.

"I know. Once you try it, you can let me know if you like it."

"Probably won't. My mom's recipe can't be topped. Cheese would make it totally different." Harper took a drink of her beer.

"I'll call you right back, Mom." She hit the end button, swung around to Harper, and widened her eyes. "What the hell, Harper. My mom just invited us to dinner. Can you stop insulting her?"

"Your mom should stop trying to outdo my mom. She's not her."

"No. She's not. But she is *my* mother and Jim's wife. You should respect her none the less. Stop punishing her because your mom's gone. She didn't make that happen." Addison swiped the beer from Harper's hand. "You should go home and unpack. Maybe I'll see you at dinner."

Harper looked confused and irritated as she headed to the door, but Addison refused to let her berate her mother any longer.

Harper gripped the doorknob and opened the door, then closed it again without leaving. She turned around. "I'm sorry. I'll do better."

"Damn right you will, and you'll apologize to my mother when we get there for dinner."

Harper nodded. "I will."

The regret in Harper's eyes stung deep inside, and when she saw the tears well in them, Addison rushed across the room and took her into her arms.

"I have so many emotions to deal with around my mom." She sobbed. "I don't mean to take it out on Patty."

"Okay." Addison squeezed Harper tighter before she released her. "We'll work on that."

Harper nodded and wiped the tears from her eyes.

When they arrived at Jim and Patty's, Harper was nervous about her apology to Patty. Addison was right. She'd been wrong in treating Patty the way she did, and she had to admit it. She felt very small and immature, but her feelings were hard to control. It wasn't Patty's fault her mom had died, and Patty did make her dad happy.

Patty was taking the baked chicken and rice from the oven when they entered. Her stomach knotted, as the dish immediately brought back memories of her mother having dinner on the table when she came inside from helping her dad with the animals or got home from her Future Farmers of America activities after school. Wonderful memories she didn't ever want to lose.

"Where are the girls?" Addison asked.

"They're in Eden's room watching TV." Patty took the plates from the cabinet and set them on the counter.

"I'll go check on them." Addison smiled and headed down the hallway, giving Harper a few minutes alone with Patty to apologize.

She took the plates, set one at each of the six place settings, and then went to the silverware drawer. "I'm sorry for what I said earlier, Patty."

Patty stopped stirring the vegetables and turned to face her. "Is it that I'm married to your dad, or do you just hate me?"

She shook her head. "No. I don't hate you. Just the opposite, and I think I'm mad at myself because I like you so much. You make me feel good, like my mom did, and in my heart I can't lose my mom—I won't let that happen. Ever."

"Oh, honey." Patty took her hands and squeezed them. "Your mom was a wonderful woman. I could never replace her. Maybe I can be someone different. Doesn't your heart have room for someone else?"

"My heart is very confused right now, and it's not only about you."

"Come here. Sit down and tell me what's troubling you." Patty led her to the table, where they sat adjacent to each other.

"It's always been my dream to own my own clinic in Denver— to run it myself. Now I can have that if I can get V to agree to let me buy her out, but it doesn't seem so important anymore."

"Then let V have it."

"I can't do that. People depend on me to keep it successful. V doesn't do any of the bookkeeping. She knows nothing about what it takes to keep the place running."

"Then become a silent partner, or split your time between here and there." She rubbed her back. "Let go. Circumstances have changed. Stop holding on to something you really don't want."

She shook her head. "You're right. I don't want it. Not the way I used to—not like this."

"Coming home has changed you this time."

She felt the tears welling in her eyes. "It's changed everything. This clinic, this town, these people." She blew out a breath. "I never thought I'd feel comfortable here."

"And Addison?"

"I'm afraid she's going to get to know the real me and change her mind." She glanced at the entrance to the hall to make sure she wasn't back yet. "She's already pissed at me for being an ass earlier."

Patty laughed. "I think she just got a huge dose of the real you, and I don't see her running away."

"Yeah, well. Not yet, anyway."

"She's a lot stronger and more tolerant than you think. Otherwise she wouldn't still be friends with Gemma."

"Why *is she* still friends with Gemma?"

"I'm not really sure. Maybe because Jessie and Brook are such good friends. Maybe because she hasn't had a strong enough reason not to be, but I see that friendship rocking soon."

They heard Addison coming down the hallway, and Patty got up and went back to the stove.

Addison went to the counter, picked a piece of cucumber out of the salad, and ate it. "Everything okay in here?"

"Just perfect." Patty smiled and handed her the salad bowls. "Take those over to the table, and then get the silverware out, please."

Addison smiled at Harper, and all was right in her world again. It was funny how one smile from her could make that happen—make her forget about all her worries.

CHAPTER TWENTY-THREE

Addison sat in the lodge watching the skiers as they came down the slope. She'd always wanted to learn to ski but had never found the right time or the right instructor. By the time she'd gotten around to it she was too embarrassed to tell anyone. So, she usually faked an ankle injury or something else.

She saw Harper through the window. She leaned her skis and poles into the rack and came toward the lodge. It had been close to two weeks since they'd started spending more time together, and it had been better than she'd expected. Harper was warm, gentle, and generous in every way. When Harper had suggested a ski day with the girls, she couldn't say no. She'd let Harper assume she knew how but made an excuse to stay in the lodge and study.

Addison quickly opened her book before Harper came through the door and walked inside. She didn't want to have to make up any excuses—just wanted to be left alone to study.

"Why aren't you skiing?" Harper slid into the chair across from her.

"Studying, as usual."

"Come on. Take a break. I can help you study later."

"My ankle kind of hurts anyway."

"You haven't said anything about that this week. You've been on your feet the whole time we've been working at the clinic."

"Probably why my ankle hurts."

"Come to think of it, I've never seen you actually ski. You were always hanging out in one of the lodges." Harper tilted her head. "You don't know how, do you?"

She chewed her bottom lip. Should she tell Harper? Riley had made fun of her the first time she found out. Would Harper do the same? She shook her head. "No."

"What? You grew up in a ski town. Why didn't you say something?"

"I just don't. I didn't want to say anything, and that's that." She slapped her book closed and got up. She shouldn't have told her.

"Hold on. Don't go." Harper popped out of her chair and grabbed her arm. "I'm sorry. I'm not making fun of you. I'm just surprised. I thought you knew how. I've seen you at the chalet up top on the mountain before. What happened?"

She sank down into the chair. "I never learned. I used to ride up on the lift, hang out in the chalet, and ride the lift back down after everyone else took the last run."

"But you own skis and boots." Harper leaned back in her chair and glanced under the table.

"No. I don't. I borrowed these from Riley." She motioned her hands in front of her. "Does this body look like I ski on the daily?"

Harper grinned. "I know for a fact that your body looks fantastic." She snagged the book from in front of her. "Why don't I teach you?"

"No. That wouldn't be any fun for either one of us." Plus, she would be embarrassed beyond reason.

Harper stood and held out her hand. "Come on. It'll be fun. I promise." The sincerity in Harper's eyes seemed genuine.

"Okay, but only for a little while. I really *do* have to study."

"You say when to stop. Then we'll come inside, warm up, and I'll help you study. Okay?"

Wow. She really was trying to help her all around. "Okay." Addison dropped her book off at the counter, where she asked them to hold on to it until she got back inside. Knowing the owners had its perks.

Harper was waiting at the door for her. "Do you need help with your skis?"

She shook her head. "I've done that a thousand times. It would look weird if I rode the lift up without them."

"Riley is the only one who knows you don't know how to ski?"

She nodded. "Yep, just Riley."

"Okay then. We'll be discreet." They found their way to the bunny slope. "If anyone happens to see us, we'll tell them you're teaching me some new tricks."

"I'm not sure that will fly, since you're an excellent skier."

"I can be a bit clumsy at times."

Just then, Addison felt her skis slide out from under her. Harper immediately dropped to the ground as well. "You're adorable when you're flustered. Always have been." She got back to her feet and reached out to help Addison up.

A rush of warmth overtook her as she clasped Harper's hand, and her frozen cheeks started heating. She didn't know why, but she still didn't expect compliments from Harper. She'd never thought Harper had given her a second look.

"Point your skis mostly parallel to the slope. You don't want to go straight down. You want to go from side to side until you get the hang of it."

Once she was on her feet, Harper moved to her side, just below her on the bunny slope and a half-ski in front of her. "Let's move out of middle traffic area and take the rest slowly."

"I don't know if I—"

"Sure, you can. I'm right here." Harper took her hand, wrapped it around the ski pole, and held it with hers. "Keep your skis about a foot apart and move with me." She gave them both a nudge with the pole, and they glided across the slope to a less active area.

Harper's confidence was clear, and it seemed to bleed into her, forcing her fear into the corner of her mind as she concentrated on her balance. They took the rope tow to the top of the slope, and with Harper's help, she was doing it—actually skiing from side to side all the way down.

Harper grinned as Addison snowplowed at the bottom of the slope and slowly slid in next to her. "That was perfect."

"Not really. I was aiming for the other side of you."

The burst of laughter that came from Harper's lips along with the smile that took over her face were incredible. The tingle raging inside her was increasing by the minute.

Harper threw up her hand for a high five, and she slapped it. "But you didn't run into me, so it's all good." She tilted her head. "Or maybe that would've been better." The wink Harper gave her sent her system into full overload.

After a few more runs, Addison raced to the bottom a little faster than she'd expected, and her ankle twisted in her boot as she plowed sideways and came to a stop. Harper slid in right beside her.

"I think I'm done for the day." She pressed her pole to the binding and tried to release one ski from her boot, but of course she couldn't be cool enough to make it happen. "I'm going to go inside and have something warm to drink."

"Sounds good." Harper pressed her pole to the binding and released one ski from her boot, then did the same for the other.

"You don't have to go in too." Harper was only being nice. "You'd probably rather get in some more skiing on the black-diamond runs. You haven't had much time to do anything like this since you arrived."

Harper shook her head but didn't smile. "No. Actually, I'd rather warm up with you, if that's all right."

Warm up with me. She tingled. She'd rather they were at her place right now, doing the warming in private. The lodge would have to do for now. "Of course." She struggled to release her skis from her boots, and without delay, Harper hit each binding with one of her poles and did it for her.

"I think that's the hardest part." Harper winked. "If you can master that, you'll do fine." She handed Addison her poles and gathered both their sets of skis. "Come on. Let's get inside. My feet are frozen." Harper leaned their skis into the rack, then took the poles from her and placed them alongside. "You did great, by the way." She turned around, and Addison could see she was sincere.

"Thanks." She warmed, heat rising inside as she stared into Harper's soft, blue eyes.

Harper put her hand on the small of Addison's back, guiding her in front of her. Addison jolted, heat searing through her, even though multiple layers of clothing were preventing actual contact. Going inside would make the heat she was feeling even hotter.

Harper scanned the room and then pointed to a small table by the window. "Why don't you snag that table, and I'll get us something to drink."

"Okay." She ripped off her coat.

"Hot chocolate okay?"

"Perfect." Jeez, she hoped her vocabulary broadened once they were settled at the table, or it was going to be a long afternoon. Why was she so nervous? They'd been getting along incredibly well since they'd taken the trip to Denver. She watched Harper at the counter, her vision clouded with some sort of social-media filter where mood music played and hearts appeared all around her. What was this woman doing to her? The moment vanished when Riley appeared in front of her.

"Already done?"

She shook herself from the clouded image. "Yep. My toes are frozen."

Riley took the seat across from her. "Mine too. I'm out for the day."

"Where's Bran?"

"Going to get in a few more runs before dark." Riley slipped off her jacket and hung it on the back of the chair. "I thought I saw you with Harper earlier."

"I've been with her all day. She taught me how to ski."

"That's awesome. I never could understand how you never learned."

"Neither could she."

Riley dug into her jacket pocket and took out a twenty-dollar bill. "So, where'd she go?"

She dipped her chin toward the concession counter. "She's getting us hot chocolate."

"Oh, shit. Maybe I should leave."

"No. Don't. I'm already in huge trouble." She hadn't confided in Riley about her intimacy with Harper, and she wasn't sure she wanted to spoil the magic between them by telling her.

Riley grinned. "Yeah?"

She nodded. "Yeah." She relaxed into her chair. "She *is not* what I ever expected."

"That's good, though, right?"

"She doesn't live here, Ry."

"Not now." She pulled her eyebrows together. "But I think you can change that."

Could she? Make Harper want to stay in Blueridge? She watched her come toward the table, and the heart filter appeared again. *Stop it right now. You're reading way too much into this.*

Harper set the cups of hot chocolate on the table. Not just two, but three cups. She put one in front of each of them. "I got you some too. I hope that's okay."

"Thank you. I love cocoa." Riley smiled at Harper. "It's the best here. The service is pretty awesome too. Isn't it, Addie?" She veered her gaze to Addison.

"Absolutely." She hoped the windburn was hiding the heat in her cheeks.

Harper pulled over another chair, took off her jacket, and hung it on the back. "I'll be right back. I ordered a couple of muffins too."

As soon as Harper walked away, Riley widened her eyes and silently mouthed *perfect*. "You have got to get that girl."

She smiled. "Maybe." Who knew that making Harper proud of her could bring her so much joy? But today it had. Harper had spent the last two hours with her on the bunny slope teaching her the basics of skiing, from snowplowing to the basic skiing stance. She'd learned to move her feet and hips rather than her arms, which made a huge difference in control. Why had she never done this before? Maybe the teacher made it so easy.

Addison's hot chocolate was almost gone when the group of kids burst into the lodge. Brook and Claire went straight to the counter, with Eden right between them. Jessie followed them in about a minute later. She couldn't help but feel a little proud of her daughter for embracing Eden and including her in her group of friends. She'd always tried to instill good values and actions in Brook. Being nice to someone was easy, and ignoring them was rude. High school was tough to begin with, and kids didn't need to make it any harder. That was something she hadn't learned early enough herself.

Brook turned around and scanned the room before she noticed them. She bumped Eden's shoulder and said something to her. Eden glanced over her shoulder and then nodded before Brook, nachos in one hand and a soda in the other, crossed the room to the table where they were sitting.

"I knew you guys wouldn't last long."

"We just got here." Addison snagged a nacho from the plate.

Brook leaned in and checked out her almost empty cup. "Right. You chugged that steaming hot cup of cocoa."

"She did. I watched." Harper grinned.

"I suppose you two had a contest." Brook glanced at her cup as well. "It looks like you won."

"They did. I watched the whole thing." Riley laughed. "It was a ridiculous spectacle."

Eden showed up behind Brook with a plate of loaded fries. Brook immediately swiped one and popped it into her mouth. Claire came next, with a personal-size cheese pizza.

Jessie appeared not to be hungry and had only hot chocolate. "You guys want to sit together? We can grab a bigger table."

"If we do, you're going to have to share." Riley circled her finger at the food. "All of that looks so good."

"You'll have to buy more when we run out."

"Didn't I buy that to begin with anyway?" Addison started to get up, but a sharp pain shot through her, and she immediately collapsed back into the chair. The nacho she'd eaten threatened to come up again.

Harper scrunched her eyebrows together. "Are you okay?"

The concern in Harper's eyes made the pain dissipate to a dull ache.

"I think I twisted my ankle the last time I fell."

"You didn't fall during the whole last hour of skiing. Why didn't you say something?"

"I was having fun, and my foot was frozen." She winced. "It didn't hurt this much."

"We need to get some ice on this, or it's going to swell once we take the boot off." She glanced at the girls. "We need to get her home."

"We just got our food." Claire was the first to complain.

"I got 'em." Riley glanced at Harper. "You go ahead and take Addie home. The girls can stay over with us."

Addison wrapped her arm around Harper's shoulder and held on tightly as they walked to the Explorer. "I'm sorry."

"What are you sorry about?"

"You were having fun, and now you have to leave to take me home. I'm so embarrassed." Addison stared into Harper's eyes. Such large, round, beautiful blue eyes.

"Don't be sorry or embarrassed. I'm fine with it." Harper hit the button on her key fob. "I didn't have to leave. I want to take you home."

"Thank you." Unable to maintain eye contact any longer without kissing Harper, she glanced away.

"No worries." She opened the door and helped her into the Explorer.

It was nice to have someone care about her—be there to take her home and make sure she was all right. Riley was a good friend and could've done it, but she wanted Harper with her—to comfort her—all the time now. Funny how things could change in only a few weeks.

CHAPTER TWENTY-FOUR

It was only a short drive, but Addison was getting drowsy by the time they pulled up in her driveway. The exercise and fresh air had gotten to her. She pulled at the door handle.

"Wait until I get there." Harper jumped out, rounded the car, and pulled the passenger door open. "Come on. I'll help you inside." She put out her hand.

"I think I can manage." Addison stood and swayed to one side. "Maybe not." She quickly grabbed Harper's shoulders. "It seems everything I do will be under your control today."

Harper raised an eyebrow and grinned. "Is that an invitation?"

"Absolutely." She pressed her lips to Harper's. "A little reward for bringing me home."

The sex between them was ridiculously hot and passionate. Even with the pain radiating from her ankle, Addison couldn't seem to get enough of Harper. She couldn't wait to have her tongue inside her again. That wasn't normal, by any means—she even appeared in her dreams. It had never happened with anyone before. The sounds of Harper's whispers in her ear, along with growling screams, would be embedded in her mind forever, and she wanted to make them happen again and again.

"Take me to bed, and get my mind off my ankle."

"With pleasure." Harper helped her inside and to the bedroom, where she lowered her gently to the bed before she helped her take off her boots and ski parka.

Addison scooted up against the headboard and watched Harper as she sat in the chair and removed her snow boots. She stood as she took off her jacket and tossed it into the chair where she'd been sitting in the corner.

"Well, don't stop there." She was hoping for a sexy show but wasn't sure Harper would accommodate her.

Harper closed the bedroom door and then started slowly removing her first layer, a fleece zippered jacket. She lowered the zipper slowly, then up a bit, then back down until the sides disconnected. She removed the jacket and dropped it to the floor. Next came the buttons of her flannel shirt, which she slowly and methodically unfastened one at a time until she reached the bottom, which was tucked into her ski pants. She tugged her shirt out, letting it hang open and loose. Right now, Harper looked sexy as hell with her white waffle-patterned Henley peeking out beneath it all.

Harper seemed to notice her reaction and grinned. "Your turn."

Addison swallowed hard and began to remove her outer layer, a pullover half-zip fleece. Her next layer came over her head with it, leaving her with only a black tank and her bra. She raised her eyebrows, indicating for Harper to continue, and she did. Harper removed the flannel, dropped it into the pile, then unzipped her ski pants and pushed them to the floor. Still dressed in leggings, she stepped out of them. Addison's anticipation was high; way too many layers of clothing were involved.

Harper pointed at her. "Do you need help with those pants?"

"Oh, yes." She unfastened them and pushed them to her knees, where Harper took them and gently guided them off, careful not to jar her ankle.

"You're killing me, woman."

"I know." She laughed. "Now take off that shirt."

Harper obliged and then quickly pushed her leggings to the floor and kicked them off before she unfastened her bra and slowly let it slide down her arms. A jolt hit her midsection, and she couldn't take her eyes off the perfect form before her until the bra hit her in the face.

"Is this my prize?" She held it up.

"Nope. Your prize is much better than that." She removed her socks before she pushed her boy-shorts to the floor and stepped out of them.

Harper's confidence and beauty amazed her. No way could Addison stand naked in front of her like that and not feel insecure. She slipped her thumb under her leggings and started to push them down.

Harper hopped onto the bed and pushed her hands away. "This is *my* prize." She slid her fingers under the waistband, ran them back and forth, caressing the skin beneath it.

Addison was completely aroused as she quickly pushed the leggings from her hips, leaving her baby-blue satin panties behind.

Harper laughed. "In a hurry, are we?"

"Jesus, you're sexy."

"You're the sexy one." Harper smiled before gently removing the leggings from Addison's legs, letting her nails glide along her thighs and then her calves. She removed only one of her socks, leaving the one on the sprained ankle. Then she crawled back onto the bed and straddled Addison before she kissed her.

Reaching between Harper's legs, Addison slid a finger through her folds and felt the wetness there. Harper moaned into her mouth, clearly as turned on as she was. She slipped a finger inside and circled her thumb within her folds. Harper grabbed the headboard and pressed into her hand as she rocked back and forth on it. She took the opportunity to suck a nipple into her mouth as Harper arched into her. Such beautiful perfect breasts that Harper hid so well under her clothing. Harper's breathing became more rapid and quickly turned into soft whimpers and then all-out breathless moans as she started to come, then fell against her, clenching Addison's hand between her legs. Her finger still inside, she continued stroking her as she held Harper tightly with her other arm until she stopped quivering.

"Oh my God." Harper let out a sexy low laugh. "I didn't mean to do that. I fully intended to explore you first."

"I'm glad you did. I really like making you come. Probably even more than I like it myself."

"We'll see about that." Harper kissed Addison hard—deep—and long while she rubbed her nipples between her fingers and thumbs. The electricity inside Addison increased as the zaps to her midsection intensified. She grabbed Harper's hips and held her close as she lifted her own hips to provide more friction. Such a delicious friction. How was she going to give this up—give Harper up? She broke the kiss and took in a deep breath.

Harper pulled her eyebrows together. "Did I hurt you? Is your foot okay?"

"No. I'm fine." She touched Addison's cheek. "You—this—us." She shook her head. "It's just so overwhelming."

"I know. I never expected it, but I don't want to go back to how we were before. Do you?"

"No." They absolutely weren't going back. She took Harper's face in her hands and kissed her. Their tongues mingled softly, deeply, and her arousal came alive again.

"Okay?"

She nodded. "Okay."

Harper smiled and kissed Addison softly as she caressed her thighs. "This position won't do." Still straddling her, Harper backed up and tugged her farther down on the bed, removed her panties, then draped each of Addison's legs over her shoulders.

"Do you know you have a freckle down here?"

"No. Where?" She lifted her head and caught the smile on Harper's face.

"Right here." She blew out a breath.

The warm air that hit her center was a tease she was getting used to, a preamble to what was to come. Harper's attention to all the right places would build quickly to the intense orgasm that would take her over the edge to a new plane, one that only Harper could take her to. She startled as Harper's tongue touched her ever so softly, once, twice—the third time with more pressure. Sweet Lord, it felt so good. She gripped the sheets and held on tight as Harper gripped her thighs and pinned her to the bed as she squirmed beneath her. She felt a finger inside her, then another—a jolt rushed through her as Harper found the right spot, continuing to work her magic on her. The low, intense rumble started deep and spread throughout her limbs as she launched into orgasm and bucked against Harper's mouth. *Oh my God—oh my God—oh my God.* Harper snaked her other hand beneath her—dug her fingers into her ass and held her there as she continued her rhythm—mouth pressed firmly against her until she was spent and dropped her hips to the bed.

Harper peered up at her, eyes smiling as she took one last swipe and watched her belly bounce. Harper liked to watch her react, and she was perfectly okay with that.

She reached out her hand. "Come here."

Harper propped a pillow under Addison's ankle before she crawled up beside her, gathered her into her arms, and pulled the blanket over them. "Now sleep, love."

She was so content and satisfied she couldn't keep her eyes open. This was the way she wanted every day to end, with Harper in her arms keeping her safe and warm. For as long as she could have her.

Addison woke to the sensation of delicate circles around her belly button. "How long was I asleep, and how long have you been awake?"

"A couple of hours, and not long." Harper slowly dragged her fingers up to one of Addison's breasts and began circling the nipple. "So when did you figure this out? You're definitely good at it."

"Not long after you left. I realized I didn't get along with you because I was afraid."

"Afraid? Of me?" Harper lifted her head, rolled a leg between hers.

"No. Afraid to be out like you. You were so brave. I couldn't imagine being anything close to that—dealing with anything like you were enduring."

"I never knew that."

"Of course not." She pulled her eyebrows together. "I wasn't going to admit that to anyone, let alone you."

"Why?"

"Because then I would've had to do something about it."

"You could've come to see me, and we could've done a lot about it." Harper nipped at her neck. "This." She moved to her breasts, took a nipple into her mouth, sucked it hard, and let it pop out again. "And this." She continued farther, stopping to swirl her tongue in her belly button. "And this." She then hovered over her center. Addison jolted at the warm breath washing across it.

"Definitely that." She arched into Harper when she took a long swipe between her folds.

"A lot of this." Harper buried herself between Addison's legs, and the cycle began again. She stiffened as the orgasm started to build, not knowing if this one would be even better than the last, as they'd all been previously. She immediately launched into orgasm and couldn't fathom why she'd lost so much time between them.

Harper slipped up beside her, laid her head in the crook of Addison's shoulder.

"I'm sorry I…" The words stuck in her throat. She so regretted that she hadn't done exactly as Harper said. All those years would've been so much better with Harper in them.

"It's okay. We're together now." Harper squeezed her tighter.

But were they really together? This wasn't the first time Addison had berated herself for not getting involved with Harper when they were younger, but this time *had* cemented what a complete mistake it had been. Admittedly, Addison's experience with women was limited, having slept with only a few here and there until she became involved with Nicki. Once she'd admitted to herself that she preferred women over men, she'd enjoyed her orgasms to the fullest. She'd thought so, anyway, but sex with Harper was different—she'd never experienced such passion and absolutely regretted missing out on it for so long.

Eden was irritated as she and Brook pulled up in front of her grandparents' house. She'd called her mom several times to pick her up at Jessie's because she really wanted to change out of her snow clothes and take a shower to warm up. Her mom hadn't answered or even texted back, so Brook had volunteered to drive her. They went into the house and straight to Eden's room, where she began shedding her ski clothes.

"I'm so glad to get those off." She dropped them in the corner and pulled a sweatshirt over her head. "Thanks for driving me here. My mom's still not answering her phone."

"Neither is mine. They're probably wallpapering again." Brook chuckled as she stripped off her clothes. "So, I guess I'll stay the night. It smells like Gran is cooking something awesome." She plopped onto the bed. "Do you have an extra sweatshirt I can borrow?"

"Sure." She took a blue one, imprinted with her school logo on the chest, from the drawer and tossed it to Brook. "They're done with that." Her stomach growled at the scent of food. After a day of skiing, she was starving.

"I don't think they are." Brook laughed loudly as she slipped the sweatshirt over her head. "When I say wallpapering, I mean sex."

Eden widened her eyes. "Seriously? They're having sex?"

Brook nodded. "Of course they are."

"How do you know?"

"Haven't you noticed the way they look at each other? My mom hasn't been this happy in ages."

"I thought they were only flirting. What the fuck? She never stops."

"Who? Your mom?"

She nodded. "All she does is embarrass me."

"Because she's into women?"

She nodded again.

"Why? There's nothing wrong with it. If I wanted to kiss you, I would." She looked at her lips and then to her eyes. "But I'm not into girls, so I won't." She glanced at her lips again. "But if you wanted to kiss me to figure out if you were, that'd be fine." She licked her lips. "I've been told I'm a pretty good kisser."

"I'm sure you are, but I'm good. Thanks."

"Really. Stop freaking out about it. Your mom has a right to be happy, doesn't she?"

"Yeah. I guess. It's just that some of the kids back home are jerks about it."

"Are they your friends?"

"No. Not really. Some of the popular kids."

"Screw them." Brook snapped her eyes back to her. "Wait. Your mom doesn't sleep with a lot of women, does she?"

"No. None since V moved out."

"V was her girlfriend?"

"Yeah." She pulled her eyebrows together. "Why all the questions?"

"Getting some background. I don't want my mom wallpapering with just anyone."

"Does your mom wallpaper with other women? Doesn't it bother you?"

"I'm fine with it. My mom hasn't really told anyone she's a lesbian yet. I mean officially, but she goes to Ouray once a week to see her," she made air quotes with her fingers, "friend in the city. She says she's picking up vet supplies, but I know that isn't all she's doing." Brook laughed. "She doesn't think I know what's going on, but she comes back all relaxed and in a great mood. I get to have the most wicked sleepover parties with my friends while she's gone." She relaxed in her seat. "She's happy. When I was little, my mom and dad were always arguing. They never got along, and I hated it. Why does it bother you so much?"

"I don't really know." Eden was silent for a moment as she thought about her mom and how happy she'd been since she'd been working at the clinic in town. "I guess my mom *has* been a lot less stressed since we got here. Well, not at first, but much better now. She's always uptight around V."

"How long was she with V?"

"About five years. Mom and I were on our own before she came into the picture."

"Just think. If our moms get together, we'll be sisters." She smiled. "Of course, I'll be going off to college next year in Boulder, so you'll be stuck living with them either here or in Denver."

"Mom says we're going back to Denver. That's not far from Boulder."

"Well, then, in Denver. I hope you have a big house for when I come home on breaks. I'll be glad to get out of this tiny town and to the big city."

She hadn't thought about being sisters with Brook and really hadn't thought that Brook would be happy about it. It was nice that she was, and they had plenty of space at their house in Denver. But Eden kind of liked it here, where she could ski and feed the chickens.

Chapter Twenty-five

Harper had already found the heating pad and situated it on Addison's ankle. She was pulling on her leggings and Henley, when someone knocked on the front door.

"Are you expecting anyone?"

"It's probably Riley." She sat up and looked around for her clothes. "Go look through the slit in the curtain by the door."

Harper found Addison's tank and fleece and gave them to her before she crept down the hallway.

Harper came racing back into the room. "It's Gemma."

She heard the doorknob rattle. "Oh my God. She's coming in." She slipped her tank over her head and put her fleece on over it.

Harper froze. "She has a key?"

"Yes. She and Riley both do."

"What should I do?" Harper rushed around the room searching for the rest of her clothes. "Where should I go?"

"Take the quilt from the bottom of the bed and run to the couch." Addison half wished she'd walked in on them. Then she'd be out and wouldn't have to worry about it anymore.

Harper gathered the quilt into her arms and sped into the living room.

Soon Addison heard the door open and Gemma's voice. "What are you doing here?"

Harper didn't answer.

"Harper. Wake up. Why are you here?"

"I took Addison home after she sprained her ankle and didn't want to leave her alone." Harper was doing an awesome job of sounding groggy. "Why are *you* here?"

"I came to check on her."

She heard footsteps coming down the hallway. She tugged the blanket up around her chest and waited for Gemma to appear.

"How's your ankle? Jessie didn't tell me until this morning, or I would've come over last night."

Thank God for Jessie. She had a sneaking feeling she'd neglected to tell Gemma on purpose. She'd have to thank her for that when she saw her next. "Harper took care of it for me. It feels much better now." That and a whole lot of other body parts she would keep to herself.

"You should've called me." Gemma glanced down the hallway. "I could've taken care of you instead of Harper."

She was about to tell Gemma way too much when Harper appeared in the doorway, fully dressed and holding an ice pack.

"If you're okay now, I'm going to head home, change, and get to the clinic." Harper glanced at her watch. "I still have an hour before we open."

"Yes. Go." Gemma shooed her away with her hands.

"I'll get there as soon as I can."

Harper pulled her eyebrows together. "Absolutely not. You take it easy today." She came closer and handed her the ice pack.

"Thank you so much for everything you did last night." She kept eye contact, making sure Harper knew she wasn't talking about anything that had to do with her ankle.

"You're welcome." Harper backed up and went to the door. "I'll check on you later."

"No need. I'll take care of her." Gemma followed Harper down the hallway.

Harper had given her a reprieve on telling Gemma, but Addison wished she were stronger and had just done it. Her secret was getting larger by the day, and soon it would become like a huge ball of rubber bands snapping back at her as she peeled away each layer.

❖

Harper was taking a break in the office to catch up on some business for the Denver clinic when her dad appeared in the doorway.

"What are you doing here?"

"We had to pick up a few things in town for the chickens, so I thought I'd stop in and see how everything was going while we were here." He glanced over his shoulder. "Seems someone's organized the lab a little differently."

"I arranged it in a more practical manner."

He smiled, moved farther into the office, and glanced at her credentials hanging on the wall. "You seemed to have settled into Blueridge now."

"What do you mean?" She had an idea where this conversation was going.

"You and Addison seem to have become rather close. So I thought you might have made a decision about the practice."

"My plans haven't changed, Dad." She glanced at the email she'd been reading. "I still have so much to do in Denver with my clinic. I can't abandon it now. That wouldn't be right, and I don't want to." She'd actually gone back and forth with the idea, even put it on paper once, but she always ended up with the same result.

"I've always planned to leave the practice to you, but if you don't want it, I'll give it to Addison."

She bolted from her chair. "She's not even a certified tech yet. You can't practice medicine through her. You could lose your license." She didn't see Addison until she'd already spun around and rushed out the door. *Fuck.* "And then Addison would never be able to get her license." She brushed by her dad and took off after her, but she was in her car and gone before she could stop her to explain what she'd meant. "You're going to have to handle the appointments until I get back."

He waved her on. "Go. I'll handle anything that comes in."

She jumped into her SUV and drove, taking the back streets as fast as she could to Addison's place. Harper was sure she'd totally misunderstood what she was saying. She wouldn't have any part in creating a situation where Addison would never be able to get her license to practice veterinary medicine. She wasn't so sure about her dad, though.

❖

Addison was almost to the front door of her house when she heard Harper drive up. She didn't want to see her—couldn't stand to see her right now. She swiped the tears from her face.

"Addie. Wait. Let me explain."

"What's to explain? You don't think I can do it." She tried to get the key into the lock.

"That's not what I said."

She spun around and put her hands on her hips. Pain shot through her ankle. It had been healing well, but the quick movement hurt like hell. "You said you're going back to Denver."

"I did say that. That's always been my plan. You know that." She tried to help Addison walk, but she pushed her away.

"Then go." She wasn't about to lean on Harper. She turned, jammed the key into the lock, turned the knob, and pushed open the door. It thudded as it slammed against the wall. "Of course you wouldn't ask me to come to Denver with you. I'm not good enough."

"What? Where did that come from?" She dropped her shoulders and closed her eyes. "I didn't know you wanted to come to Denver with me."

"I don't. Not really. Especially not now."

"Addie." She grabbed her from behind and held her closely, wouldn't let her go. "I had no idea you were even thinking of leaving Blueridge." She kissed her on the sweet spot behind her ear. "It's not that I don't think you're good enough. You're excellent at caring for animals, but you're not licensed to practice." She squeezed her tighter. "If Dad puts you in that position, the board will take away your license before you even get it. You might never be able to practice at all."

The spring so tightly coiled inside her unwound, and her body felt soft and pliable, like it was meant to be part of Harper's. The impact she had on her was simply mind-blowing.

"You have to believe me. I have so much confidence in you, but you're not there yet. I don't want him to ruin your chances of becoming a wonderful veterinarian."

She twisted in Harper's arms, turned to see tears streaming down her face. She meant everything she'd said. "I believe you." She pressed her lips to Harper's and kissed her softly, sweetly, then held her in her arms. "I don't know what to do."

"You're going to finish the program you're in and then look at your options for the future."

"Is one of those options you?"

"I think so. If you want me to be."

"I do. Very much so." She wanted it all—Harper, the license, the clinic—but she wanted it in Blueridge, not Denver.

Chapter Twenty-six

Harper's phone buzzed in her pocket, and when she took it out and looked, she was surprised to see V's name on the screen. She pushed the ignore button, not in the mood to talk to her this morning. It immediately buzzed again, and a text came through from V.

I'm ready to make a deal with you.

She waited, watching the bubbles on the screen. It appeared V wasn't finished with her message.

It might not be what either of us wants, but I'm willing to compromise.

She immediately went to her contacts and hit the button for V, who answered after the first ring. "Compromise how?"

"I'll let you buy me out, if you pay me enough to establish another clinic."

"You have got to be kidding." No way was she going to do that—no way could she afford it. "You're the one with the money here."

"That might be true. But if you want *this* clinic, that's what I want."

"I'd expect you to sign a non-competition agreement. You wouldn't be able to open a clinic within a fifty-mile radius."

"That won't be a problem."

"It takes a lot of work and dedication to open a clinic. Why would you want to do that? You don't even like going to work."

"I don't, really. It's Brandy's idea. She's been helping out at the clinic."

"You brought your new girlfriend into *my* clinic without asking me?" She took a breath in through her nose to calm herself. Arguing with V while she had a deal on the table was a bad idea.

"It's *our* clinic. She's licensed, and I needed help after you left. Besides, it's not like you haven't moved on. Don't think I didn't see what's going on with Addison when you showed up here."

"Addison has nothing to do with this." Had she said something to V?

"Really? Cause if I know you as well as I think I do, you're probably planning to bring her into the practice soon." She laughed. "If I weren't happy for you, I'd be jealous."

V was right. She was planning on doing something with Addison, but she wasn't sure what yet. She wasn't sure about anything where Addison was concerned, other than she was falling in love with her. "Yeah, well. You know me. I don't go all in very often."

"I know that too well."

"Not all my fault. I tried my best." V was a huge flirt, and Addison had never felt totally secure in their relationship.

"Not faulting you for it. I made my share of mistakes, but you were always more involved with the clinic than you were with me." V was silent for a moment. "Will it be different with her?"

"It already is." She glanced up and saw Addison come into the lab. "I'll think about it and let you know." She hit the end button and slid her phone into her lab coat.

"You look like you got some bad news. Who was that?" Addison pulled her eyebrows together.

"On the contrary. V wants to sell me her half of the clinic."

"Are you going to do it?"

"She wants a lot of money for it. I don't have enough to cover it." She probably wouldn't be able to get a loan for that much either, now that V had let business decline.

"You can always sell to her, can't you?"

She blew out a breath. She'd never even considered that option before, but with Addison standing in front of her asking the question, she wasn't sure now.

"Never mind. You shouldn't have to think about it for that long." She pinched her lips together into a flat smile. "I know where you stand on that." Addison went through one of the exam-room doors.

Her stomach clenched as she leaned against the counter. The weird thing was that she didn't really know where she stood on anything anymore. She'd told Addison a few days ago that she was an option in her life, and she'd meant it, but selling to V wasn't something she'd considered. Her next steps would definitely take some serious thought.

❖

Instead of having lunch with Addison, Harper made up an excuse and went to the sporting-goods store to talk to Pete. When she entered, she searched the aisles for him. It wasn't a huge store, but big enough to avoid someone if you wanted. She took out her phone and hit Pete's number.

"Where are you?"

"In the office. Where are you?"

"In the middle of the clothing section. I'll be right there." She rushed to the back of the store and went through the double doors to the hallway that led to the office.

Pete met her at the door. "I didn't expect to see you today. What's up?"

"I need to talk to you about the clinic. V called me with a deal, and I'm afraid I've hurt Addison."

He opened the door wider, and she saw Olive sitting behind the desk.

"I'm sorry. You're busy."

"No. Not at all." Olive stood and started around the desk. "I was just leaving."

She put her hand up. "Please stay. I can use your thoughts on this situation too."

"Okay. You want a bottle of water?" She went to the mini refrigerator in the corner behind the desk.

"Sure."

Olive took out a bottle and handed it to her before she sat in one of the padded, leather club chairs on the other side of the desk and patted the arm of the one next to her.

"So what did V offer?" Pete wandered around the desk and sat behind it.

"She offered to let me buy the clinic."

"That's what you want, right?" Olive raised her eyebrows.

She nodded. "She wants more money than I can afford." She twisted the cap off the water and took a drink as she contemplated her next words. "Addison asked me if I was willing to let V buy me out."

"And?"

"And I didn't answer."

"Because?" Olive watched her intently.

She shrugged. "Because I don't know if I am or not."

Pete leaned back in his chair and smiled. "Wow. That's a change from when you got here."

Olive narrowed her eyes at Pete and then focused her attention back on Harper. "What are you unsure about?"

"This is the first time since I split with V that I've even considered selling to her, but I can't tell Addison that. It wouldn't be fair if I told her and then didn't do it." She shifted in her chair. "I've put so much work into that clinic, I can't bear to see V ruin it."

"She's already doing that, right?" Pete was only stating the facts.

She nodded. "She told me today that her girlfriend is working there now. No one at the clinic said a word to me about it." She shook her head. "I thought they were my friends, but it's like they're all against me." Maybe it ran better without the tension.

"I totally understand your dedication to the clinic, but where does that leave you with Addison?" Like Pete, Olive was always straight to the point.

"Some things happened between me and V during our relationship that left me reeling. Some were my fault, and some were hers." She sighed. "I want to do things right this time. I'm really scared I won't."

"Sometimes you need to have a bad previous relationship to have the good one that comes next." Olive rubbed her shoulder.

"You really think that?"

Olive nodded. "Falling in love with the right person is easy. It's getting past all the wrong ones along the way that's hard. You have to be alive and growing in a relationship. If you aren't, then why stay?"

She had never really conceptualized it that way before. "I really believe she's the one. I think about her face when she tells me serious things—how intense she is. Those thoughts morph into her giddiness when she lets go. When I—" she thumped her fist into her chest "—make her let go." Pete cleared his throat, and her cheeks heated. "I'm sorry. I know that's too much information."

"Not at all." Olive took her hand. "I'm happy you finally see her." She smiled at her as though she'd known it all along.

"I do." She shook her head. "I've completely fallen for the smile she forms when she thinks no one is watching. You know, the one she doesn't know she makes." She let out a sigh. "She's so beautiful all the time. Even when she's intense—out of control—angry—kind, so many different emotions hit me right in the heart—right where I live. I can't get her out of my mind." She truly believed she was becoming a different person because of Addison. How could she let that go?

"You need to tell her that."

"What part?"

"All of it—everything you just told us. Otherwise she's not going to understand why you keep going back and forth, why you make the decisions you make. If she is truly the one, you can't exclude her from those uncertainties. She needs to know everything that happened with V and the clinic, and where you're at with V now. And you absolutely have to tell Addie how you feel about her."

"I'll try." She stood and went to the door. "Thank you for listening."

Olive followed her out. "Of course. We're always here if you need us." They both stood in the doorway as she made her way into the store. She didn't know if she could do what Olive suggested, still afraid she'd hurt Addison with her indecisiveness. She didn't want to tell Addison anything without making up her mind and taking action first. V wouldn't wait forever for an answer, and she needed to make plans quickly.

❖

The clinic wasn't as busy as Harper would've liked when Gemma came whirling through the door. That was one woman she preferred to avoid, both in high school and now. The fact that she was Jessie's mother made that impossible. Gemma had a passive-aggressive way of making everyone feel inferior, and she hoped she didn't make Jessie feel that way. Harper had learned to block her out long ago, but Addison had remained her friend over the years, and she still seemed to have some weird control over her. She had no idea why Addison needed to please Gemma, even if she was her friend.

"You really need to come to the house and work out with me." Gemma gave Addison the once-over. "It looks like you've put on a few pounds."

"I don't have time for that. I barely have enough time for work and school."

Harper came out of one of the exam rooms. "What don't you have time for?"

Gemma moved her fingers in the air, circled them, then pointed up and down Addison. "Don't you think Addison could use a little workout? She seems to have put on a few pounds."

"I think she looks incredible just the way she is." She winked at Addison. "Why is it any of your business anyway?"

Gemma stared at her. "She's not gay, you know." She spoke with such conviction, Harper wanted to drive a dagger right through her little bubble and spill the news out onto her like rainbow glitter from a balloon—that would stick to her forever. Then she would never forget.

She glanced at Addison, saw the panic on her face. "Isn't that a shame."

"Whatever made you decide to become a vet?" Gemma scowled. "Working with animals is so…" she seemed to shiver…"unclean."

"You cannot seriously believe that." She couldn't understand how anyone could dislike animals so much. "Animals are beautiful creatures who provide comfort and love, when treated properly."

"I've never known one that has been any of those things." Gemma shook her head as though she was trying to clear a bad memory from her thoughts. "I don't even like Jessie working here, but she insists."

"Leave her alone, Gemma." Addison's voice was firm.

"Why are you still defending her like you did in high school?" The hold Gemma had on Addison was unbelievable.

Harper was unaware that it was this strong. "Did you ever think maybe it's you and not the animals? You certainly could learn a thing or two about love. It shouldn't come with strings and conditions."

"I don't have any conditions around my friendship." She pulled her eyebrows together and scowled. "Ask Addison."

Addison was silent. "You do kind of like things your own way."

"I can't deny that, but that doesn't depend on my friendship."

"When we were younger, it sorta did."

"Jesus, Addie. I think I've grown up quite a bit since high school."

"Have you?" Harper raised her eyebrows. "Doesn't seem that way to me, or you wouldn't be standing there telling Addie she needs to work out."

"Tell me, Harper. Do you get much business? I mean, being a lesbian and all?" Classic Gemma—change the subject.

"Contrary to your narrow-minded thinking, most people looking for a veterinarian don't check the gender-preference box first. They don't care that I'm gay." Harper wasn't about to let Gemma get away with her ridiculous ideas about Addison or herself. Only one of the reasons she couldn't stay in this town—why she left in the first place. Gemma's small-minded thoughts only cemented that conviction firmer.

Gemma narrowed her eyes. "I'm leaving now." She glanced at Addison. "We'll talk about this later." She was acting like a parent scolding her child after she'd mouthed off in public. Gemma spun and went out the door.

"Someone should put a muzzle on her." Harper watched her leave. "Gemma is right—I don't belong here." She walked to the lab. "I can't stay here—it has too many boundaries, too many rules I don't live by anymore. I belong with my friends—my family in Denver. They don't judge me. Never have. This town, the way people look at me, act around me, is oppressive."

"That's not true. Everyone here has been nothing but welcoming to you—grateful even. If someone hasn't, tell me who, and I'll set them straight."

She couldn't help but smile at Addison's persistence. "Maybe you've been wearing those tinted glasses for too long."

"Please don't make a decision based on the remarks of a stuck-up woman whose main goal in life is to be the star of another housewives' reality TV show."

"Really? She wants that?"

Addison nodded. "Been submitting ideas and begging to get a show here for over a year."

"Oh my God. Have they even considered it?"

Addison flattened her lips and shook her head. "Not enough wives who don't work or are interesting enough to make them even think about it. Thank heaven." She chuckled. "That'd be just what we need—a bunch of spoiled rich girls taking over the town. They're looking at Telluride, though. Maybe she'll pick up and move there."

"Woohoo. I'd cheer for that."

"I know she's a bitch sometimes, but she's been very generous with her philanthropy in town, and she's convinced her husband to let the kids who live in town ski free. They all get season passes until they're out of high school and have jobs so they can afford the lift tickets."

"I'm glad to hear she has a heart, even if it's the size of a tiny nugget of rhodochrosite buried deep in the mountains."

"My biggest regret in life is having let her have so much influence over me and my life choices when I was younger."

"You would've done things differently?"

"Absolutely."

"For example?"

"I would've gone to veterinary school right out of high school. Gemma didn't think it was an acceptable job for someone in our group. Still doesn't, really. I should design clothes, own a boutique, or even be in marketing to help her with advertising the lodge." She looked at her hands. "More importantly, I wouldn't have ignored you."

"You really regret that?" Considering Addison's behavior in front of Gemma today, Harper still wondered.

"Yes. Very much so." She blew out a breath. "If I hadn't, we could've had a nice life together, and as it stands now, I don't know if that can happen. At least not here."

"So what do we do now?"

"I don't know." She fell into her arms. "I only know I don't want to lose you."

She held Addison tight, thought about the obstacles in their way. Were they really obstacles or just minor roadblocks they could get past with a little effort? They had to find some way to make this work.

CHAPTER TWENTY-SEVEN

Harper parked in the visitor space in front of Colorado State University Veterinary Teaching Hospital in Fort Collins. The schedule at the clinic was light for a Friday. Nothing but wellness checks, so she'd slipped out early this morning and left word that she was needed at her clinic in Denver. She checked her email on her phone quickly before she got out of the car and headed toward the entrance to find the administrative offices. Even though she kept in touch with Lisa, her former instructor and now the director of the teaching hospital, it had been quite some time since she'd visited her on campus. She'd actually taught a few courses as an adjunct instructor when she was first trying to get her clinic off the ground. She'd declined multiple offers in recent years from Lisa to continue to teach, even only one class a semester, but Harper found that she didn't want to teach animal medicine, at least not in a classroom setting. After rejecting all Lisa's offers, she was grateful Lisa had free time to fit her into her schedule.

She entered the hospital and followed the signs to the office of the director of teaching. Still the same path she remembered. The doctors she passed as she walked seemed much younger than when she went to school here. The familiarity of the place made her rather nostalgic, but she certainly didn't miss the stress of the schoolwork. The hours Addison put in studying and doing homework indicated the classes hadn't gotten any easier.

"Hi. I'm Harper Sims, here to see Dr. Darby."

"Yes. She's expecting you." The woman hopped out of her chair, headed to the door, and opened it. "Dr. Sims is here."

When she entered the office, Lisa stood and came toward her. Harper had forgotten how stunning she was. About five feet ten inches tall, Lisa carried herself with a distinct walk of confidence, an aura Harper also strived to present but had never really mastered. Her jet-black hair flowed elegantly across the shoulders of her pink shirt. Her appearance wasn't the only reason she'd been able to move up quickly into the director position. Lisa was smarter and more compassionate than anyone she knew.

Lisa met her halfway across the room and swept her into a hug. "It's so good to see you again. It's been far too long." She held her at arm's length. "You look really good."

"Thanks. You don't look so bad yourself." She dragged her eyes away from Lisa's baby-blue eyes that were accented by perfectly arched brows and glanced around the room. "You've come a long way since being my favorite instructor." She remembered being able to watch Lisa lecture for hours, which was saying something, because she hated lectures.

"You say that now, but I don't think that was the case when you were taking my classes."

"Probably not, but you pushed me to learn, and I'm a better doctor because of it."

"It's getting pretty deep in here." Lisa motioned for Harper to sit before she rounded the desk and sat. "Now I know you must want something."

She laughed. "I do, but everything I said is true." She flopped into the chair in front of the desk. Lisa had been instrumental in her decision to take on the clinic in Denver when the previous doctor retired. She'd advised her on how to get the loans and what she could do to improve the clinic to gain more customers. Turns out that a dwindling customer base had been the least of her problems.

"How's your practice?"

"It's good, but I've been in Blueridge running my father's clinic for the past couple of months."

"Why is that? Is your dad okay?"

"He had a heart attack. He's been having issues for quite some time and hadn't told anyone. He still needs time to recover."

"Oh my gosh. That's horrible. I'm so sorry."

"Thanks. He's getting better. But I can't seem to get out of Blueridge. I kind of met someone."

"Well, why would you want to leave if you did that?"

"I thought it could be different, but it's not. The town is too small, and people talk too much. The woman I met isn't really out. She is with her family, but not with some of her friends and other people in town."

"Really? I thought most lesbians were at least out with their friends. It's the twenty-first century, for heaven's sake."

"I know, but it's her news, and I can't fault her for not wanting to share her lifestyle with some of these people."

"What are you going to do?"

"Well, that's part of the reason I'm here. She's taking online classes at the Community College of Denver, and after she finishes this semester, she'll have her associate degree in veterinary medicine."

"And you want her to enroll here?"

She nodded. "Besides being the best, it's the only veterinary college in the area. She's not sure she wants to continue her education right away. I've talked to her about the risks of waiting, but…" She shrugged. "Long story short, she doesn't want to leave Blueridge."

"She'll have to leave at some point if she wants to go further with her education. We don't have many online classes in the program. She'll have to take classes on campus, here in Fort Collins, That's at least seven hours from Blueridge."

"I know. I was hoping you could give her a recommendation. Maybe help get her enrolled in whatever online classes that *are* offered so she won't have to move here right away."

"What's her name?"

"Addison Foster."

Lisa scribbled the name on a sticky note. "Has she registered for the summer or fall semesters?"

"I don't think so. I really don't know."

Lisa picked up the laptop from the side of her desk, opened it, and began typing. "I don't see that she has." She typed more on the keyboard. "We still have room in some of the classes for the fall semester." She glanced up at Harper. "Will she be going full-time?"

"I think that would be best. Don't you? She works a lot of hours at the clinic now. I thought she could help out at my clinic in Denver to earn some extra cash."

Addison could live with her and Eden. The house was big enough for Brook to live there too, if she decided to go to college here as well. Wow. She was really getting ahead of herself. She was packaging herself up a ready-made family, and she didn't even know what Addison's plan was. She'd expressed her desire to attend the university to further her education and become a veterinarian, but they'd never discussed a time frame.

"She's smart and really wants this, right? She's not going to change her mind halfway through the program, is she? It's difficult, even for the smartest students. You can attest to that."

"She's very smart, and dedicated." She held up her hand. "I swear. I wouldn't ask if I didn't know she could do it." Whether she wanted to was yet to be seen. A whole lot was riding on this decision, and it wasn't all about education.

Lisa reached into her drawer, took out a folder, and flipped through it, then removed one page and added another. "Okay." She handed it to Harper. "Here's the information packet. The website is listed on the first page. Have her fill out the application online and let me know when it's submitted. I'll get with the Vet Prep Program advisor to see if she's a candidate, and she'll have to take a full load of classes for the program. If not, I'll make sure she enrolls in the proper classes for her first semester to get her on the road to her bachelor's degree. When the time comes, she'll have to interview for the DVM program."

Harper grinned. "Have I told you that you were my favorite instructor?"

"Uh-huh, and now I'm your favorite director. Just make sure she doesn't let either of us down. Okay?"

"She won't. I promise." It seemed like everything was coming together. Harper could go back to her clinic, and Addison could come live with her and attend the college. They could be together and happy in Denver. She wasn't going to think about all the details yet. They were already making her head spin. She needed to stay the course and believe it would all work out.

"You might owe me a class or two for this one, or at least some time at the hospital. We have plenty of interns that can use the guidance of a seasoned DVM."

"I'll gladly pay up."

Lisa grinned. "Addison must be pretty special for you to agree to teach again. I know how much you hated it."

"I think she is, and I didn't hate it. I enjoy practicing medicine more." Addison was indeed special. In fact, Harper thought she was the one woman who would remain in her life. It seemed like she always had been, but she couldn't help but be nervous about the whole thing. She'd never completely gone all in on a relationship before, and Addison seemed to be defining the rules. Control was totally out of Harper's hands on this one.

"So what's your dad going to do about his practice? Are you planning to take it over someday?"

"He's got a lot of years left in him, so I don't think that will be anytime soon. Besides, I don't really want to leave my practice in Denver." She didn't plan to move to Blueridge right now, possibly not at all.

"Is V still a partner in the practice?"

"Yeah. I can't afford to buy her out right now, and I'll be damned if I'll let her have it. I worked really hard to get it up and running, not to mention rebuild the clientele."

"So, you're planning to bring Addison into it with V?" Lisa raised her eyebrows. "That'll be a cozy threesome."

"Foursome. Her new girlfriend's already working there."

Lisa raised her eyebrows. "Really?"

"Yeah. Don't even get me started on that." Once she was back in Denver, she hoped V would get tired of working with her and move on to a practice of her own with her new girlfriend.

"Sounds messy and uncomfortable. Maybe you should look past your feelings about the practice in Denver…" Lisa hesitated… "and the one in Blueridge and decide what you want in the future you'll be sharing with Addison."

"Maybe I should." She smiled but still didn't see a future for herself in Blueridge at this point. "Can I buy you some lunch?"

"You'd better." Lisa closed her laptop. "There's a new little sandwich shop just off campus that has fresh-baked baguettes and a whole pastry case of desserts. I can't get enough of them. I've tried almost every sandwich on the menu."

"Do they have a good Reuben?"

"The best."

"Spicy mustard?"

"Absolutely. None of that thousand-island-dressing stuff."

"Lemon tarts?"

"And croissants, and eclairs, and chocolate cream pie, and—"

"Okay. I'm already hungry. Let's go." She popped out of her chair.

When they arrived at the restaurant, the scent of fresh-baked bread wafted into her nose. It smelled like heaven. When it came to overindulgence, bread was her downfall. She could never resist it in a basket, on a sandwich, or toasted with garlic. That last choice didn't bode well for dating, so on the occasion she did have a date, she tried to steer clear of Italian restaurants. Of course, that was difficult in Blueridge, considering there were only a few restaurants, the best one so far being The Bistro.

The place was small and busy. A few parties were before them and quite a few after them. People were lining up outside. Thankfully, they'd arrived close to eleven a.m. and were ahead of the crowd. It wasn't a fancy place. It was the kind where you ordered at the counter, then found a table, and they brought your food to you.

"Why don't you go snag us a table, and I'll order? What kind of sandwich do you want?"

"I'll have the turkey-and-avocado panini, no bacon."

"No bacon?" She couldn't disguise the shock in her voice. "Who doesn't like bacon?"

"Me." She grinned. "I'll take a Pellegrino Limonata to drink. I'll grab it from the cooler."

"Ooh, that sounds good. Get one for me too."

Lisa nodded and headed for the cooler, taking the drinks from it, and then she moved on to a table for two against the wall.

Harper ordered the sandwiches—a Reuben for herself and the turkey and avocado for Lisa—then snagged two bags of chips and went to the table. "You like regular, right?" She tossed the bags of chips in the center of the table. "I got barbecue too, just in case."

"Both are good with me."

"Good. Then we can share." She sat and scooted her chair closer to the table. "Glad you got a spot away from the window. I hate it when people watch me eat."

"Same. Not my first visit here." Lisa laughed. "So tell me more about Addison. How did you meet her?"

"I actually grew up with her."

Lisa raised her eyebrows. "Seriously?"

"Yeah, but she wasn't gay then." She tore open one of the bags of chips, took a chip, popped it into her mouth, and slid the bag across the table.

"And she figured that out when?" Lisa took one and ate it.

"Sometime between when I left town and came back this time." She ate another chip and swallowed. "Seems she knew that about herself all along, but was afraid to come out."

"She came out for you?"

"God, no. She's been out with her family for a while—was actually seeing someone casually who lives in Ouray." Her drink hissed when she opened it. "Kind of a once-a-week visit when she went to get supplies for the clinic."

"So, nothing serious, then."

The waiter delivered their sandwiches and took the number from a holder on the table. "Everything look okay?"

They both checked their food and nodded.

"I don't really know, but Addison doesn't pick up supplies anymore." She took a bite of her Reuben sandwich. The flavors of warm corned beef and homemade sauerkraut filled her mouth. It was as good as Lisa had said. "Oh my gosh. This is delicious."

"Told you."

"I might have to come see you more often."

"We can hit this again when you start teaching."

"Clinicals only." At least then the students would be involved rather than falling asleep while she lectured.

"Deal." Lisa grinned as she wiped her mouth. "I actually wasn't going to hold you to it."

"Damn. I should've kept my mouth shut." She took another huge bite. She hadn't realized how hungry she was. She'd left home this morning before sunup. "It'll all be worth it to help Addison. I can't wait to get home to tell her."

Lisa finished chewing the bite she'd taken and swallowed. "Are you sure you're staying in Denver?"

"Of course." She pulled her eyebrows together. "Why?"

"You called Blueridge home."

Wait. A chill shot through her. Did she do that? "Just a slip of the tongue. Denver is my home and has been for a long time." And it was going to stay that way.

Lisa chuckled. "It sounds like your home is going to be wherever Addison is."

"Maybe so." If she let her heart lead, that was completely true, but her head knew she would have to leave too much behind in Denver. At least right now.

"I'll see if there are any open vet-tech positions at the college," Lisa said. "She'd get a break on tuition for herself and her daughter, if she decides to choose CSU as well."

"That would be great." She grinned and pushed her plate away. "You are definitely my favorite director." She couldn't contain her excitement. Everything seemed to be coming together.

"I'm glad I cemented that title." She finished the last of her drink. "Now you for sure *have* to teach. No backing out."

"I will. I promise."

Lisa glanced at her watch. "Sorry to cut this short, but I need to get back for a meeting." She stacked their empty dishes.

"Let me get that." Harper stood and took the dishes to the drop-off.

As Harper pulled up in front of the college, Lisa reached across and clutched her hand. "Listen. It doesn't sound like you've had a discussion with Addison about your plans for yourself or her." She squeezed her hand and then let it go. "Remember that two people are involved in your relationship, so be open to Addison's wants." She shrugged. "And needs. They might be different from yours." She got out of the car and walked toward the building.

As Harper left Fort Collins heading for her clinic in Denver, the words Lisa said about sharing a future with Addison popped into her thoughts. What would a future with Addison be like? A house full of animals, dogs, cats, and chickens in the yard? Grandkids someday? Or just grandpups?

She took in a deep breath. She was getting way ahead of herself and needed to stay in the present. She hadn't even shared any of her plans with Addison, not even what she'd arranged today at the college. She couldn't wait to tell her. Hopefully, Addison would be as excited as she was. Their happiness was only a few steps away, she hoped. Getting Addison to take them would be the challenge.

Chapter Twenty-eight

When Harper entered Addison's house, she was grinning like she'd just won the lottery.

"Well, you look happy. I guess everything went well in Denver?"

"It went exceptionally well." Harper handed her the folder she was carrying. "I got this for you."

"What is it?" She flipped open the folder and saw the CSU logo on the first page.

"It's enrollment information for the College of Veterinary Medicine at Colorado State University."

"Why do you have it?"

"On my trip to Denver, I drove up to Fort Collins to see my friend Lisa. She was one of my instructors, and now she's the director of the teaching hospital." Harper continued smiling like she'd solved all their problems. "She said to go to the website, fill out the application, and submit it, then let her know. She'll see if she can get you into the Vet Prep Program. It's accelerated and will start you on your way to being a DVM faster."

Heat invaded her neck. "Why in the world would you do something like that without talking to me first?"

"I thought that's what you wanted?"

"I do, but not now. Not when Brook is going to be just out of high school and starting college herself. She wants to go to Colorado University."

Harper pulled her eyebrows together. "Didn't she apply to Colorado State too?"

"Yes. But we've decided on Boulder. The curriculums were similar, but Boulder is closer to Blueridge."

"I'm sure Brook can find a similar degree program at Colorado State. They have an engineering college, performing arts, natural resources, even business, if she wants to go that route." They'd talked about so many things, she'd thought Brook was looking at engineering, but had no idea what direction she had chosen. "They also have a really cool student center. I really think she'll like it there."

"I can't afford to go to college at the same time as Brook. I haven't even paid off the new laptops I bought last year. Plus, the veterinary college is in Fort Collins. That's an hour away from Denver."

"I thought we'd find a house somewhere in between, maybe Mead. It's kind of small, or maybe Longmont, which is a lot larger. Lisa is checking to see if they have any vet-tech jobs on campus. If she can find one, you'll get a break on tuition for you and Brook. It's a teaching hospital, so most likely they'll need replacements for graduates in the fall. Brook can live on campus at CSU."

"Another expense I can't afford." Between her anger and surprise, her head was spinning. "I can't believe you've made all these decisions without talking to me."

"I was trying to surprise you."

"Well, clearly you did." This was unbelievable.

"Don't you want to be with me?"

She blew out a breath. "Of course I do, but I don't want to uproot everything I have here. I'm not ready for that now."

"Well, I'm not ready to live here. I have a home and a practice in Denver. I can't afford to let that go." Harper turned and went out the door, slamming it behind her.

Addison paced the room, not knowing what to do. She had a plan for her life, and it didn't include leaving Blueridge—moving to Denver or any other city. She couldn't leave her mom and Jim or the clinic. The customers and animals needed her here.

The door opened, and she braced herself for Harper again, relieved when Brook came in.

"Mom. Are you okay?"

"No. I'm not."

"What's going on? I just saw Harper getting into her car. She wouldn't talk to me. She looked upset. I think she was crying."

Her gut tightened at the thought of Harper crying, but she was upset too. "I'm sorry she's crying, but she should've thought about that before she planned our future without me."

Brook came closer and stood in her path. "What did she plan, Mom?"

"She wants us to move to Denver with her. Go to school at CSU."

"What's wrong with that? I was thinking of going there anyway."

"What?" This was news to her. "I thought you had your mind set on Boulder."

Brook shook her head. "The more I compared them, the more I like CSU. They have an awesome engineering college. In fact, the whole college is fantastic."

"Why didn't you tell me?"

"Whenever we talk about it you get really stressed." Brook smiled slightly. "You and Harper are a great match."

"Ya think—how did you know?"

"It's been pretty obvious since you stopped going to," she made air quotes with her fingers, "pick up supplies in Ouray."

She shook her head and blew out a breath. "You knew about that too?"

"I'm not an idiot, Mom." She scrunched her forehead. "You could've just told me."

"I guess I should've." She should probably tell everyone.

Whether Brook changed her mind or not, she was still angry—no, furious at Harper for going behind her back and contacting her friend at the college. Who made decisions about someone else's life without telling them? How could Harper expect her to uproot everything and comply with whatever she had planned?

❖

Harper got into her car and drove. She needed to be anywhere but there. How had everything gotten so heated? All she was trying to do was make things easier for Addison, who'd hated everything she'd done. She'd thought they were on the same page about a future together, but now she could see that wasn't the case. Apparently Addison wanted Harper to make all the concessions, and she just couldn't do that. Addison at least needed her to meet her halfway.

She took her phone from the console and hit the number for Pete, who answered immediately. "Hey, what's up?"

"Are you at the store?"

"No. I'm off today. We're at the house."

"I need to talk to you."

"You okay?"

"No. Not really." Everything felt raw, like Addison had reached down her neck and torn out her heart.

"Well then, come on over."

Pete's door was open when she got there, and he was sitting in his chair in the living room. On the table next to him sat two beers, and he held one up as she entered. "Sounds like you might need this."

"Thanks." She took the beer and sat on the couch, still thinking about how everything had gotten so out of control. Pete wasn't one to push, so he waited for her to spill what was going on. "You know how Addison is about to finish her associate program to become a vet tech?"

He nodded. "Been working on it for a while now."

"She's been talking about going to veterinary school once she's finished, so I thought I'd help her out. I went to see the director of the teaching hospital where I graduated. I know her, and we talked about the program and Addison's options. Bottom line, she said she might be able to get her into an accelerated program and that she'd look for a job for her on campus."

"Sounds like a great deal."

"I thought so too, but Addison got so angry with me for not talking to her first. I was trying to surprise her."

Olive entered from the hallway. "I'd have been pretty pissed off too."

"Why?" She shrugged. "Explain that to me?"

Olive sat on the couch, and Pete immediately stood, went into the kitchen, got a beer from the refrigerator, and brought it to her.

Olive looked up at Pete. "Thank you, baby." She took a swallow and set the beer on the table next to her. "I'm going to be blunt with you, Harper." She flattened her lips. "You whirled into town and took over your dad's practice. Pretty much took charge of everything. You two were at odds with each other, and then something happened, and you and she are suddenly doing whatever." She flipped her hands up.

"Right." She had no idea where Olive was going with this.

"So you're here, you two are playing house together, and everything's good. Do you think maybe she got the impression you might stay? I certainly asked Pete that very question."

"I never said I was. I always planned to go back to Denver, but I guess we never really sat down and discussed it seriously." She'd assumed Addison knew that.

"Do you see what I'm getting at here?"

She nodded. She hadn't meant to give anyone that impression.

"*Now*, you go to CSU and make decisions about what's going to happen next for both of you *and* Brook. All the events that have happened since you got here have been out of Addison's control."

"That's not completely true. The decision to get involved with each other wasn't just mine."

Olive raised an eyebrow and tilted her head. "With the sparks flying between you two, do you really think she had a choice there?"

"No." She shook her head. "It just happened." She didn't have a choice either.

"And here you are in an impossible situation."

"I didn't think about it like that."

"How would you feel if she started talking to V about you selling your half of the practice to her?"

"That's totally different. That's a financial situation that's not really her business."

Olive smiled. "And getting a job on campus isn't?"

"Shit." She closed her eyes briefly. "What do I do now?"

"I suggest you think about what you really want and if you're willing to compromise to get it."

"I can't move back here." She shook her head. "Not now. I have too much at stake in Denver. My home—my practice. Eden's school."

"Then I guess you have your answer." Olive rubbed her hands down her thighs and grabbed her knees before she picked up her beer and took a swig.

Her stomach bottomed out, and she'd never felt such heaviness on her chest. She'd made stupid assumptions, and none of them had proved to be true. The future she envisioned with Addison wasn't going to happen anytime soon, and possibly not at all. The reality of it almost crushed her. She really had no one to come home to anymore. Here or in Denver.

Later that evening, Harper called Lisa to let her know her plan had backfired. The phone rang a couple of times before Lisa answered. "Hey. How'd the surprise go?"

"It didn't. Addison's not ready to start the program yet."

"Oh. What's her time frame?"

"She didn't have a time frame." She blew out a breath. "I don't know if she wants to continue with her education." She shouldn't have assumed she did.

"Well, I can understand that. Entering the program can be overwhelming, especially considering Addison's daughter will be starting college at the same time."

"I don't think she will, and right now I don't know if we're still together. She was so angry at me for talking to you and arranging things for her."

"It can't be that bad."

"I'm afraid it is. The ball's in her court. I'll let whatever feelings I have go, if I have to. I've done it before." Too many times.

"Stop that self-sacrificing bullshit, and go all in on this with her. If she's who you want, make the changes. Become a silent partner in your Denver practice—move to be with her. Your dad's going to retire someday, and you'll have his practice."

"That's a long way off, and what about Eden?"

"She'll be fine. She's only in her sophomore year. You've already said she loves it there."

"I'll give it some thought. I probably need to leave her alone for now. See if she comes around."

"Don't wait too long. You don't want the gap between you to get too large. My offer to help still stands, if Addison changes her mind."

"Thank you for that. I really appreciate everything you did." She hit the button and dropped her phone to the counter.

Harper's Explorer was behind the clinic when Addison pulled up. The knot that was finally beginning to loosen in her stomach tightened again. It had been several days since Addison had seen her. She'd needed some time to get her anger under control. She was still a little puzzled with herself at why she hadn't been able to get past Harper's actions. They weren't selfish, just unexpected. She realized she was only trying to help, but the fact that Harper hadn't even consulted her, asked what she wanted, was unacceptable. She refused to be in a relationship like that—ever.

She got out of her car and noticed suitcases loaded in the back. Her stomach was in her throat now. How could Harper think of leaving town without even telling her? Another unilateral decision made.

The door opened and Harper emerged. She stopped short, appearing startled. "I didn't think you'd be here this early."

"You're leaving?"

Harper nodded. "I'm heading back to Denver. V is down with the flu, and Dad said he's well enough to come back to work. You and he can handle it now." She tossed a bag into the back of the SUV. "Just picking up a few things." She headed back inside.

She followed Harper inside, unable to say anything—not knowing what to say. She went about her business in the front. Was she really going to let Harper go? Leave it up to Harper to make this decision for them? After all that they'd shared? She picked up the small plaque on her desk that said, *If you love someone, set them free. If they come back they're yours; if they don't they never were.* She tossed it into the trash, then rushed to the back of the clinic, where Harper was loading a few last items into her Explorer.

"Harper. Wait."

Harper didn't look at her. "I'd rather skip this part." She continued to gather her things, then brushed by her out the back door and carried them to the SUV.

Addison grabbed her arm and spun her around. "You can't skip over it—I won't let you. Whatever this might be between us—however you might feel—this is still our moment—good or bad."

Harper shook her head as she stared at the ground. "I can't, Addie. It's too hard."

She dipped her head to make eye contact and made Harper look at her. "Too hard to leave or too hard to admit you don't want to?"

"Both." She tossed some things into the back of the SUV. "You're right. I don't want to leave, but I have obligations in Denver, and I won't live in the closet here. I can't—even with you."

Harper really did care about her, even after the shitty way Addison had treated her. Addison hadn't considered that she was part of the roadblock. Could she have enough confidence in their love to make Harper stay—or to leave and pursue her education? She rushed to her, put her arms around her. "I can change. I promise. I don't want to hide either." A car drove by, and she instinctively released Harper.

"But you do."

"You can't expect me to unlearn years of behavior in a few months."

"No, but I can expect you to compromise." Harper gripped the top of the liftgate. "I know I was wrong not to talk to you about my visit with Lisa, but I was trying to find a way for us to have a future. I have a business in Denver—a stable practice that I built—a life I need to get back to living—a life I love."

What could be more special than the life she'd been living right here, with Addison? She couldn't suppress the tears spilling from her eyes any longer and held her tighter—pressed her face to Harper's back. "I love you, Harper. Please don't go."

"You know where I'll be. We can make this work if you want it." Harper twisted around, took Addison's face in her hands, and kissed her gently, sweetly before she released her, slammed the liftgate closed, and got into her SUV.

Addison knew when Harper kissed her that she was already holding back, and it was all her fault. She swiped the tears from her eyes as she watched Harper drive away, then turned and walked back into the clinic. It was all on her now. She had some serious decisions to make.

CHAPTER TWENTY-NINE

Addison had hardly slept last night. The tour of the college yesterday afternoon had been nice, yet seemed extremely long. It probably wasn't, but Addison hadn't been able to concentrate on much of anything since Harper had gone back to Denver a little over a week ago.

When they first arrived on campus, they'd slowed as they passed a group of students on the lawn having class outside. The instructor had come over and asked if he could help direct them to the administration building. Brook couldn't contain her smile when he motioned for a cute young man from the class to show them the way.

Brook was very social, and it seemed the young man was as well. They'd walked through one of the common areas to get a feel for the atmosphere. There were so many students, some huddled in groups studying, some alone in chairs reading. Brook knew right off the bat that she'd fit right in. They were able to find the counselor's office easily after the young man left them inside by following the signs posted on the walls and pillars as they walked. The college was everything Brook said it was—beautiful and full of amenities. It quickly became clear why she wanted to go to school here. Addison hadn't expected it, but it was Brook's choice to come to CSU in Fort Collins instead of CU in Boulder, and Brook seemed to be ecstatic about it.

Addison had no idea how she was going to approach this morning's conversation with the director of the veterinary teaching hospital. Dr. Darby had been very gracious on the phone when she'd called but reluctant to commit to what Harper had discussed with her. She'd guessed Harper had already told her about Addison's reaction. She hoped she could sway Dr. Darby to give her another chance.

Once they left the hotel, they took the short drive to the hospital. Addison was glad to see it was only about five minutes away from the main campus. She'd been stressing about being so far away from Brook when she started in the fall. If Addison decided to enroll at the veterinary college, she'd be ridiculously close. Probably closer than Brook wanted.

She parked in the lot, and they walked through the double doors at the main entrance. Then they stopped at the desk where a woman was sitting.

"Hi. I have an appointment with Dr. Darby. She said to have you call her when I arrived."

"Your name?"

"Addison Foster."

"One moment." She picked up the phone, hit a few buttons. "Addison Foster is here to see you." She listened for a moment. "Will do." She hung up the phone. "She'll be right out."

"Thank you."

After a few minutes a tall woman with jet-black hair came down the hallway. She smiled as she grew closer. "Good morning, Addison." She extended her hand. "Lisa Darby. It's so nice to meet you."

Addison shook it and was surprised at the strength of her grip. "Good morning, Dr. Darby. This is my daughter, Brook." She motioned to Brook, who was turned the opposite way, scoping out the area.

Brook spun around and shook Lisa's hand. "Hi."

"I hear you're going to be attending CSU. What program are you in?"

"Engineering."

"Oh. Which track?"

"I'm starting with civil, but I'm interested in several of them and haven't made up my mind yet. My advisor said the first year is the same for most, so I can switch if I want before next year."

"Well, let me know if you decide to switch to biomedical. We do a bit of crossover in that program."

"I will." Brook smiled.

Lisa glanced back at Addison. "I've heard so much about you, I feel like we should be friends."

"I didn't realize you and Harper were that close." In fact, she hadn't even heard about Lisa until a couple of weeks ago.

"We've been friends for a long time. I think, right after she became a student here. That was so long ago, it's hard to remember." She tilted her head. "She seems quite taken with you. I hope you two can work things out."

Apparently, she knew a whole lot more about her than she thought. Harper must have confided in her about her reaction to her plans, which she was still embarrassed about.

"That's why I'm here. I'm afraid I reacted badly to her surprise. I hadn't had a chance to think it through—process all the information she gave me."

"And now that you have?"

"It's a pretty solid plan. I hope it's not too late."

"You won't know until you talk to Harper, but knowing her for as long as I have, I think she might be open to it."

"Please don't tell her I've come to see you." She'd already made that request when they'd spoken on the phone, but she wanted to make sure she was the one to tell Harper about her change of heart—to apologize for the way she'd behaved. "We need to sit down and talk about the logistics of it all."

"I think you'll find she's a wonderful mentor."

"Yes. I already know that. She's been very helpful in my current studies."

"Right. She mentioned you were completing your associate degree at the community college. What is your grade point average there?"

"Currently, 4.0, but the past few weeks have made it hard to concentrate, so I'm not sure what it will end up at."

"I'm happy to put in a good word for you when it's time to apply for the medical college."

"Honestly, I don't want any special treatment. I'd like to get in on my own."

"Then I have every confidence you will. Even without the transfer policy between Denver Community College and CSU, your GPA alone would get you into the undergraduate program. And your dedication will keep you there." Lisa raised an eyebrow and whispered, "We'll rethink that recommendation when it's time to move up to the graduate program."

"Sounds good." She knew that was the hurdle she'd have to get past. From her research she'd learned that only ten to fifteen percent of students who applied got accepted. A letter of recommendation from Lisa would be beneficial. By then, Lisa will have known her long enough to give it based on firsthand information, not just as a favor to Harper.

"So, why don't I give you a tour of where you'll end up eventually." Lisa led them on a tour through the hospital.

The hospital was so much larger than she'd imagined. Learning here would be much more beneficial than at the clinic back home. They started in radiology, then moved to the large-animal area and out through the breezeway to the barn. It was huge.

"Are you interested in large-animal medicine?"

"Yes, but I'm afraid there's not much call for it in Blueridge. The clinic has several large-animal clients, but the majority of the patients are small."

"Well, you'll eventually learn a lot about both here, during your rotation."

"I've seen some of both at the clinic, so I'm excited for it all. Dr. Sims, Harper's dad, is kind of a vault of knowledge and experience. Nothing really stumps him. He pretty much knows everything." She'd gone back and forth between treating small animals and horses. In the end she hoped to be able to take care of both.

"That's good to hear. Small towns need doctors who can field cases from all types of animals."

Next they toured the humane-society area, where plenty of dogs and cats were waiting for homes. She wouldn't be able to work here and not take at least one of them home. She hoped Harper was prepared for that probability. She shook her head.

"What?" Lisa asked.

"I was thinking about whether Harper would be upset if we adopted a dog or a cat."

"Seriously?" Brook's eyes widened. "We could adopt one of each."

"Well, the last time she adopted a dog, it didn't turn out so well. She had to give it back to the owner."

Lisa pulled her eyebrows together. "What happened?"

"The owner hadn't really given her up. Her boyfriend did it because he didn't like dogs."

"That's horrible."

"Yeah. For both the owner and Harper. She'd had Daisy for quite a while."

"She'll be fine, Mom. We'll surprise her one day."

"No. Absolutely no more surprises." She laughed.

"Oh, right." Brook grinned. "Gotcha. Besides, Eden will probably want to help me pick them out." It seemed the choice was now out of her hands.

When they got to the small-animal-medicine area, Lisa went straight to a man who was making notes on a chart.

"I hear you have a couple of vet techs graduating this year."

"Yes, several actually."

"Addison will be attending, and I believe she's looking for a job." Lisa raised her eyebrows and looked at Addison.

"Yes. I am."

"Oh." He raised his eyebrows. "Do you have any experience?"

"I currently work at a clinic in Blueridge."

"Perfect." He took a small pad and pen out of his pocket. "Write down your phone number and email address, and I'll have HR send you the application information."

She took the pad from him and jotted down her information, her hand shaking as she wrote. This all seemed to be happening so fast. She needed to take a breath and realize this was a good thing—everything happening was good.

They'd spent the better part of an hour touring the facility before they landed in Lisa's office. They'd visited several different areas, including dentistry, cardiology, and oncology. Everything she'd seen solidified her decision to move forward.

"I can't thank you enough for this, Dr. Darby."

"Please, call me Lisa." Lisa took a few bottles of water from the mini fridge in the corner of the office, handed them each one, and kept one for herself before she sat in the chair behind her desk. Addison and Brook each took a chair on the other side. "Are there any other questions I can answer for you?"

"No. I'm a bit overwhelmed right now." She twisted the top off the water and drank. The cool water tasted good, helped decrease the heat she was feeling from her nerves. "At my age, going back to school at a college of this caliber is terrifying. The rest of the students are young and smart, with perfect memories."

"And sometimes arrogant attitudes." Lisa laughed as she spoke. "I know it's a lot to process. Life choices always are." She glanced at Brook. "What do you think about it all?"

"It's awesome. I'm proud of her for going back to school."

Warmth spread in her chest. Those words made the challenge worth it. "It's something I've always wanted to do, but I have to admit my brain has been on overload since I started."

"Well, don't let that stop you. That's not any different from anyone else's brain in the program."

"We should probably let you get back to work." They needed to get on the road too. She stood, and Brook followed suit.

Lisa rounded the corner of her desk and offered her hand. "It really was nice to meet you, and I hope to see you again soon."

"Same here."

Lisa opened her door and let them out. "Straight down this hallway will take you to the entrance. Have a safe drive home, and tell Harper I said hello."

"Thank you. I will." Next, she had to work out how she was going to tell Harper. No time like the present. She would stop in Denver at Harper's clinic before the drive home.

"Mom. This place is awesome."

"It is pretty nice."

"You have to go here."

"Well, I wouldn't go here right away. I'd have to finish my bachelor's degree first."

"Still. The whole place is better than I expected, and you'll be really close to me."

"Aw." She wrapped her arm around Brook's shoulder and squeezed. "You do love me, after all."

"You'll still have to stay out of my social life. I'm kind of an adult now."

"Kind of?" She hit the button on her key fob, and her car chirped.

"When I want to be." Brook laughed as she got into the car.

Addison slid into the driver's seat. "I guess that means I don't have to be a parent all the time either."

"Deal."

She glanced over her shoulder as they drove off. She hoped this would be her second home for the foreseeable future, this and Harper's house. If she'd still have her.

Chapter Thirty

A s the sun came up over the horizon, Harper saw its rays land on the town she grew up in—her town. The next exit led her home. Only this time she had no doubts about where she wanted to be and who she wanted to be with. Addison was her home, and it seemed she always had been. She would find a way to make this work even if she had to commute to Blueridge on weekends. She refused to let Addison go without a fight. Addison was right. Even though she was only trying to help, she'd overstepped by miles. Once she'd had time to think about it, Harper realized she would've been just as upset—probably more.

She pulled up to Addison's house but didn't see Addison's car. She'd headed out late the night before to avoid traffic, as she usually did, and was hoping to catch Addison before she left for work at the clinic. She glanced at Eden, who was asleep in the passenger seat, and then killed the engine. She quietly got out of the car, went to the front door, and knocked. No answer. She knocked again, then tried to look inside through the window. The shades were partially closed, but she still couldn't see any activity inside. It was only six thirty in the morning. Where could she possibly be? There must've been an emergency or something. She got into her Explorer and took off toward the clinic. Maybe she could help. When she drove to the back of the clinic where they all usually parked, she didn't see any cars. She swung around front—still no cars.

Next, she drove to the only other place she thought Addison could be, Dad and Patty's. A rush of heat filled her. Maybe something had happened to one of them. She pressed her foot to the gas and sped down the road. The house looked calm as she pulled up the gravel road, and Addison's car wasn't there either. What the hell was going on?

She shook Eden. "Wake up. We're here."

Eden rubbed her eyes. "I thought we were going to Addison's first."

"We did. She's not there." She got out of the SUV and went to the front door.

Eden followed her. "I hope there's breakfast."

The front door was open, but the glass storm door was locked, so she rang the doorbell.

Patty came to the door quickly. "What on earth are you two doing here?"

"I'm looking for Addison. Is she here?"

"I'm afraid not. She's took Brook to tour the college yesterday."

"Seriously." She raked her hand through her hair. Her timing sucked.

Patty nodded. "Left yesterday before first light. Spent the night there."

"What are you making for breakfast, Gran?" Eden pulled open the refrigerator.

"Whatever you want, darlin'. Your grampy is out collecting eggs, if you want to help."

Eden flew out the side door without another sound. It was amazing how much she loved those chickens.

"What time do you expect them back?"

"Not until later today."

Patty poured Harper a cup of coffee and handed it to her. "Is everything all right?"

"No, but I plan to make it better." She didn't want to get her hopes up until she'd had a chance to talk to Addison.

Eden came through the door with a basket full of eggs. "Looks like we're having a good breakfast."

Her dad followed Eden in and gave Harper a hug. "It's good to see you."

Patty opened the refrigerator and took out a few things for breakfast, then went to the stove. "I'll get the bacon on. Who's on toast duty?"

"I got it." She went to the breadbox and took out the loaf of bread. Harper didn't know if she could wait for Addison to get back. Six and a half hours meant she wouldn't be here until the afternoon, unless she left early. If she headed back to Denver, she might miss her altogether, so she was going to have to stay until Addison and Brook returned.

Patty finished scrambling the eggs and filled everyone's plates with eggs, bacon, and the toast Harper had made before she slid a plate of food in front of Jim.

"Looks like I've got myself some extra help at the clinic today." Jim dug into his eggs.

"Anything major scheduled?" She might as well help. She needed something to occupy her time. She took a couple bites of her eggs, and her stomach rumbled.

"Nothing major, but a full schedule as usual." He pushed some eggs onto his toast and took a bite.

"Jessie's coming in early since Addison's out, and I thought I'd go up and handle the front counter." Patty sipped her coffee. "I'm sure you're tired from the drive, so Eden can help me in the front or help Jessie in the back while you take a nap."

"As long as she doesn't make me do the dirty work," Eden said.

"I think you're out of luck on that one, but maybe you two can share it."

She frowned and rolled her eyes. "Fine. But I get to feed the chickens tonight."

"You got it."

"You okay with that?" Jim asked.

She realized her dad was staring at her. "What?" Harper hadn't heard a word they'd said, too worried about what Addison's reaction would be when she arrived. She hoped it would be more accepting than before. If not, she would be at a loss on what to do next.

"Eden's going to help at the clinic while you take a nap."

"Great. She can do cleanup."

Jim laughed. "That's what I was just telling her."

"Sorry. I'm a little distracted. I have a couple of patients I need to check on in Denver." She left the table, went outside onto the back porch, and took out her phone. She looked at her favorites, contemplated whether to call Addison, and then hit the button. The call went directly to voice mail, which was probably a good thing. She didn't know what she was going to say, and winging it on the phone was a bad idea. Addison would be able to escape the conversation by simply hanging up. She didn't want to make it that easy for her to ignore her. She hit the end button without leaving a message.

Her dad appeared from the doorway with two cups of coffee and came toward her, handed her one. "You okay?"

She set the cup on the porch railing and shrugged. "I don't know. That all depends on Addison, I guess."

"So what's your plan when she gets here?"

"I'm going to beg her to try to make it work."

"Okay. You want to tell me what happened between you two."

"I asked her to go to school and live with me in Denver."

"Doesn't sound like a bad idea to me."

"I assumed some things I shouldn't have without consulting her."

"And now?"

"If she doesn't want to go to school, that's her choice, but I love her, Dad, and still want to be with her." She couldn't stop the tears streaming down her cheeks. What would she do if Addison wasn't willing to compromise? Did she really want to know?

Jim set his coffee on the railing and gathered her into his arms. "For what it's worth, she's been miserable since you left. I think she loves you too."

"That's what I'm counting on." That was the only reason she had hope. She was prepared to up-end her life to compromise if Addison was willing to meet her halfway.

❖

Addison was more nervous than she'd anticipated when she pulled into the parking lot of The Total Pet. It was midday, and she fully expected Harper to be immersed in patient care. She parked the car and gripped the steering wheel.

"Do you want me to come in with you?" Brook stirred. She'd been sleeping for the past hour.

"No. I need to do this alone." She needed to gain the courage to face Harper after the way she'd reacted to her surprise. Every time she thought about it, her stomach clenched. She'd realized she'd been shortsighted about their whole relationship. Expecting Harper to pick up and move—leave everything in Denver behind—was a ridiculous ask. She was mortified and ashamed that she'd treated Harper with such anger.

Customers sat scattered around the waiting room. Four, maybe five, people in seats with several dogs and one or two cats waiting to be seen. She closed the door and went straight to the counter, waiting for the girl to look up.

"Hey." She heard Jeremy's voice from the hallway and smiled when he approached. "What are you doing here? Is Dr. H with you?"

"No. I'm here to see her."

"She's off today." He glanced over his shoulder as V came out of an exam room.

This wasn't working at all how she'd planned. Harper wasn't here, and she really didn't want to talk to V.

"I'll catch her at home."

"She's not there either." V's voice was low as she came to the counter, then scribbled a few notes into the chart she was carrying. "She's left town for a few days. Not sure when she'll be back." She handed the chart to Jeremy. "Can you give this one a rabies and a Bordetella vaccination. They're planning to board her next week."

"Sure thing, Dr. V." He took the chart and went into the back to the lab area.

"Do you know when Harper will be back?"

V shook her head. "Nope. She said she needed to get out of town. I'm not sure what you did, but she's been pretty upset." She clenched her lips together. "Won't even talk to me about buying the clinic now. Guess she's in Denver to stay."

"I guess she is." She took in a breath, tried to keep the tears from welling in her eyes. "Don't tell her I stopped by. I'll catch her another time."

"Got it." V turned, plucked the chart from another exam room door, and went inside.

She rushed out, reached her truck, tugged open the door, and slid into the driver's seat. When she got into the car, a wave of helplessness overtook her, and she couldn't stop the tears.

Brook raised the seat back up. "What's wrong? What did she say?"

"She's not there. She's gone somewhere to get away from everything—to get away from me." She swiped the tears from her cheeks. "I've totally messed everything up."

"Call her." Brook handed her the phone.

She took it, almost pressed the button for Harper, but then dropped it into the console. "I don't want to do this over the phone. I need to apologize to her face-to-face. That's why we stopped here." That's why she'd ignored all Harper's calls earlier. Had she been calling to tell her she was leaving town?

"When is she going to be back?"

"A couple of days. They don't know for sure."

"So you'll come back in a couple of days." Brook said it like it was a no-brainer.

She would do that, but waiting a few more days would be torture. Too much time to rethink all that had occurred over the past week—to reconsider her choices. She didn't want to do that again.

They were over halfway home when Addison hit the button on her phone for the clinic, and the call came through the speakers. She knew her mom would be there helping cover various tasks while she was out. Jim was great at doctoring but horrible at doing lab work and keeping the front office running. Jessie would do a lot of the work in the lab, as well as cleaning the exam rooms.

"Happy Tails. Can I help you?" Her mother's voice was cheery, as always.

"Hi, Mom."

"Hi, honey. Are you on your way home?"

"Yep. All finished. Brook will be officially attending CSU in the fall."

"That's wonderful. Tell her congratulations for me."

"Tell her yourself. You're on speaker."

"Congratulations, Brook. I know you're going to do so well there."

"Thanks, Gran. It's the best place ever. You're not gonna believe all the stuff they have there."

"We can't wait to hear all about it." Patty was silent for a moment. "Come straight to the house. I'll have dinner ready when you get here."

"That's sweet, Mom. It'll be a few more hours. We're about halfway there."

"Sounds like perfect timing. We'll see you when you get here. Drive safely."

She hit the hang-up button on her steering wheel. Her mom was always good about having meals for them when they came in from trips and at least a couple of other days during the week. She would miss that when she moved.

❖

They were almost through with their day at the clinic, and Harper was thankful they were busy. She hadn't had time to think about Addison. She'd already seen a dozen patients, and a few people were still in the waiting room. People had been popping in without appointments to have their pets seen by her. It seemed they'd heard she was in town and were happy about it.

She glanced at her watch. She'd been making notes on a patient chart when Patty got the call from Addison earlier. Harper's pulse had raced as she waved her arms at Patty and told her not to tell Addison she was there.

She didn't want to explain to Patty why she didn't want Addison to know, so she made up something about her not wanting Addison to worry while she was on the roads in case they were slick. A lame excuse, since they hadn't had snow in weeks. Still, she didn't want her to hurry and have something go wrong. She refused to say the word accident out loud, because that would be a bad omen. Not that she believed in those, but still. She was actually kind of surprised Patty didn't already know what had happened between them.

Harper was worried. It had been over six hours since they left Boulder. "They should be home by now. Can you call Addison and check on them?"

Patty looked at the clock on the wall. "When she called, she said they'd been on the road for a few hours, and they were making good time. Even so, they won't be here for at least another forty-five minutes or so." She picked up a stack of files and took them to the file cabinet. "They shouldn't be too late, though. Might even show up here before we close. Your father and I have made the drive to Fort Collins a few times. It's never much more than seven hours. Once you make it through Denver, it's usually smooth sailing."

"Fort Collins? I thought they were going to Boulder."

Patty shook her head as she filed. "Brook changed her mind. She's going to Colorado State in Fort Collins. Addison called that friend of yours at the veterinary college. She planned to meet with her while they were there." She pulled her eyebrows together. "I thought you knew."

Harper's mind spun. Why hadn't Addison called her—told her Brook was going to CSU? "No. She didn't tell me anything about it." Her pulse raced at the thought of Addison changing her mind. Knowing Addison was even thinking of going to the veterinary college made it hard to control her happiness.

"I hope I didn't ruin a surprise or something."

She immediately took her phone from her pocket, found Lisa in her contacts, and hit the screen.

Lisa didn't answer until the fourth ring. "Hey. I'm about to go into a meeting. Can I call you back?" She sounded rushed.

"You didn't tell me that Addison was coming to see you today."

"Well, I didn't know until after we'd spoken last."

Harper's throat tightened. "Why did she come to see you?"

"I can't talk to you about Addison. She asked me not to mention it to you." She heard voices in the background. "I have to go."

"Thanks. Sorry for holding you up."

Lisa didn't respond, and the phone went dead.

That news gave her a boost. Now all she had to do was keep herself occupied until they arrived. She took the patient folder from the next exam room, checked the reason for the appointment, and went inside.

The next hour dragged on like pouring molasses in the dead of winter. Every time she came out of an exam room, she hoped to see Addison, but no luck yet. She was at the counter finishing her notes on the last patient of the day, a cute little cocker spaniel with ear issues, when she heard the door open. She continued writing but was prepared for one more patient if necessary.

"You're here." Addison's voice seemed softer than usual. More beautiful even.

She snapped her head up and nodded. "I've been waiting for you." She swallowed hard. "I don't like the way things ended when I left." She didn't move closer. "I think we should find a way. Whether it's me trekking back here on the weekends or you coming to Denver. I want this—us to work." She shrugged.

"Me too." Addison took a few steps. "I've been thinking a lot about what you said—what you did for me."

"We can just try it out. You can come stay with me in Denver whenever you want." She swallowed again, trying to keep her emotions controlled. "We can split the time between here and there."

"Wait. I need to tell you a few things." Addison put up her hands. "First off, I'm sorry for the way I acted before. You were only trying to do something nice for me, and I was an ass. Second, I've enrolled at CSU, and I might have a lead on a job at the hospital." She glanced at her mother. "So I'll only be able to help out here depending on my class schedule, and possible work schedule at the hospital, if I get the job. Otherwise it will be whenever I can get back home."

"Jimmy can handle the clinic now." Patty moved closer. "I'll be here with him, and we also have Jessie."

She glanced at Brook. "What happened to Boulder?"

Brook jumped up from the chair she'd slipped into behind the counter. "I decided to go to CSU. They have an awesome engineering program. We visited yesterday and talked to a counselor. I'm already enrolled."

"I want to go to CSU too." Eden chimed in.

"You have a few more years of high school to figure that one out."

"Can I stay with Gran and Grampy this summer?"

"I don't know. You can be a handful sometimes."

"Moi?" Eden acted surprised. "I promise I'll be on my best behavior."

"That's a big responsibility. I don't know if Patty and Dad will want to do that."

Jimmy came out from one of the exam rooms. "She'll be fine with us. Patty doesn't let her get away with any more than I did you." He winked at Patty. "Right?"

"Right." Patty smiled.

Addison shrugged. "Brook was my last excuse. I think I was afraid of change. So if you agree, I can go to school during the week, and we can come back here on the days we can manage to help out."

Harper didn't respond. She only stared at Addison, unable to believe that everything she'd hoped for was coming true.

"Listen. I know it might be a little crazy at first, and it would definitely take some getting used to. We'll probably be exhausted, but—"

"You'll give it a shot?" She couldn't hide the excitement in her voice.

Addison nodded as she closed the distance between them. All the weight from Harper's shoulders released. This was her path, her woman, her life. No one in the world made her feel safer than Addison did.

She fell into their embrace and kissed Addison deeply. Letting all of her emotions take her as Addison held her, she felt tears running down her cheeks as Addison covered her lips with soft, gentle kisses. It didn't seem as though Addison cared who was watching.

She stared into Addison's eyes. "I'm sorry I left the way I did." She blubbered as the words escaped her lips. "I was afraid you didn't want me."

Addison squeezed her tighter and whispered in her ear, "It's okay, baby. I want you every day for the rest of my life. I love you." She took Harper's hand. "Come on. Let's go home."

She turned to everyone else. "I'm done for the day."

Patty smiled. "Okay. See you tomorrow."

"We'll see. Harper and I have a lot of catching up to do." Addison glanced at Harper and grinned. "Brook, you and Eden are with your grandparents tonight."

Everything was right in Harper's world again. She'd never felt this good about any other decision she'd ever made.

EPILOGUE

Addison stood in the kitchen of their new house, wondering where she was going to put her cookware. Would it be next to the gas stove, closer to the double ovens, or somewhere else completely? Maybe hanging over the island in the middle. She didn't have all that much, which meant they would definitely have some empty cabinets at first. It was much larger than the kitchen at Harper's house on the south side of Denver, and three times bigger than her kitchen in Blueridge. When Harper had said she'd found them the perfect house, she certainly hadn't expected this huge, gorgeous place with a pool in back. The girls were going to love that. She glanced around the open living space. It was perfect. A split-bedroom layout with three bedrooms, four baths, and an office they could share for work and school.

The past six months had been nothing but surreal. She and Brook had gone from living alone in Blueridge to being part of a full-blown integrated family with Harper and Eden in Denver. She was relieved they all got along really well. So far.

Harper came through the door with a box of kitchen items and slid it onto the counter before she trapped Addison in the corner of the counter. "What are you thinking?"

"I'm never going to be able to fill this kitchen."

"You don't think so?" Harper backed up and pulled open the lower cabinet next to the stove. "These will take up some space, won't they?" It was a brand-new set of pots and pans.

"Oh my gosh." She tugged the box from the shelf, and Harper helped her lift them to the counter. "These are expensive. I can't believe you bought these."

"A new kitchen needs new cookware."

"How did you know which ones?" She'd been wanting this set forever, but hadn't been able to justify the cost.

"I have my contacts." Harper grinned.

"Riley or Gemma." It had to be one of them.

"You're going to think this is funny, but it was actually Gemma. Riley had no clue." Harper pulled open the box, took out the first pan, and handed it to her.

"Gemma? Really?" She held the pan against her chest like it was a new puppy.

"Yeah. I don't know what you said to her, but she's been really nice to me since you told her about us."

"I just made her realize what's important in life." She'd given Gemma an ultimatum. If she wanted to be in her life, she had to accept that Addison was in love with Harper. She was happy, and somewhat relieved, when Gemma had chosen to remain her friend and curb her judgmental attitude.

Harper continued unpacking the cookware. "And don't think you're going to get away with doing all the cooking. I expect some lessons."

"You can be my sous chef." She set the pan she was holding on the counter and tugged Harper to her. "And keep me company while I cook."

Eden came through the door and dropped another box on the counter. "I can do that."

"Nope. The job's already mine." Harper kissed Addison—sent her further into the dreamy state she'd been living in for the past six months.

"Ew. Can you guys take that somewhere else?" Eden rolled her eyes.

Brook came in not far behind. "Maybe we should go somewhere else tonight, so these two can wallpaper."

Harper scrunched her eyebrows. "This place is perfect the way it is." She looked as confused as Addison was.

The girls laughed. "Okay, but we're still going to find somewhere else just in case."

"Do you think we'll be able to stay here tonight?" The movers were supposed to bring the beds, but they weren't in the first load.

"I'll make sure of it. Even if I'm up all night making sure it happens."

She laughed. "That's my plan, whether you get them set up or not."

"See. Wallpapering." Brook grabbed Eden's hand and tugged her out the door.

Addison finally got what they meant, and her cheeks warmed. "Definitely wallpapering in the bedroom tonight." She squeezed Harper tighter as she laughed. "We're going to give that room a lot of makeovers, for sure."

"Thank God it's at the other end of the house from the girls." Harper kissed her, and her whole world spun. Her fairy-tale life had finally come true.

Addison didn't know why it had taken her so long to be happy. Maybe she'd been waiting for Harper all along. Thankfully, Harper seemed to have been waiting for her too.

THE END

About the Author

Dena Blake grew up in a small town just north of San Francisco where she learned to play softball, ride motorcycles, and grow vegetables. She eventually moved with her family to the southwest where she began creating vivid characters in her mind and bringing them to life on paper.

Dena currently lives in the southwest with her partner and is constantly amazed at what she learns from her two children. She is a would-be chef, tech nerd, and occasional auto mechanic who has a weakness for dark chocolate and a good cup of coffee.

Books Available from Bold Strokes Books

Coming to Life on South High by Lee Patton. Twenty-one-year-old gay virgin Gabe Rafferty's first adult decade unfolds as an unpredictable journey into sex, love, and livelihood. (978-1-63555-906-4)

Fleur d'Lies by MJ Williamz. For rookie cop DJ Sander, being true to what you believe is the only way to live…and one way to die. (978-1-63555-854-8)

Guarding Evelyn by Erin Zak. Can TV actress Evelyn Glass prove her love for Alden Ryan means more to her than fame before it's too late? (978-1-63555-841-8)

Love's Falling Star by B.D. Grayson. For country music megastar Lochlan Paige, can love conquer her fear of losing the one thing she's worked so hard to protect? (978-1-63555-873-9)

Love's Truth by C.A. Popovich. Can Lynette and Barb make love work when unhealed wounds of betrayed trust and a secret could change everything? (978-1-63555-755-8)

Next Exit Home by Dena Blake. Home may be where the heart is, but for Harper Sims and Addison Foster, is the journey back worth the pain? (978-1-63555-727-5)

Not Broken by Lyn Hemphill. Falling in love is hard enough—even more so for Rose who's carrying her ex's baby. (978-1-63555-869-2)

The Noble and the Nightingale by Barbara Ann Wright. Two women on opposite sides of empires at war risk all for a chance at love. (978-1-63555-812-8)

What a Tangled Web by Melissa Brayden. Clementine Monroe has the chance to buy the café she's managed for years, but Madison LeGrange swoops in and buys it first. Now Clementine is forced to work for the enemy and ignore her former crush. (978-1-63555-749-7)

A Far Better Thing by JD Wilburn. When needs of her family and wants of her heart clash, Cass Halliburton is faced with the ultimate sacrifice. (978-1-63555-834-0)

Body Language by Renee Roman. When Mika offers to provide Jen erotic tutoring, will sex drive them into a deeper relationship or tear them apart? (978-1-63555-800-5)

Carrie and Hope by Joy Argento. For Carrie and Hope loss brings them together but secrets and fear may tear them apart. (978-1-63555-827-2)

Death's Prelude by David S. Pederson. In this prequel to the Detective Heath Barrington Mystery series, Heath discovers that first love changes you forever and drives you to become the person you're destined to be. (978-1-63555-786-2)

Ice Queen by Gun Brooke. School counselor Aislin Kennedy wants to help standoffish CEO Susanna Durr and her troubled teenage daughter become closer—even if it means risking her own heart in the process. (978-1-63555-721-3)

Masquerade by Anne Shade. In 1925 Harlem, New York, a notorious gangster sets her sights on seducing Celine, and new lovers Dinah and Celine are forced to risk their hearts, and lives, for love. (978-1-63555-831-9)

Royal Family by Jenny Frame. Loss has defined both Clay's and Katya's lives, but guarding their hearts may prove to be the biggest heartbreak of all. (978-1-63555-745-9)

Share the Moon by Toni Logan. Three best friends, an inherited vineyard and a resident ghost come together for fun, romance and a touch of magic. (978-1-63555-844-9)

Spirit of the Law by Carsen Taite. Attorney Owen Lassiter will do almost anything to put a murderer behind bars, but can she get past her reluctance to rely on unconventional help from the alluring Summer Byrne and keep from falling in love in the process? (978-1-63555-766-4)

The Devil Incarnate by Ali Vali. Cain Casey has so much to live for, but enemies who lurk in the shadows threaten to unravel it all. (978-1-63555-534-9)

His Brother's Viscount by Stephanie Lake. Hector Somerville wants to rekindle his illicit love affair with Viscount Wentworth, but he must overcome one problem: Wentworth still loves Hector's brother. (978-1-63555-805-0)

Journey to Cash by Ashley Bartlett. Cash Braddock thought everything was great, but it looks like her history is about to become her right now. Which is a real bummer. (978-1-63555-464-9)

Liberty Bay by Karis Walsh. Wren Lindley's life is mired in tradition and untouched by trends until social media star Gina Strickland introduces an irresistible electricity into her off-the-grid world. (978-1-63555-816-6)

Scent by Kris Bryant. Nico Marshall has been burned by women in the past wanting her for her money. This time, she's determined to win Sophia Sweet over with her charm. (978-1-63555-780-0)

Shadows of Steel by Suzie Clarke. As their worlds collide and their choices come back to haunt them, Rachel and Claire must figure out how to stay together and most of all, stay alive. (978-1-63555-810-4)

The Clinch by Nicole Disney. Eden Bauer overcame a difficult past to become a world champion mixed martial artist, but now rising star and dreamy bad girl Brooklyn Shaw is a threat both to Eden's title and her heart. (978-1-63555-820-3)

The Last First Kiss by Julie Cannon. Kelly Newsome is so ready for a tropical island vacation, but she never expects to meet the woman who could give her her last first kiss. (978-1-63555-768-8)

The Mandolin Lunch by Missouri Vaun. Despite their immediate attraction, everything about Garet Allen says short-term, and Tess Hill refuses to consider anything less than forever. (978-1-63555-566-0)

Thor: Daughter of Asgard by Genevieve McCluer. When Hannah Olsen finds out she's the reincarnation of Thor, she's thrown into a world of magic and intrigue, unexpected attraction, and a mystery she's got to unravel. (978-1-63555-814-2)

Veterinary Technician by Nancy Wheelton. When a stable of horses is threatened Val and Ronnie must work together against the odds to save them, and maybe even themselves along the way. (978-1-63555-839-5)

16 Steps to Forever by Georgia Beers. Can Brooke Sullivan and Macy Carr find themselves by finding each other? (978-1-63555-762-6)

All I Want for Christmas by Georgia Beers, Maggie Cummings, Fiona Riley. The Christmas season sparks passion and love in these stories by award winning authors Georgia Beers, Maggie Cummings, and Fiona Riley. (978-1-63555-764-0)

From the Woods by Charlotte Greene. When Fiona goes backpacking in a protected wilderness, the last thing she expects is to be fighting for her life. (978-1-63555-793-0)

Heart of the Storm by Nicole Stiling. For Juliet Mitchell and Sienna Bennett a forbidden attraction definitely isn't worth upending the life they've worked so hard for. Is it? (978-1-63555-789-3)

If You Dare by Sandy Lowe. For Lauren West and Emma Prescott, following their passions is easy. Following their hearts, though? That's almost impossible. (978-1-63555-654-4)

Love Changes Everything by Jaime Maddox. For Samantha Brooks and Kirby Fielding, no matter how careful their plans, love will change everything. (978-1-63555-835-7)

Not This Time by MA Binfield. Flung back into each other's lives, can former bandmates Sophia and Madison have a second chance at romance? (978-1-63555-798-5)

The Dubious Gift of Dragon Blood by J. Marshall Freeman. One day Crispin is a lonely high school student—the next he is fighting a war in a land ruled by dragons, his otherworldly boyfriend at his side. (978-1-63555-725-1)

The Found Jar by Jaycie Morrison. Fear keeps Emily Harris trapped in her emotionally vacant life; can she find the courage to let Beck Reynolds guide her toward love? (978-1-63555-825-8)

Aurora by Emma L McGeown. After a traumatic accident, Elena Ricci is stricken with amnesia leaving her with no recollection of the last eight years, including her wife and son. (978-1-63555-824-1)

Avenging Avery by Sheri Lewis Wohl. Revenge against a vengeful vampire unites Isa Meyer and Jeni Denton, but it's love that heals them. (978-1-63555-622-3)

Bulletproof by Maggie Cummings. For Dylan Prescott and Briana Logan, the complicated NYC criminal justice system doesn't leave room for love, but where the heart is concerned, no one is bulletproof. (978-1-63555-771-8)

Her Lady to Love by Jane Walsh. A shy wallflower joins forces with the most popular woman in Regency London on a quest to catch a husband, only to discover a wild passion for each other that far eclipses their interest for the Marriage Mart. (978-1-63555-809-8)

No Regrets by Joy Argento. For Jodi and Beth, the possibility of losing their future will force them to decide what is really important. (978-1-63555-751-0)

The Holiday Treatment by Elle Spencer. Who doesn't want a gay Christmas movie? Holly Hudson asks herself that question and discovers that happy endings aren't only for the movies. (978-1-63555-660-5)

Too Good to be True by Leigh Hays. Can the promise of love survive the realities of life for Madison and Jen, or is it too good to be true? (978-1-63555-715-2)

Treacherous Seas by Radclyffe. When the choice comes down to the lives of her officers against the promise she made to her wife, Reese Conlon puts everything she cares about on the line. (978-1-63555-778-7)

Two to Tangle by Melissa Brayden. Ryan Jacks has been a player all her life, but the new chef at Tangle Valley Vineyard changes everything. If only she wasn't off the menu. (978-1-63555-747-3)

When Sparks Fly by Annie McDonald. Will the devastating incident that first brought Dr. Daniella Waveny and hockey coach Luca McCaffrey together on frozen ice now force them apart, or will their secrets and fears thaw enough for them to create sparks? (978-1-63555-782-4)